STROKE OF DEATH

Shampa Roy has taught in the Dept. of English, Miranda House, University of Delhi for over three decades. Her academic writings – articles, book chapters and translations – have appeared in various international journals and edited anthologies. She has co-edited and contributed to *Towards Freedom: Critical Essays on Rabindranath Tagore's Ghare Baire/The Home and the World* and *'Bad' Women of Bombay Films*. She is also the author of *Gender and Criminality in Bangla Crime Narratives* and *True Crime Writings in Colonial India*. *Stroke of Death* is her first novel.

STROKE OF DEATH

Shampa Roy

hachette
INDIA

First published in 2024 by Hachette India
(Registered name: Hachette Book Publishing India Pvt. Ltd)
An Hachette UK Company
www.hachetteindia.com

1

ISBN 978-93-5731-618-7 (Paperback)
ISBN 978-93-5731-314-8 (eBook)

Hachette Book Publishing India Pvt. Ltd
4th/5th Floors, Corporate Centre,
Plot No. 94, Sector 44, Gurugram 122003, India

Typeset in Ibarra Real Nova
by Mukul

Printed and bound in India by
Manipal Technologies Limited

MIX
Paper | Supporting responsible forestry
FSC™ C043100

To Professor Sisir Kumar Das, who helped 'decolonize' my thinking in so many different ways

PROLOGUE

RAJAPUR, A VILLAGE IN (WHAT WILL SOON BE) EAST BENGAL

October 1904

Sarala Dasi's corpse had lain undiscovered for more than twelve hours. And had it not been for some boys chancing upon it while playing truant from the village school, it would have probably remained unseen for much longer. Her body lay on its stomach, the smashed head twisted to one side. On the deserted path that connected the local zamindar's estate, the Rajbari, with the rest of the village. Sarala, a cook and household help at the Rajbari, took that path once a week to walk back to the village. By the time her lifeless form was spotted, flies had already begun swarming all over it, playing a grotesque tune to accompany the stench of death. All else forgotten, the boys gaped with horror-filled fascination at the dead woman's splayed limbs, the open wound at the back of her head, where blood and brain matter had coagulated, and the sightlessly staring milky eyes. Then one of them saw a fly crawl out of her eye, recoiled and threw up his last meal.

A spell seemed to be broken, and all the boys screamed in unison and ran towards the village, clutching their dhotis, to raise an alarm.

When Daroga Bansidhar Gupta arrived on the scene, he fought hard to control his nausea as the acrid smell of blood, urine and rotting flesh assailed his nostrils. Every time something like this happened, he would chide himself and try to bolster his courage, but invariably, his knees would tremble and bile would tickle the back of his throat. Finally, when he could no longer go on pretending to assess the surroundings, without running the risk of being thought a coward by his junior officer, he dropped to his haunches with a sigh to get a better view of the dead woman's face. 'Bloody hell!' he exclaimed as he flapped his hands to move the flies. 'Isn't this Sarala Dasi? Isn't she a cook at the Rajbari? Why, who could have done this to the poor girl?' Then the corpulent daroga stood with some effort, pulled at his robust moustache and thought plaintively, *Lord, help me! How am I ever going to get to the bottom of this?*

The evening just before having her head bashed, Sarala Dasi, in yet another instance of life's cruel ironies, had felt her entire being swell with a rare sense of happiness. This despite the fact that the morning's flurry of activities had left her feeling exhausted and tetchy. For kitchen hands like Sarala Dasi, the approaching Durga Puja celebrations meant monstrous amounts of work in the Rajbari kitchen. There was the incessant pounding, grinding, mashing, chopping and slicing of various kinds of spices, vegetables and fish. Then the scouring and scrubbing of heavy brass and copper utensils till every muscle hurt. Eyes and throat would burn with the thick smoke coming out of the large stoves. And all this accompanied by the head cook Kamini's angry glare and oft-repeated warnings about the reprisals that would follow any mistakes in the kitchen. Sarala had to bite her lips to prevent a fitting rejoinder from flying out of her mouth. She often fantasized about killing the battleaxe! If there was a *boti* big enough to do the task, Sarala would have happily sliced the woman into pieces like the aubergine she was about to chop.

By late afternoon, Sarala had felt a headache chafing the back of her eyes and announced that she would return the next day after visiting her house in the village. Ignoring Kamini's huff of annoyance, she had stalked out of the kitchen and then walked slowly to her favourite place on the estate, the little pond, the *pukur*. That was where she would often go to rest her aching limbs and calm her agitated mind. It also happened to be the beginning of her favourite time of the day. The time when the sun, just before fading gradually, proclaimed its presence in a dazzling display of colours. Ma had once told her that it had a special name – *godhuli* or the hour when the cows returned home, stirring up dust with their restless hooves – and little Sarala had smiled dreamily. Sitting on the banks of the pukur, she stretched out her legs and felt the water lapping against her feet. All around her, cicadas had begun their choric chirping. Frogs croaked at regular intervals, and tiny insects could be seen hovering right over the still surface of the pond water. Even the harsh cawing of the crows seemed to meld perfectly with the sweeter sounds of birds returning to their nests. It made her believe that life was full of possibilities. With a rapturous smile on her lips, Sarala leaned back on her hands, shut her eyes and inhaled the fragrance of the *shiuli* flowers that magically appeared at this time of the year to herald the arrival of the goddess. After a while, she placed her chin on her knee and thought about her precious secret, hugging it to herself.

Until now, there had been little in Sarala's brief life to give her true happiness. Memories of her childhood made gall rise to her throat. Her parents had never made the slightest effort to hide their disappointment at having a daughter instead of the son they had always longed for. As they saw it, she was a *hotobhagi*, an accursed girl who had survived at birth by not allowing her male twin to breathe. All those years ago, while they had waited with bated breath for the midwife to revive their son, it was their wretched daughter's lusty cries that filled their ears. And the cries had continued to rend the air for a long time, a loud and insistent echo of their own sense of devastation and loss.

Not surprisingly, therefore, soon after she turned eleven, they felt euphoric about being able to marry her off to a middle-aged man of the right sub-caste of brahmins. A grey-haired, hollow-cheeked Nobin Chandra, who was unabashedly besotted with his lissom mistress, a Boishnobi* called Haridasi. His wife he only saw as fit for endless cursing, pummelling, kicking and slapping. Thankfully, he did her a favour and died four years into their marriage. Sarala could still recall the day when the news of the accident and of his death arrived and flooded every pore and crevice of her tormented fifteen-year-old body and mind with relief.

With nothing but her tiny marital home to call her own, Sarala's initial relief, however, had been quickly replaced with worries about finding a way to make ends meet. Her ma and baba all but abandoned her after offering injunctions about the life of a virtuous widow. *Don't even dream of eating fish*, her mother had warned her through pinched lips. Sarala had nodded mutely while swallowing back the screams

* A Boishnob or Boishnobi refers to practitioners of Vaishnavism in Bengal. Associated with the worship of Radha and Krishna, Vaishnavism was hugely popular in the nineteenth century amongst prominent Hindu houses as well as amongst men and women of non-dominant castes.

of frustration building up inside her. Why? She wanted to yell. What on earth does fish-eating have to do with a dead husband? I began eating fish long before I met him! So why, even in death, does this man have the right to take away everything that gives me pleasure in life? But she had kept quiet and watched her parents leave.

Strangely, help had come from a completely unexpected quarter. Out of the blue, her husband's mistress, Haridasi Boishnobi, had paid her a visit one day, gauged her situation with large, intelligent eyes and then brought her the offer to work in the Rajbari kitchen.

That was how Sarala Dasi had landed up at Zamindar Ballabh Ray's estate a year ago. A whole year ago! How time had flown! The first day that she had seen the imposing mansion with its seemingly endless grounds, it had left her feeling giddy with terror. Little by little, she got used to it. To the sheer scale of the place with its pond and gardens, its impossibly sturdy yet graceful pillars, maze-like corridors and courtyards, tall alabaster sculptures and latticed brickwork. To the people living in it. And then, just when she assumed that her arid life was going to centre around the endless drudgery in the Rajbari kitchen, something unexpected had happened. Something she didn't think was written in the destiny of a hotobhagi.

With a smile, Sarala heaved herself up from the steps of the pukur. She could see someone walking towards her. A tide of jubilation rose inside her. Her life, Sarala felt confident, was on the brink of a great change.

Later, with the feeling of happiness still lingering, she walked towards the village, like she did every week. After every five days, she would return to her tiny house in the village. To clean it and then rest for a day before returning to the Rajbari. Walking on that desolate path usually made her jittery because of all the stories she had heard since childhood, of *brohmodottyi*, the demoniacal ghosts of brahmins, lurking in the trees and ready to pounce on unsuspecting travellers. But that evening, it felt as though she were treading air. The leaves she clutched in her hand made her feel invincible. She was loved, they told her, their rough edges rubbing against her palm. She had put a few in her mouth, but she wanted to feel the rest in her hand. She found herself humming a long-forgotten tune under her breath.

Just then, a slight noise made her stop. What was that? A trapped bird fluttering its wings? The sinister presence in the trees that she had heard about? Or just her mind playing tricks on her? She needed to walk faster, not stop and wonder. And that's when the blow seemed to come from nowhere and put paid to all of Sarala Dasi's dreams. She felt as though her head was exploding into a thousand fragments as she pitched to the ground. Then, just before drawing her last ragged breath, Sarala glimpsed a face peering down at her. A set of familiar eyes was watching her die with an unwavering expression. That was no ghost! She knew the owner of that face. *But why?* was her baffled thought before darkness descended and Sarala's mind lost its ability to make sense of anything forever.

1

AN INSPECTOR ARRIVES

When Inspector Dhananjoy Lahiri of the Detective Department of Calcutta Police alighted from the train that had brought him from the bustling city, where he lived and worked, to the quiet village of Rajapur, nothing could be further from his mind than a homicide investigation. It was at his boss Mr Smithson's behest that he had had to plan this holiday, and his boss had made it quite clear that his instructions were not to be taken lightly. The superintendent of Calcutta Police had noticed the growing shadows under the young detective's eyes – legacies of sleepless nights – and the slight tremor in his hands. He knew they were signs of the hidden toll that battling the forces of darkness was taking on his best and favourite recruit. Without further ado, he insisted that Dhananjoy take a month-long break during Durga Puja. The idea had filled the young detective with feelings of bewilderment. A break? How on earth was he going to live without what Smithson had termed 'the relentless pressures of working as a detective in this wretched city'? What was he supposed to do if he could not puzzle over enigmatic clues, pursue intractable leads or go off on wild goose chases? But Smithson had been firm. He needed to get away from it all for a while. Dhananjoy had had no choice but to rack his brains for a place to visit. And that's when Rajapur had sprung to mind.

Rajapur! The village where he had spent his childhood. The village he had not visited in over fifteen years, despite all the promises he had made to his childhood friend Bansi, now Daroga Bansidhar Gupta of Rajapur Thana. Bansi had even stopped writing to him for a while when Dhananjoy could not make it to his wedding. At long last, it seemed to Dhananjoy, the time had come to make good on all those promises. Revisiting Rajapur after more than a decade, he hoped, would provide the much-needed panacea for his ills. Crime-solving would have to be set aside for a while.

And yet, one of the first things he heard as he got off the train in the evening and scoured the small platform to see if Bansidhar had come to meet him was the word 'murder'. The rural railway station was utterly different from the one at Howrah from where he had started his journey. That had been a swirling mass of passengers, porters, food and magazine sellers and beggars. A maelstrom of sights, sounds and smells that left one's senses reeling. Here, besides him and a skeletal stray dog searching for scraps of food, there were just two men on the near-deserted platform. They were talking in agitated voices, and there was no doubt that the one word he heard being used repeatedly was 'murder'. Feeling Dhananjoy's eyes upon them, the men stopped and turned around to cast curious glances in his direction. One of them then walked up to him and asked whether he needed any help. Strangers were a novelty in Rajapur, and the gentleman who asked the question stared intently at the newcomer.

And then, after scanning Dhananjoy's face for some time, he exclaimed in a loud voice as though he had just won the lottery, 'As I live and breathe, it's Dhananjoy, is it not? Pandit moshai's son? Arre, no wonder you seem so familiar! You look so much like your father, Dhirendra Lahiri. Our

Pandit moshai. Tall and lean like him. Same eyes as him! I remember the hair as well!' Chortling gleefully, he pointed at Dhananjoy's abundance of wavy hair, which had always defied the ministrations of a comb. 'I was a few years senior to you in school, but we were all taught maths by Lahiri Pandit. And who can forget those lessons and the canings that accompanied any mistakes? I had heard that you were going to pay us a visit. You have come to visit your old friend Bansi, right? Our Daroga Bansidhar? By the way, I'm Ahir. Ahir Bhattacharya. I'm the station master here. Welcome, welcome back to Rajapur.' Dhananjoy had nearly forgotten that in a village, secret threads of communication bound every household. In a place like this, it would be nigh on impossible for a stranger to slip in unnoticed. Everyone knew everyone else, and if a stranger was spotted, the locals felt entitled to know every little detail about him and probably also that of his forefathers. Once Dhananjoy confirmed that Ahir was right in his conjectures, he found his hand seized and pumped with great enthusiasm.

The other gentleman had been standing at a distance and picking his teeth, his eyes trained on the duo. When Ahir waved to him, he joined them and was introduced as Ahir babu's cousin from a neighbouring village. After some initial pleasantries, they both looked at Dhananjoy with keen interest and asked, 'Now that you are here, Dhananjoy babu, are you going to help our Bansidhar in his investigations?'

In response, Dhananjoy could only look at them blankly and ask, 'What murder? What investigation?'

Taken aback by his genuinely perplexed expression, the two men exchanged glances and then launched excitedly into a lengthy description of the murder that the entire village was abuzz with. The body, it seems, had been found that very morning. A woman's body at that! A cook at the Rajbari. Their garbled account of the incident was rounded off by

Ahir babu's cousin's ominous proclamation about the Rajbari estate. It sounded like something he said often and with relish. Shaking his head, he asserted after spitting out a few bits of betel leaf, 'The Rajbari is accursed, I tell you, Dhananjoy babu. Not a year passes without some incident that leaves everyone reeling with shock.'

'But, Ajay, that's not necessarily a bad thing for us, is it?' the station master countered with a cackle. 'Where would we get all our fodder for gossip and speculation if it were to become a quiet, uneventful place? Fodder we can chew on for months and months? We would probably all die of boredom, don't you think?'

After a while, sensing Dhananjoy's growing restlessness, Ahir said, 'You must be tired after your journey, Dhananjoy babu. Look at us, jabbering away. But Bansi isn't here yet. Maybe there's something holding him up. I have a suggestion. Why don't I ask my assistant, Panna, to accompany you to the daroga's house? It's not that far.'

Several minutes later, as he walked to Bansi's house accompanied by a dour-faced Panna, who had clearly not appreciated being hauled away from whatever he was doing and sent off to chaperone a strange man from the city, Dhananjoy wondered what could possibly have prevented his friend from coming to the station. Was it because of the case that Ahir and his cousin were talking about? Or could it be that Bansi's wife, Saroja, didn't share her husband's enthusiasm about having a random stranger rattling about their house? What if she was a strict follower of the purdah, and resented the very thought of having to welcome a man who wasn't actually a relative? In the city, he had begun to see a few ladies running the gauntlet of mockery and censure, and emerging out of the veil. Some, he had heard, entertained their husband's friends at home. A few bold ones had even started travelling on the train with their husbands or crossing the seas with them. He truly admired them. But how could he possibly expect the same behaviour from a young woman who had never stepped out of Rajapur? How thoughtless of him not to consider these things till now. Had he unwittingly ignited a domestic spat in his friend's house? Is that what had prevented Bansi from coming to the station? Preoccupied with his misgivings, Dhananjoy started a little when Panna pulled up short in front of a house and shouted, 'O Bansi dada, look who's come here all the way from Calcutta to see you.'

And then, to Dhananjoy's immense relief, a young woman, her head covered with the end of her sari, walked out into the courtyard to greet him with a broad, welcoming smile and said, 'Thakurpo, your friend has told me so much about you. He misses you a lot. Why did you take so long to come and meet us?' And with that, she proved all his worries to be unfounded. The mystery of Bansi's absence at the railway station was also soon solved. Daroga Bansidhar, it seemed, had gorged on *luchi* and halwa in the afternoon and, not surprisingly, by the evening, had been prostrated by a terrible pain in his stomach.

With a glint of amusement, Saroja said, 'Ever since your letter arrived, he has been on pins and needles with excitement. Running around and preparing for your visit. But then, there was the murder scene he had to visit in the morning, and when he returned, he just couldn't stop eating.' She continued with a heavy sigh, 'You know, Thakurpo, some people sink their worries in drink. Your friend drowns his in food.'

~

Upon seeing his old friend after fifteen years, all that Bansidhar could muster was a wan smile and a half-hearted embrace before going back to clutching his rather substantial stomach and importuning his dead parents to come and rescue him from the pain. He was sprawled on a *takhtaposh*, moaning, 'Baba go, Ma go,' and vowing from time to time that he would never touch another luchi again in his life.

Dhananjoy was sat next to him in a chair, with his arms folded and a small playful smile on his lips. Glaring at him, Bansidhar bleated, 'Is the hoity-toity inspector from Calcutta amused at my suffering? Is it not enough that he has deigned to visit his oldest and closest friend after fifteen long years? Must he then add insult to injury by cackling shamelessly at my pain?'

Trying in vain to control his laughter, Dhananjoy comforted his offended friend. 'Oh, no, no, not at all. I'm very sympathetic, Bansi. After all, it's not every day that one gets to hear of such Herculean feats! Sixteen luchis, Saroja boudi informs me! You are a true marvel, my oldest and dearest friend! So what if there's a bit of stomach ache? Think of it as a small sacrifice at the altar of the great luchi!'

Bansi continued glowering at his friend. 'Is it my fault that your boudi makes luchis only once in a blue moon? Of course I end up overeating. You know about my weakness for the wretched things.'

Somehow, Bansi managed to look both angry and woebegone. Dhananjoy burst out laughing as he sat watching his childhood friend. 'Yes, Bansi, I know about your weakness for food. That's something I have not forgotten in all these years. But I can also understand why Saroja boudi makes luchis only once in a while.'

Saroja peeped into the room upon hearing her name and then said in an emboldened voice, 'Yes, Thakurpo, please tell your friend that his gluttony will be the end of him someday. I have given up trying to knock sense into his head. Can you see that belly of his? People laugh behind his back and say that the *chor-dakat* of Rajapur sleep peacefully because they know Daroga Bansidhar will never be able to chase them with that huge paunch.'

Bansidhar grimaced as a fresh wave of pain hit him and then huffed like a fractious child. 'Must you also start? Aren't I being punished enough as it is? O Ma, go! Go away now. Let me talk to my friend. His Highness has come to visit me after fifteen long years. Leave us in peace, will you?'

Saroja bristled. 'Who's talking to you? Can't I have something to say to my Thakurpo? But since I'm here, let me tell you, Daroga babu, you are going to get thin gruel for the next two days. Don't even think of protesting. I'll start adding an extra day of gruel for every word of protest that comes out of your mouth. Everything else that I make in the kitchen will be for Thakurpo. He could do with a bit of fattening up. I don't think he gets the time to eat in Calcutta.' And with that, Saroja flounced out of the room.

Sitting near Bansidhar, Dhananjoy felt a little dazed by the fact that he was seeing him after more than a decade. His puny childhood friend had gained a fair bit of weight in the intervening years. But he could still catch glimpses of the round-faced boy he had left behind. All those years ago when most of the other boys of the village pathshala would give Dhananjoy a wide berth or trouble him for being the fearful Lahiri Pandit's son, Bansi, for some reason, had decided to stick by the tall, thin boy's side. He felt protective towards the earnest boy who was slightly younger than him. They had become inseparable – *manikjor* as they were called by the people of the village – and remained so till that fateful day when Dhananjoy left the village with his uncle.

'Can't bear that thin gruel,' Bansi said with a grimace. He looked at his friend and said in a low voice, 'You know, Joy, I would probably not have eaten so much had I not been to the scene of a murder in the morning. I can't describe to you what I felt when I saw that poor, helpless woman lying there on that path like a discarded sack of potatoes. Her legs exposed for the world to see. Those unseeing eyes, the blood. That horrific smell. I didn't really know her well. Heard she had started working as a cook at the Rajbari. But no human being deserves that kind of an end, don't you think, Joy?' After a few minutes of silence, he continued in a sad voice, 'I know what you're thinking. That as a daroga, I should be used to such sights by now. Impervious to them. But I can't put in words the way that body lying there moved me. Young girl, not even twenty, killed and tossed aside like garbage. Why would anyone do that? How can there be such cruelty in this world? I really could not get the image out of my head. And that's why, like a fool, I turned to food for solace. I need to toughen up, right? Do you think there'll ever be a time when I'll be completely indifferent to such things, Joy?'

In truth, Dhananjoy knew exactly what his friend was talking about. In their line of work, every so often, there were things they desperately wished they could unsee. Times when the horror of the scene made it impossible to behave simply as a dispassionate finder of clues like that wretched literary detective everyone raved about. The haughty, all-knowing Sherlock Holmes. Dhananjoy had tried reading a few of the stories and given up in exasperation. No detective worth his salt could remain that detached and clinical. Bansi's distress took Dhananjoy back to the case of the missing children that he had recently solved in Calcutta. Those tiny, frail bodies, murdered and buried callously near the river, had all but wrecked him. At the scene of the crime, he felt grateful that his face had not revealed the emotions that churned his insides. And when he managed to find and arrest the monster responsible, he had assumed that would end all the pain. But then, after a few days, it was as if his body began to rebel. Every so often, he would find himself perspiring and dry-mouthed, or rubbing his eyes furiously to remove the terrible images that lurked somewhere in his peripheral vision. The images even erupted in his dreams so that he began to dread sleep.

Drowning himself in work, Dhananjoy had decided, was the best solution. Work would keep him busy, and in time, the images would fade and take with them the nightmares and the bouts of panic, terror and breathlessness. But the symptoms of his unspoken anguish were in no hurry to fade and did not escape Smithson's attention. Dhananjoy had had a bad feeling when summoned to the boss's office.

With a sombre face, Smithson addressed his brightest recruit. 'Look, Lahiri,' he said, 'you know that I consider you one of my most valuable detectives. There are others who can work hard, find clues, pursue leads like bloodhounds, but you... you, young man, have that something extra that gives you an edge over the others. The bloody Frenchies even have a phrase for it. This indescribable quality that only some people have. In a detective, it is that instinct, a pull of the gut, if you wish to call it that, which separates a great one from just a good one.'

Living as he did in a region known for colic diseases and diarrhoea, Dhananjoy suppressed a smile at the thought that 'pull of the gut' could have very different meanings here. In any case, no such pulls were required – metaphorical or literal – for Dhananjoy to realize that the fulsome praise carried a sting in its tail. He braced himself for whatever unpleasant news Smithson was about to throw at him.

'And that's the reason, Lahiri, I'll have to insist that you take a breather. All these gruesome incidents in this infernal city, all the corpses that you have been seeing on a regular basis... I have a feeling all of it is beginning to get to you.'

He had raised his hand to silence the hot words of protest rising to Dhananjoy's lips. 'No, Lahiri, no. You'll have to do this before it destroys you completely. Believe me, it is for your own good.'

Why, Dhananjoy thought glumly, must people always say that while administering a bitter pill? I'm quite capable of thinking of my own good, thank you very much. If he had his way, he would ban that line from ever being uttered.

Smithson got up from his chair and ambled across to one of the tall windows and looked out at the city that filled him with exasperation and affection in equal measure. After asking Dhananjoy to sit down, he stood with his back to the young Bengali inspector. Dhananjoy was left facing the huge portrait of Stuart Hogg, the founder of the modern Calcutta Police, that was hanging in the room. He couldn't help admiring the man in the portrait for having thought of a separate Detective Department for the Calcutta Police, but those eyes always left him feeling a little unsettled. Dhananjoy examined his hands intently to avoid Hogg's gaze. His ears were trained on what Smithson was saying. 'Lahiri, I've never told anyone about this, but when my brother returned from his stint in the Boer War, he was almost unrecognizable. Do you remember, I had gone to England three years ago to meet my family? More than anything else, I wanted to meet my brother. My brave brother, my hero! What I saw left me aghast. It was like a different person had come back from the war. Three missing fingers, and that was not even the worst of it. His suffering was unimaginable.'

Smithson's voice faltered for a bit under the weight of those memories, but he carried on after a while. 'Breathlessness, hand tremors, nightmares accompanied with soul-wrenching screams. I even saw him trying to gouge his own eyes out because he said he wanted to be rid of the horrific things seared in his eyelids.' Turning towards Dhananjoy, he added softly, 'The reason I'm telling you all this is because police officers also go to a battlefield of sorts every day, don't you think? We see the worst of humanity. The mind needs to recover, Lahiri. Give it some rest. Take some time off. Trust me, there's no shame in it. You can't keep looking into the mouth of hell and expect to remain unscathed. I know you think that working like a bloody machine will make everything all right, but that's not going to do the trick. Besides...'

Smithson stopped again and walked towards where Dhananjoy was sitting. Drawing up a chair close to the detective, Smithson sat down with a loud sigh. Dhananjoy quite liked his boss. Unlike many other British officers that he knew, Smithson never held forth pompously about India's so-called advancement as the result of the efforts of the British. Nor did he believe that civilization had arrived in this country when the ships of the East India Company reached its shores. Not surprisingly, his boss didn't have too many friends amongst his peers. Dhananjoy could clearly see the bags and folds of exhaustion under the eyes of the man who sat in front of him. In the last couple of years, Smithson seemed to have aged a fair bit. His stoop had become more pronounced, and Dhananjoy was certain his forehead hadn't had all those sharply scored worry lines when he had first met him a few years ago. Or the lines that fanned out from the sides of his mouth. Being without any real friends in this strange city would do that to anyone, Dhananjoy thought. That and the mounds of papers and files piled on his boss's table. But why was he looking so grim? He shifted in his seat as he waited for Smithson to speak. Was there something worse that his boss had to tell him?

'Besides,' he continued with a slightly distracted air, 'there's something big brewing on the political front. Between you and me, Viceroy Curzon is bad news. He is both ignorant and arrogant. I have a bad feeling about the kind of things he and his man, Risley, are plotting for Bengal. And for once, pardon me for saying this, Lahiri, even the lugubrious Bengalis seem to have been shaken out of their usual torpor. Champing at the bit to go beyond petitions and pamphlets. Mark my words, there's a storm gathering on the horizon. And when it finally breaks and hits us, I want you by my side, refreshed and ready for action. Chin up, Lahiri. I'm only asking you to take a holiday. Not sending you to the gallows, for god's sake. Go somewhere, get out of this city of dreadful night! It's an order.'

And then, as Dhananjoy was leaving the room, his head whirling with all that he had just heard, Smithson quipped, 'That was Kipling, by the way! Just in case you thought I was turning into a poet in my old age.'

'Sir?' Dhananjoy asked, blinking with confusion.

'That bit about Calcutta as the city of dreadful night. That's Kipling. Apt, isn't it? Go now, before I insist you take a leave of two months. Go celebrate Durga Puja with your family or friends. And try not to sulk and ruin everyone's fun while you're at it.'

'Right-ho, sir,' he said and left the room hurriedly before Mr Smithson could spring any more surprises on him. He felt Hogg's censorious eyes boring into his back as he stepped out of the room.

And so, Dhananjoy knew only too well about the melancholia that had settled around Bansidhar after seeing the brutally bludgeoned body of the young woman. He placed a gentle hand on his shoulder and said, 'No, Bansi, you must never think of outgrowing this side of your personality. It is true that as investigators we must be practical and rational and all the rest of it, but unless we can feel for the victim, what would be the point of being a police officer?'

Bansidhar clutched the hand that was placed on his shoulder. That lean frame, the bright eyes, the unmanageable hair were all so familiar despite the lapsed years. He looked at his friend imploringly.

'Please, Joy, promise me that you'll help me solve this murder. To be honest, I'm not really cut out for such things. At best, I can handle petty thefts or cases of extortion by those *bajaria* crooks who operate in local bazaars and haats. Maybe even some rare case of dacoity. But murder? And on top of that, the victim was a cook in the Rajbari kitchen. Which means I would have to question the high and mighty people of that mansion. Do you really think they will be amenable to the idea of talking at length to someone like me? Orre baba! I need you by my side, Joy. We talk of your achievements with such pride here in Rajapur. I brag to everyone that the famous detective inspector in Calcutta is my best friend. Oh, Ma! Ma Durga! Save me from this pain. Oh!' The pain couldn't have arisen at a better time, giving Bansidhar the opportunity to look pathetic as he grabbed his belly and writhed dramatically.

Keeping his expression as neutral as possible, Dhananjoy patted Bansidhar's shoulder and asked him to rest. Then he stepped out of the room, saying he wanted to sit in the courtyard for a while and smoke a cigarette.

2

A DECISION MADE, AN INVESTIGATION BEGINS

Sitting in the *daaoa*, or courtyard, Dhananjoy gazed at the coconut trees looming like tall, elegant giants over the house and swaying ever so gently. A warm breeze stroked his face. Except for the slight noises made by insects and small animals, there was complete silence. Living in Calcutta, Dhananjoy had all but forgotten what this impenetrable quiet could feel like. And then, as he marvelled at the utter stillness of his surroundings, a couple of bats startled him by making a loud, whirring noise before wheeling away into the night sky. And weren't those fireflies glittering near the bamboo tree? With a smile, Dhananjoy realized that the stillness was illusory; it hid a world of multitudinous noises and movements from the inattentive human ear and eye.

Part of him was still finding it hard to believe that he was back in Rajapur. That peaceful village with its pukurs, trees, his old pathshala, temples and a mosque. It was where Dhananjoy had spent the first decade of his life. Bansi and he – like most other boys in the village, including the station master who had recognized him on the platform despite all the years that had gone by – had studied in the pathshala attached to the Kali temple. Dhananjoy's father was one of the feared pandit moshais. Why was he back here after more than a decade? Was it to test that cliché about time being the greatest healer of wounds? To see whether the memories that he kept a tight lid on still had the power to sting and hurt, like bees released from captivity?

It was close to sixteen years ago that a ten-year-old Dhananjoy had left the village to spend his Durga Puja holidays with his maternal uncle, Nilu Mama, or Mamu as he called him, in Calcutta. While he was in Calcutta, the monstrous cholera epidemic had struck some villages, including Rajapur, and, amongst many others, had claimed Dhananjoy's ma and baba as its victims. When a grey-faced Nilu Mama had given him the news, the ten-year-old Dhananjoy refused to accept what he was saying. What did he mean? Ma and Baba were no more? Had turned into stars who could only gaze down at him from the distant skies? How could that be? Hadn't he seen them just a week ago, smiling at his excited preparations to leave for the big city with his uncle? When it had finally sunk in that he would never see or touch them again, he had felt like breaking everything around him to assuage the pain in his heart. Had his parents sensed the advancing jaws of death and sent him away? Were they protecting him and preparing to face the impending horror themselves? These were questions that began to haunt him afterwards. But in the midst of his crisis, Nilu Mama was the one who had held him close, and assured him that he would never desert him. The two of them had clung to each other like two sailors holding on to a single rock after every familiar fragment of their ship had floated out of sight.

The little boy's wounds had taken a long time to heal to the extent that they could, and Mamu, true to his word, had always been by his side with a heart full of unconditional love. It was he who made sure Dhananjoy had the best education possible at a missionary school in Calcutta, encouraged his nephew's interest in science and not demurred when Dhananjoy had announced he wanted to work in the police department. Perhaps he understood that his nephew saw it as a way to expiate his irrational guilt at not having been around when his parents had suffered and died.

'That's an interesting choice of career, Joy,' Mamu had said. 'I am so glad you have thought of a path for yourself. I can't say I fully understand your reasons for choosing this profession. But that's not important. You have my blessings. I won't insult your intelligence by pointing out that you'll have to work under a British boss, and it may not be a pleasant experience. You know that already. Nor do I need to tell you that it'll be a job full of challenges and risks of the kind that'll be beyond the imagination of most people. But promise me one thing, Joy. Promise me that you will not judge or condemn anything that you come across in your line of work, based on conventional opinions. Right or wrong is not always a simple matter of black and white, son. Truth can be a many-splendoured thing.'

'Isn't it love that's supposed to be many-splendoured, Mamu?'

'Aah, Mr Smarty-pants! So, you do listen when I quote literary lines.' Mamu had smiled and reached up to pat his cheek. 'Your face is usually so impassive that I assume you switch off mentally while your old man rambles on.'

'I remember it because I have always wondered why a man so full of erudite quotes about love has never been able to bring home a wife,' Dhananjoy had said teasingly.

'Arre, what do I need a wife for? Don't you see how happy I am with my life? I have you, I have my friend Rahmat with whom I can sit and talk for hours and I have Robi to cook for me. Why do we need a woman to come in and disrupt this wonderful set-up? The only woman to be welcomed in this house will be your rosy-cheeked bride.'

Dhananjoy couldn't help but laugh when he heard this. Lately, he felt sure that the reason his mamu had never married was because he had taken on the responsibility of raising his orphaned nephew. He winced when he remembered the vicious tantrums he had thrown as a child, to deal with his grief, and how patiently his uncle had managed them. No newly-wedded wife of his uncle's would have hung around to put up with that intemperate child.

'Don't change the subject,' Mamu was saying. 'Leastways, remember what I just said.'

'That's going to be a tall order, Mamu! A police officer must uphold the law.'

'I know that. But just because Lady Justice is blindfolded doesn't mean you can't keep your eyes and mind open. Just something your old mamu wants you to bear in mind.' He had then embraced his nephew, given him his blessings and added, 'Try not to be too hard on yourself, Joy. Some things will always be out of your control.'

A few days ago, when he had told Mamu about his decision to take some time off from work and visit Rajapur, Mamu had reached up to pat his cheek and said with his usual perspicacity, 'You have a good boss in that Smithson, Joy. I am so glad he has asked you to go on a holiday. The grey hollows under your eyes were beginning to worry me as well. And don't try to tell me it's your own decision because I may be growing old, but I am not yet senile.'

~

When Dhananjoy walked back into the house, he could see Bansidhar was fidgety and restless. Clearly, he was dying to find out what his friend had decided. The police detective from Calcutta had thought long and hard about Bansi's request. He felt caught in the crosshairs of his friend's plea and his boss's injunction. But ultimately, the decision he made was not a very difficult one to arrive at. He knew Smithson had been right about his needing a holiday, but his mind craved stimulation that only solving a murder could bring. Surely, his boss didn't want him to return to Calcutta with an atrophied brain rather than a well-rested one.

'Look, Bansi, I'll help you if you want me to. But not in an official capacity. Please keep me away from all kinds of paperwork. I—' Before he could finish the rest of his sentence, Dhananjoy found himself almost knocked over by a fierce bear hug.

'Hurray! I knew it! I knew you wouldn't disappoint your oldest friend.' Stomach ache forgotten, Bansidhar beamed and clapped his hands loudly. When Saroja heard her husband's juvenile expressions of delight in the kitchen, she shook her head and smiled while she sat on her haunches to grind the spices for a special fish curry for Dhananjoy.

~

And so, the very next day, the two friends set off to examine the place where Sarala's corpse had been found. As soon as Bansidhar had announced in the morning that he was feeling fine, Dhananjoy had said in a firm voice that they must not delay the investigation. Bansi's shoulders had slumped a little, but he could see from the set of his friend's jaw that his mind had been made up.

From what Dhananjoy could gather from his exchange with Bansidhar on the way to the scene of the crime, expecting a rich harvest of clues from that place was going to be futile. Nevertheless, he wanted to get a sense of where the body had lain. There had been some rain in the night, and by now, other pairs of feet would have tramped all over the path. Thankfully, it was not a path many people took, so it wasn't going to be a completely hopeless situation.

Bansidhar informed him that when he had done some preliminary enquiries, right after the discovery of the body, he had been told that Sarala was last seen a couple of days ago while walking out of the *dokhin dorja*, or southern gate, of the Rajbari to take the path leading to the village. The dokhin dorja was what the men and women who worked in the mansion used, Bansi informed his friend. Puti, another maid in the zamindar household, had told one of Bansi's *jamadar*s, amidst loud sobs, that Sarala and she had chatted for a while just before the latter set off for the village. The last thing Sarala had said to Puti was that she wanted to reach home before dark. She was afraid of ghosts and terrified of being set upon by vengeful spectres on that path. That was the last time Puti or anyone else could remember seeing the slain girl. Lathiyal Ramhari had also been near the gate and seen Sarala leave.

Of all the people in the Rajbari, only Rakhal babu – Thakurani's brother-in-law – had left the mansion at four p.m., in order to walk to the station and catch a train to Calcutta at five-thirty or so. Seeing Dhananjoy's nonplussed look, Bansidhar explained that Thakurani was what everyone called the zamindar's wife, Radharani. Rakhal babu had, of course, used the *uttor dorja*, or northern gate, as was customary for the family. Later, he had been seen boarding the train by both Panna and the station master, Ahir. So it seemed he had some kind of an alibi.

It took the two policemen about an hour to reach the spot where the young woman's body had been found. On the way, the Calcutta detective, not used to the unpaved *mete rasta* of the village, stumbled once or twice and nearly fell.

Bansidhar couldn't contain his amusement when he heard his friend muttering curses. As they walked, the village daroga slipped effortlessly into the role of guide and pointed out various places where, he said, the two of them had played as children or simply idled away the afternoons. 'Remember that field, Joy? We used to play ha du du there.' Dhananjoy nodded, although much of what Bansidhar was talking about had actually become a blur in his mind. But he didn't mind the sound of Bansi's voice and his descriptions of the places Dhananjoy had left behind all those years ago.

When his friend's voice suddenly petered out, he realized they had reached the crime scene. It was a narrow path flanked by different kinds of trees and dense foliage. Placing his hand on Bansidhar's shoulder, Dhananjoy said, 'Bansi, you can't be silent now. Walk me through everything you saw yesterday. Close your eyes and try to remember all the details of the place when you came here and saw the body for the first time. Don't leave out anything.' When he saw the daroga scratching his head nervously, Dhananjoy told him to take a few deep breaths.

'It's all right. Sit down and think about what you saw. No doubt it was an extremely unpleasant sight. But you need to go back and dwell on it for a while. For the sake of the investigation. Meanwhile, I'll look around and see if anything unusual catches my eye.'

Daroga Bansidhar nodded forlornly and sat under an enormous mango tree to collect his thoughts. The very thought of recalling the scene of the crime made him queasy, but he knew he had to do it. After anxiously primping his drooping moustache for a while, the daroga shut his eyes and cast his mind back.

For any passer-by in the next hour, the two policemen would have presented an intriguing sight. The tall one, with his wild hair and glinting spectacles, bounded about looking closely at bushes, hunkering down to lift things from the ground, or at times even lying down to search for invisible things. Every so often, he would make notes in a red notebook. The short, portly figure, on the other hand, just sat very still with his eyes closed, looking for all the world, like a meditating sanyasi.

In the end, Bansidhar felt quite pleased with what he could remember and report to his friend. Once his eyes were closed and his mind focused, he could recall the way the body was lying, how the hands were placed, which side the head was turned, where the wound had been and how much blood had seeped into the ground. Dhananjoy absorbed all that he said silently and pronounced after some reflection, 'Based on what you're saying, I would conclude that the poor girl was attacked from behind. Someone had crept up behind her while she was walking and then, *Bam!* The weapon hit her head, and she fell to the ground. There are no drag marks. So, she was attacked and killed right here as she was hurrying back home. Which way did you say was her head placed, Bansi?'

Bansidhar shut his eyes once again and then pointed his finger in the direction of the village.

'Why is that important, Joy?'

'I'm just trying to be sure of the direction she was walking in when she was struck. If, as you say, her head pointed that way, and she fell as a result of a surprise blow from the back, isn't it most likely that she was walking in that direction?'

Dhananjoy pointed towards the bamboo grove in the distance, beyond which lay the village. 'One tends to fall on one's face when struck from behind. That means she was definitely moving away from the zamindar's house and going towards her house in the village, right?'

'That's right.'

'So, the chances of the killer being from the Rajbari are the highest, don't you think? I don't see any other house between the estate and that bamboo grove. Would you say this path stays fairly deserted in the late evenings?'

'Yes. There are quite a few stories about brohmodottyis that are supposed to emerge at night and hang around in some of the bel trees here. Few people use it after sunset. To be honest, it's a path that is rarely used by villagers. So, it is used pretty much by the men and the women who work in the Rajbari. Joy, what do you think could have been used to bash her head?'

'The doctor who examined her body should be able to give us some idea about that. In fact, I would like to take a look at the corpse myself.'

Bansidhar looked a little crestfallen. 'The body had already started decomposing, Joy. We had to send it off for cremation. Our village doctor – Daktar babu – doesn't really have any means of preserving corpses. But we are fortunate that Daktar babu, Annada Charan Bandopadyay, practised medicine in Mymensingh before coming here. While he was there, he became familiar with the process of post-mortem.'

'In that case, it's imperative we have a chat with Annada babu. But, here, first take a look at what I found. See these leaves that were left in the depression made by the body? Is there anything you notice about them?'

Daroga Bansidhar looked thrown by that question. What could he possibly tell his friend about those leaves? 'N... no, not really!' Bansi stuttered. 'Why? What's so special about these leaves?'

Dhananjoy made an impatient noise at the back of his throat. 'You need to look carefully at things, Bansi. Do you see any trees or plants around here with leaves of this kind? Look around you.'

'Oh!' Bansidhar's eyes widened as realization dawned. He licked his lips and said, 'Yes, yes, now I see what you mean.

These leaves don't seem to have come from any of these trees or plants. So where did they come from? Do you think the leaves will lead us to anything important?'

Dhananjoy was brushing off mud and stray leaves from his kurta. 'Who knows?' he said. 'As of now, everything that doesn't quite fit in with the surroundings here is important for us. For all you know, it could be utterly useless. On the other hand, it could help unlock some part of the mystery. We have to be patient, Daroga moshai.'

'I understand. Now what? If you feel there's nothing more here, we could stop for a bit and have the *khoimakha* that Saroja has packed for us.'

'All right, let's finish the khoimakha. But after that, you will not think about food for some time.'

Bansidhar looked at his friend sheepishly. Joy was in his element, and food would have to be forgotten for a while. With a sigh, the daroga of Rajapur decided that the gurgles emanating from his stomach would have to be silenced with just the khoimakha. He said in placatory tones, 'Achha, achha, calm down. It's just that I can't think very clearly if I don't eat for too long. Let's finish this quickly, and after that I think I know where you would want to go. To visit the doctor and quiz him about Sarala's corpse, am I right?'

Dhananjoy smiled and punched his friend's shoulder playfully. In a voice that mimicked Smithson's, he said, 'Well done, Daroga Bansidhar! You do have the makings of a fine detective, after all.' And then, even as the two of them laughed, Dhananjoy remembered something. 'On the way back, take me to a local haat. I want to buy a sari.'

Bansidhar looked utterly bewildered. 'A sari? What for? Will we be needing one for our investigation? Are you thinking of donning a disguise of some kind? You can count me out if that's the case. Daroga Bansidhar is not going to wear a sari, come what may. Not even for an investigation. No way.' Bansi shook his head in a manner that showed his fierce determination.

'No, you idiot! For Saroja boudi. With Durga Puja coming up in a few days, the least I can do is buy her a sari. I should have brought one from Calcutta, but then, everything happened in such a rush. Besides, I was also thinking of feasting on some *mishti* and *kochuri* at the haat. Can you think of someone better than my friend to guide me through the local delicacies?' Dhananjoy added the final bit with a knowing smile, which deepened when he saw the glow of pleasure on his friend's face.

3

ANATOMY OF A MURDER

The walk to Daktar babu's house was a pleasant one, and Dhananjoy found himself relaxing as he inhaled the fragrance of the earthy petrichor and gazed at the wide expanse of azure skies. The call to prayer from a mosque nearby filled the air. They had already walked past two pukurs, one of which he vaguely remembered as the *dhhopapukur*, the pond used for washing clothes. Bansidhar reminded him that was where they had learnt to swim and discovered their love for water games. And even as he spoke, a raucous group of boys ran towards the pukur and jumped in with the kind of reckless abandon and laughter that only children are capable of. Soon, their gleeful faces could be seen bobbing in the waters, their wet hair gleaming in the sun. One of the boys grinned at them cheekily and then stuck his tongue out before ducking back into the waters.

When the two men passed a *dighi* bursting with lotus and *shapla* flowers, its unsullied perfection took Dhananjoy's breath away. There was one spot in the water that was not covered by the shimmering blooms (since the water in that part of the dighi, Bansidhar explained, was quite deep), and a lungi-clad man was fishing in it. Catching sight of them, he craned his neck for a better view and then raised a scrawny arm and waved. Bansidhar waved back at him and explained, 'That's Hakim chacha. Even though he's a doctor of sorts, his true passion is catching fish. He can sit there waiting patiently for ages. Even the ducks floating on the dighi have got used to him. But it's better we don't stop to talk to him. The sun will have set by the time he finishes telling us about the different kinds of baits he prepares for the fish here. Three years ago, when Annada Charan had come here, Chacha was dead against his setting up a dispensary in Rajapur. This was despite the fact that it was Thakurani herself who had written to Annada babu and brought him here. He's her first cousin. Hakim chacha tried spreading canards about him. But now they have become such good friends. That happened after Annada babu treated Chacha for the painful sores on his feet. They even consult each other at times. And...' Bansidhar suddenly stopped talking when he noticed that his friend was sitting on his haunches, gazing at the pink lotuses moving in the breeze. After a while, Dhananjoy reached out with a tentative finger to stroke the petals and marvel at the iridescent raindrops balanced perfectly on the round, fan-like leaves. Just as his finger reached the petal, a dragonfly rose and flew away with a whirring of its transparent wings.

Dhananjoy was mesmerized by the watery field of flowers. When did he last have the time to look so closely at something so perfect in its beauty? All he ever did was stare at mutilated bodies to see what clues they could yield. He had made sounds of impatience earlier when Bansidhar had suggested they should walk slowly so Dhananjoy could take in some of the beauty that his childhood village had to offer. Why dawdle to look at ponds and trees? He had simply wanted to reach the dispensary as quickly as possible and talk to the doctor. And yet here he was, unable to resist the pull of that very beauty that he had been so quick to dismiss. But the idyllic charm was not all that the village had to offer, Dhananjoy reminded himself as he stood and brushed off the soil stuck to his dhoti. After all, wasn't he out to investigate the cold-blooded murder of a young woman in these gentle environs?

While crossing what used to be the village school, the pathshala, bittersweet memories of being fed by his mother and walking to school with his father made tears well up in Dhananjoy's eyes. His breathing accelerated as he recalled having little lumps of rice and dal put in his mouth by his mother. She would watch him eat with a tender smile on her face. He could almost feel her fingers as they brushed aside the locks of hair that fell untidily on his forehead. His parents did not have much money, but he had always felt loved and cherished. Dhananjoy shook his head, as if to get rid of all the painful thoughts. Where had they suddenly come from? Without warning, the long-buried emotions had worked their way up from the bottom of his consciousness. When Bansidhar turned to look at him, he quickly averted his eyes and pretended to cough. 'Wasn't there a turmeric field right next to our school?' he asked in a strangely hoarse voice. Realizing that his friend needed some time to steady his emotions, Bansidhar hastily launched into a long and animated description of the place.

'Yes, yes, Joy! You remember that? It was owned by Jaymohan Ghosh. That's gone now, as you can see. Jaymohan khuro died, and his sons sold the land. There's a brick kiln in its stead. That place there, where you can see all those *bherenda* plants growing, was where we used to sit for our classes.'

Bansi's artless prattle had the desired effect. Looking much calmer, Dhananjoy asked, 'Is that a temple on the other side?'

'Yes, that's a small temple dedicated to the Goddess Kakaichandi. She looks a lot like Kali, but the villagers believe this goddess protects travellers who have to navigate difficult terrains and inclement weather. Legend has it that several decades ago, a traveller, while returning home in the dark, lost his way in a forest and appealed to the goddess and she appeared in front of him as a girl. Apparently, she then struck stones together to create light for him and illuminated the entire forest.'

'That's an interesting story. Do the villagers actually believe all that?'

With a wry smile, Bansidhar said, 'As much as you would believe Pythagoras's theorem that Pandit moshai talked about in his classes.' Dhananjoy couldn't help laughing uproariously at that. He remembered how tough his father's classes were for most of his classmates at the pathshala.

Bansidhar watched his friend laugh and then wondered whether Dhananjoy might be interested in finding out about the state of his *bhhite*, his childhood home, built by his grandfather. Most of it had decayed and disintegrated or succumbed to a rapacious pipal tree that had all but consumed it. But parts of it had withstood the ravages of time and seemed to stand as a sad memorial to a beloved home. Every time Bansidhar walked past those ruins, he would stand still and remember running around in the courtyard of that house with Joy. But just now, having seen the depths of pain on his friend's face and his futile struggles to hide his emotions, the daroga decided that it was best not to bring it up unless Dhananjoy asked him about his old house.

The rest of their journey to the dispensary was completed by both men in a pensive frame of mind. The silence was broken only when Annada Charan's dispensary loomed into view. Bansidhar said, 'There he is. There's Annada babu. Oh, he's talking to Sijad. Remember we saw Hakim chacha a little while ago? Sijad's his grandson.'

'Does he work at the dispensary?'

'Not quite. Hakim chacha wants him to become a doctor like our Daktar babu and get a degree from Calcutta Medical College. And Sijad is completely obsessed with the idea of moving to Calcutta. He becomes all dreamy-eyed at the mere thought of spending his life in that crowded city with all the excitements it has to offer. Personally, I've never been able to understand the charm. Why would anyone want the dust, smoke and jostling crowds of a city when they can have all this?' Bansi had spread out his arms to indicate that by 'this' he meant nature's bounty all around them. 'But to each his own. So, you'll find Sijad hanging around the dispensary quite often and picking Annada babu's brains. There, Daktar babu has seen us. Look, he's waving.'

Annada Charan had an open and friendly face, although a pugnacious jawline and the dark furrows from the corners of his nostrils to the corners of his mouth hinted at a life that had thrown several challenges and disappointments his way. He couldn't have been more than forty, but his hair was already thinning and streaked with grey. With a beak-like nose, small, darting eyes and quick movements, he gave Dhananjoy the impression of a bird dressed in a crumpled dhoti and *chadar*. After the introductions were over, he led them inside, to a sparsely furnished, small room built next to the dispensary. Beside a large almirah bursting with medical books and journals, the room had two chairs and a stool. Despite its size, it was a clean, cheerful room with a large window that allowed sunlight to stream in and light up all the corners. Bansidhar insisted that Daktar babu and their guest from Calcutta sit on the two chairs. He sat on the stool, while young Sijad rolled out a *madoor* and sat on it. Dispensing with any further niceties, Dhananjoy turned to the doctor with his questions.

'Tell us, Annada babu, what were your thoughts when you examined the corpse?'

Rather than feel offended, the doctor smiled at the young man's impatience. 'I can see that Dhananjoy babu believes in getting straight to the point.' After that, he continued with a solemn expression, 'To be honest, Dhananjoy babu, I was devastated to see the young woman with her head smashed like that. I have seen Sarala off and on, ever since I came to this village. In fact, a couple of months ago, she had come to me with an injured foot. She had stepped on something sharp near the staircase inside the Rajbari – if my memory serves me right, a nail – and the bleeding just wouldn't stop. She was quite brave, didn't even wince when I administered the tincture. It didn't take long to heal after I took care of it. And now this! She didn't deserve to be killed and left on the road in that manner. No one left in her family to mourn her death either...'

The doctor fell silent for a while but then collected himself and said, 'Pardon me, my mind had wandered off. Let's get down to business. Who knew when I came here from Mymensingh that I would be asked to perform an autopsy here. I thought my autopsy-performing days were over. You know, Dhananjoy babu, the surgeon I aided in the Mymensingh Hospital was a complete bastard. Pardon my language, but no other word would describe him better. A fellow called Dr Compson, who hated Indians. For no reason. He just did. I once saw him kick a ward boy with his booted foot till the poor fellow's spleen was ruptured. How, it made you wonder, could a doctor be so cruel? Aiming his kick where he knew it would do the maximum damage. Mind you, this same doctor's face crumpled with sympathy when injured British soldiers were brought in. But then you realized that the answer was easy. He didn't really see that native boy as a human being. And do you know what he hated more than Indians?'

After asking the question, Annada babu stopped and looked at each member of his audience for effect. To

Dhananjoy, he seemed more than ever like a bird turning its head this way and that, searching for a worm, beady eyes shining brightly. When there was no answer forthcoming, the doctor continued dryly.

'Well, if there was one thing he loathed more than Indians, it was Indian doctors. The very idea of young Indian men with medical degrees made him seethe with resentment. But there's no denying that he was an absolute wizard with the scalpel. I owe my own skills with the scalpel, such as they are, to that scoundrel. His autopsies were conducted with such precision and attention to detail. It really was like watching an artist at work. But I'm glad Radhu wrote to me and asked me if I would be interested in opening a dispensary here for the people of Rajapur. I call Radharani Radhu. That's Thakurani I'm talking about, Dhananjoy babu. She's my first cousin. I think most people here have forgotten she has a name other than Thakurani. Anyway, it was she who wrote to me. Little did she know that she was the one doing me a favour. I would have given anything to get away from that monster. Sorry, I know I'm getting carried away. Anyway, it's because of what I learnt from him that I could perform Sarala's autopsy. It brought back so many memories. I'm sure Dhananjoy babu wasn't expecting to find someone like me in this neck of the woods. Let's hope my autopsy-performing skills haven't rusted and I can give you some helpful information.' He exhaled loudly through his mouth, cracked a few knuckles and then began, 'All right. Enough chit-chat. Now for the corpse. Sijad, can you please get me the blue notebook I keep on my study table?'

When the earnest young man got him the notebook, Annada Charan quickly riffled through the pages and then, after clearing his throat, began to speak. Dhananjoy had his own red notebook ready and sat bolt upright with a fiercely attentive expression on his face. Looking at him, Bansidhar suddenly had a memory flash of his friend sitting in a similar way in the pathshala. Unblinking like the Mahabharata's renowned Arjun, who had gazed with fierce attention at the eye of the fish. Other boys would twitch and stare wistfully out of windows, at the fields outside. But not Joy.

Berating himself for letting his mind wander at such a crucial moment, Bansidhar focused on what the doctor was saying. 'I examined the body quite carefully and made notes of the possible things that might help your investigation. For one, the state of decomposition suggested that she had been dead for close to a day before the body was found. I'm afraid I can't be more exact than that. The next thing is that she was struck on the back of her head. I am certain that the murder weapon was a brick. After looking at the wound quite carefully, I managed to retrieve tiny shards of one. She seems to have been completely unprepared for the blow. The position of the wound suggests that the killer was taller than her. But then, Sarala was a short, slight person. Most people, especially men, would have been taller than her. Her assailant arched their arm back powerfully and brought the brick down on her head. My conjecture is he might have made some slight noise to stop her in her tracks. And when she stopped, the blow fell with perfect accuracy. Even if she survived for a couple of minutes, she wouldn't have been in any state to move. No signs of struggle. I searched her fingers to see if there were any defensive wounds. Couldn't find any. No broken fingernails either to suggest she fought her assailant. The killer sneaked up on her from behind like a coward and then hit her with the brick with all his might and finished her off. Suggests a lot of rage.'

'And yet the violence was not really of a frenzied kind, don't you think?'

'Why do you say that, Joy?' Bansidhar asked.

'Well, simply because there was only one blow. Would an out-of-control killer have stopped at one? Wouldn't there have been repeated blows or kicks to the head? Nothing of the sort here.'

'That's true. And yet, the one blow was a fairly powerful one. Her skull had caved in slightly because of the impact.'

From the corner of his eyes, Dhananjoy could see young Sijad squirm. He looked pale. The lurid details of the autopsy were probably hard for him to stomach. Dhananjoy turned towards him and said, 'Maybe Sijad can join us some other day. We need to keep this information to ourselves, don't we, Bansidhar?'

The young man looked quite relieved at being given this opportunity for a dignified exit. After darting a look at the doctor, he sprang up, bid them all a hurried farewell and then left the room hastily.

'Before you go on, Daktar babu, can I ask you a couple of questions?' Dhananjoy leaned forward in his chair with eyes that seemed to glitter through his spectacles.

'Yes, of course. Go ahead.'

'Are you completely certain that the assailant was a man? Could a woman not have done this? Are you saying we should rule that possibility out entirely?'

Annada Charan raked his hair with his fingers and gave the question serious thought. 'So, you want to know if it would have been physically possible for a woman to have struck this fatal blow? Or are you asking me if I think a woman could be capable of this kind of rage?'

'Well, now that you say it, why don't you answer both those questions.'

'My answer would be yes. Yes, I feel a woman can become as angry, as vengeful, as desperate as any man. I know we would like to believe that womenfolk are gentle and capable of only the most delicate sentiments, but since you ask, I think women can also feel murderous rage, as much as men. Doesn't happen often, thankfully. They have enormous reserves of patience.

But given the right motivation, who can tell? As I said a few minutes ago, Sarala was fairly petite. Quite a few women would have the required height and strength to kill her with a brick. Especially since the assailant took her by surprise.'

'Really, Annada babu?' Bansidhar yelped with horror. 'You feel that a woman could have done this?'

'Why so shocked, Bansidhar? Think of our goddesses. We seem to have no problem worshipping violent women. Durga, Kali, Chamundi. Surely if we can imagine our goddesses as killers... Anyway, I am a man of science. Dhananjoy babu asked me a question, and I feel it is my duty to answer it in the most rational manner possible. In fact, I will be adding something in a bit, from my findings, which will strengthen what I've just said. But first, let's hear what Dhananjoy babu's second question is.'

'I wanted to ask you this. Can we say with a fair amount of certainty that this is premeditated murder and not one committed in a sudden fit of fury?'

Annada Charan smiled. 'From what I've heard, Sarala would take that route while going back home on a fixed day. Once every five days, I am told. Looks like her killer was aware of that. Seems unlikely that someone would just lurk there on the off chance that she would walk by. If you're asking me, I don't think this was spontaneous or unplanned. Quite the opposite, in fact. The rest, of course, will be Bansidhar's and your job to find out.'

Dhananjoy folded his arms. 'There's another possibility, though. She might have met her killer in the dark somewhere and then started walking away. It could have been a meeting which ended in an altercation. Maybe the killer didn't like what she had to say and decided to follow and attack her. You are certain it was just one blow that killed her?'

'Yes, fairly certain. I examined the wound quite carefully. It was one crushing blow that killed the poor girl.'

Annada Charan gazed at them for a few moments and then said, 'Well, you have your work cut out, don't you? But let me add a couple of things that will stir things up a bit more.'

'What? There's more?' Bansidhar's voice came out like a strangled squeak. Consternation was writ large on his face.

Dhananjoy's eyes, however, were glinting with something akin to excitement even though he forbore speaking. Annada Charan could see, with a certain degree of wry amusement, that, unlike his friend, the inspector from Calcutta liked complicated puzzles.

'Two things. From my examination of Sarala's stomach contents, it was clear to me that someone had tried to poison her.'

Bansidhar couldn't contain himself when he heard this. 'What! What do you mean, Daktar babu? Poison? But Sarala died of a blow to her head, right?'

'Yes, yes, Bansidhar, she did. And yet I would be lying if I didn't report all my findings, wouldn't I? There were some poisonous leaves in her stomach. Dhatura, if I'm not mistaken.'

Bansidhar turned to Dhananjoy with the look of someone completely at sea.

'Joy, what does this mean? Why would someone try to poison that poor widow and also hit her on the head?'

Dhananjoy tapped his chin as he thought of what the doctor had revealed. 'Unless there were two killers. Two people who wanted her dead and went about it in different ways. Or a killer who wanted to be doubly sure? Belts and braces?' His mind raced and then shifted inexorably to the next question. 'Daktar babu, is this why you haven't dismissed the possibility of a woman being the killer? Because the poisonous leaves could have been easily administered by a woman? And made Sarala that much easier to attack?'

Annada Charan smiled approvingly. 'That's right; that's exactly what I meant. But the amount was not much. I would imagine it would have made her slightly groggy or given her a pleasant kind of light-headedness.'

'Yes, I see what you mean. Oh, wait, Annada babu, can I show you something?'

Dhananjoy drew out a few leaves from between the pages of his red diary and showed them to Annada Charan. 'Do these look familiar in any way?'

'Of course! The very leaves that I found in her stomach. Dhatura. You found them near where her body had lain?'

Dhananjoy nodded.

'Nothing about this case seems very straightforward, does it? The leaves weren't even concealed as part of some food that she ate. This suggests that she might have taken them herself. Why, though? In any case, that's not what killed her. The blow did. The leaves, as I said, would have just made her somewhat unsteady on her feet.' After saying all this, Annada Charan made to get up from his chair, but Dhananjoy said quickly, 'Wait, Daktar babu, didn't you say you had two things you wanted to tell us?'

'Indeed, I did. But don't you think we all deserve a little tea break? Our friend here is looking quite ashen-faced. What do you say, Bansidhar, to a cup of aadaa chaa?'

4

REVELATIONS AND RESOLVES

'Oh, yes, yes! Please let's have some tea.' Bansidhar puffed his cheeks and blew out a long and loud breath. He could feel the blood beating in his ears and his palms getting clammy. While one part of Bansidhar felt guilty at having lumbered his friend with a case at a time when he was meant to have a holiday, another part felt happy that he was able to enlist Joy's help. This case was doing his head in. Give him a common robbery any day over this. So many unanswered questions! What did it all mean? He definitely needed some nourishment before the doctor gave them what he hoped would be the final shock of the day.

Annada Charan made the tea himself and was surprisingly fussy over serving it to them in the right cups and saucers. In the tiny kitchen area that he had created in the room, he paced about, looking for appropriate crockery. Finally, bone china cups were located, and tea was poured out. Some savoury snacks – *nimki*s – and biscuits were arranged on a saucer and kept on the table. Bansidhar could see Dhananjoy's leg jiggling up and down with mounting impatience. Daktar babu knew he had a captive audience and had decided to string the suspense out for a bit. After making quite a production of the tea-making and serving, he finally settled down in his chair with a satisfied smile.

And then, between sips of tea, he said to the two police officers, 'Okay, I think I've tortured Dhananjoy babu long enough. It is time to reveal my final discovery. I also found that Sarala Dasi was pregnant. Close to three months. Give or take.' After saying this, he sat back and added, 'That's all. That would be the sum and substance of my findings.'

Even Dhananjoy was brought up short by this piece of information. Bansidhar, who had been holding his breath while the doctor spoke, released it slowly upon hearing this. The biscuit he had dunked in the tea was forgotten, and it fell back into the hot liquid with a tiny plop. Normally when this happened, the daroga would feel miserable. But on this occasion, it barely registered with him. After looking blank with shock for a while, his face soon became distorted in an expression of revulsion. 'She was a brahmin widow! Pregnant! How could she? Utterly disgraceful.'

With a tightening of his jaw, Annada babu countered, 'I am a man of science, Daroga babu, and for me there is nothing unnatural about this. Whatever the shastras might say, how can a young, healthy woman not have or not want to fulfil normal physical desires? But maybe I'm getting ahead of myself. She could also have been forced. Who knows what happened? I can only tell you what I found in the autopsy.'

'Tell me, Daktar babu,' Dhananjoy asked the doctor, 'would Sarala have gone to someone to get her pregnancy confirmed? A dai in the village, perhaps? I'm assuming she didn't come to you?'

'No, she didn't come here.' Annada Charan scratched his throat and added, 'She might have gone to a local midwife. There are a couple of them in the village. Why do you ask?'

'Just wondering how she was going to deal with her pregnancy. Was she thinking of an abortion? We will need to talk to the midwives and see if she had approached anyone.'

'She might even have gone to a dai in a different village,' Bansidhar suggested. 'Taken Haridasi's help. The Boishnobi goes everywhere and knows all kinds of people. If Sarala wanted a quiet abortion and to avoid public calumny, she might have done just that. I will try to find out. Haridasi can be quite elusive, though. Gadding about and never in one place for long. She hasn't been seen in the village for some time now. But I will get my men to start searching.' The news of Sarala's pregnancy had suddenly made Bansi rancorous towards womankind. Lip curled, he added, 'I'll never understand women!'

When Dhananjoy's brow continued to remain furrowed, Bansidhar asked him what was bothering him.

'I am wondering if this was the reason why Sarala got killed. Wouldn't the people of the Rajbari be paranoid about a scandal?'

The doctor dug the heels of his hands into his thighs and rose from his chair with a grunt. 'That will thankfully be Bansi's and your job to find out. My work finishes here, gentlemen. I hope I have been of some help. Bansi, my friend,' he said, clapping him on the shoulder, 'try not to look like the skies have fallen on your head.'

Bansidhar managed to produce a watery smile. The doctor was right. His head was spinning after hearing everything that had been said. All he wanted to do now was go home, eat and lie down for a while. It felt as though he had been thrown into a boat, without oars, on a river with strong currents and whirlpools. How was he going to solve the murder of a young, pregnant widow who had worked in the Rajbari? The very thought of unearthing scandals and secrets in that place made panic bubble within him. Why was Ma Durga doing this to him on the eve of her grand arrival and Puja? He felt deeply relieved when the doctor indicated that he had nothing more to add. The two policemen thanked Annada babu and set off for the haat.

Standing at the door of his dispensary and waving farewell to the two men, the doctor also heaved a sigh of relief. He felt troubled by the fact that he had not been entirely truthful with them. Well, he straightened his back and assured himself that as far as his autopsy findings were concerned, there was nothing he had concealed. Wasn't that all they were interested in? They only saw him as a reliable dispenser of medical information about the body. And he had fulfilled that role. His face, he hoped, had successfully camouflaged his panic when Sarala's pregnancy was being discussed. Or was he betrayed by that damned telltale twitch of his left eyelid? Those piercing eyes of the Calcutta detective seemed to miss little. Feeling a wave of exhaustion rise through him, Annada Charan rubbed his brow wearily before going back inside his dispensary.

~

Dhananjoy had seen the expression of suppressed anxiety on Bansidhar's face and decided that he needed to take his friend's mind off the investigation for a while. They would visit the haat so Bansi's mood would lighten. The haat, when they reached it, was heaving with people. Dhananjoy almost ground to a halt in despair when confronted by the sea of humanity. But once he got over his initial annoyance at being jostled and elbowed, he began to take the crush in a good spirit. It was part of the mood of that pullulating hub of commerce. He observed the myriad activities around him with keen interest and felt it all seemed vaguely familiar. The sounds, sights and smells – the neatly arranged shoes, lamps, knives, bangles, umbrellas on sale, oleographs of languid European women cheek by jowl with prints of Hanuman carrying the mountain, acrobatic men with heavy loads balanced on long sticks on their shoulders, astrologers and soothsayers waiting patiently with their caged parrots, the flute seller shouting for attention, handkerchiefs with Queen Victoria's face printed on them, young men buying soaps and pomade, sounds of fierce haggling over prices of lungis, dhotis and *gamchha*s – everything filled him with a sense of déjà vu. And exhilaration. He had always thought he had an insuperable aversion to crowded places. But being in the haat was lifting the corners of his mouth, and he couldn't shake off a strong feeling that he had spent some happy moments in a similar place at some point in his life. Could it have been with his father?

It took longer than they had expected since neither of the men could decide which sari Saroja would like. It was only after the surly stall-owner wagged his finger and sprayed them with flecks of spit as he shouted, 'Hurry up, will you? Am I supposed to waste the entire day selling one sari to the two of you?' that they hurriedly settled for a red one with green stripes. The excitement of the thronging crowds of shoppers and hagglers was quite infectious, and Dhananjoy noticed that by the time they finished eating the kochuri and mishti, his friend looked like his usual buoyant self. The earlier panic had ebbed.

But while they were in the haat, at some point, Dhananjoy had begun to have a strange feeling of being watched. Although, every time he turned around, he couldn't be sure. Was it that man with his head wrapped in a turban? Or the one with the flamboyant eyebrows and moustache, who melted away into the crowd as soon as their eyes met? Was his imagination going into overdrive, or was the man sitting and feeling the cloth of the displayed dhoti darting looks at him from time to time? When he shared his unease with Bansidhar, his friend brushed it off with a laugh. 'Arre baba, so many people in the village know that you are here. It's not every day that we get inspectors visiting us from Calcutta, do we? Can you blame people for gaping a little? Some might even be trying to connect you to the child they had seen all those years ago. And then, there are those who will stare at anyone who looks like an outsider.'

Was that all that it was? Nothing more than curious stares? Why then was the hair standing at the back of his neck telling Dhananjoy otherwise? Or was it simply another attack of panic like the ones he had begun to experience in Calcutta? The feeling of unease was forgotten for a while when he had his toes trod on. The irate words that sprang to his lips had to be swallowed when he realized that in the constantly moving crowds of people, there was no one individual he could buttonhole and curse.

But the uneasy feeling of being shadowed returned as they walked back home in the dusk, with Bansidhar chattering nineteen to the dozen and telling him about the ways in which the village was gearing up for the Durga Puja celebrations. Unlike in the morning, when his friend's voice had helped take the edge off his pain, in the growing darkness, Bansidhar's monologue did little to ease his alarmed palpitations.

Before long, a three-quarter moon began to cast eerie shadows. The mighty trees that had seemed so reassuring in the morning now appeared full of menace. The shrill chorus of the cicadas started to press down on them from all sides. The dark seemed to be throbbing with all kinds of invisible, sinister creatures. Was that a snake he could feel slithering slimily over his toes? While Bansidhar remained blithely unconcerned, Dhananjoy felt his body tense. He clenched his fists to stop a slight tremor that he could feel starting in his fingers. And it was while he was making an effort to calm his nerves and listen to Bansidhar's words that it happened! A large stone seemed to come flying out of nowhere and hit Dhananjoy on the back of his shoulder. '*Uff, Ma*,' he cried, clutching the spot where the stone had hit him, and slumped to the ground.

'What! What was that! Who's there?' Bansidhar cried out and then began looking all around him to see where the stone could have come whizzing from. But before he could make any attempt to nab the stone-thrower, a figure dashed out from behind one of the trees and scampered off into the darkness, right before their stunned eyes. Dhananjoy could feel blood oozing out from the wound and soaking the sleeve of his kurta. It had also started hurting like hell. Wincing with pain, he said, 'Bansidhar! Let him go. I think we need to go back home. There's no way you will be able to catch him in the dark.' Bansidhar helped his friend up, and the two of them managed to hobble back to the house.

Grabbing a lantern, Bansidhar rushed off to fetch Annada Charan and when Daktar babu came and saw what had happened, he muttered, 'You've had a very lucky escape, Dhananjoy babu. If the stone had hit you on your head...' Hearing this, Bansidhar wrung his hands and looked like he was about to burst into tears. Saroja, who had been listening to the doctor's voice from outside the room, walked in, her head covered with the end of her sari, and said in a low voice, 'Daktar babu, why don't you explain to me what medicines and balms need to be administered to Thakurpo? I'll make sure he's on his feet as soon as possible.'

'Yes, Saroja ma, I think that would be a good idea. Your husband looks more rattled than the patient himself. I will show you exactly how to take care of the wound. The cut is superficial, thankfully, but it does need attention. Today is Chaturthi, the fourth day of Durga Puja, am I right? I have a feeling that by Ashtami, the eighth day, our friend here will be up and about. But only if you take adequate rest, sir. No gallivanting around looking for clues and leads.'

'Have you seen Boudi's grim face? I am pretty sure gallivanting is not going to be much of an option.' Dhananjoy looked at the doctor with a weak smile.

While leaving, Annada Charan turned to Dhananjoy one last time and said, 'So, Dhananjoy babu, what do you think? The news that you are here sure seems to have put the wind up some people. In the words of that great detective everyone talks about... what's he called? Holmes? The game is afoot.'

Dhananjoy mustered a smile and said, 'Yes, Annada babu, the game sure seems to be afoot. And according to my Mamu, that line is originally from a Shakespearean play.'

'Aah, is it? Why am I not surprised? Most memorable lines in that language are, aren't they? Anyway, you need to be careful. Take rest now. I'll come and check up on you after a few days.'

~

On the morning of Panchami, Dhananjoy woke up to some strange sounds that he couldn't recall ever hearing before. The shoulder wound was still aching, and the unrelenting banging made his heart pound. What was it? When Saroja came to his room with a cup of tea, she took one look at his mournful expression and giggled helplessly. 'Thakurpo, I'm sure you have heard this noise in your childhood. On the fifth day of the Puja, the women of the village get together and pound *chnire*, or flattened rice, and all kinds of other stuff on the *dhhneki*.* That's because from Shashti till Lakshmi Puja, the

---

* Dhhneki refers to a husking pedal, usually operated by women with their feet. *Dhaaki* refers to the person who plays the musical instrument *dhaak* during Durga Puja.

dhhneki can't be touched. They have to finish all the pounding by tonight. So, all of them keep at it tirelessly. But don't worry, you won't hear this tomorrow.' And then, just when Dhananjoy slumped back onto the pillows looking relieved, she added with a mischievous smile, 'From tomorrow, you'll only hear the *dhaaki* playing the *dhaak*.' She left the room quickly after that, shoulders heaving with laughter, leaving him to clutch his head and groan.

But despite the medley of sounds, by Ashtami, Dhananjoy did start feeling much better. Annada Charan had been right in his prognosis. When Dhananjoy mentioned this to Saroja, she beamed delightedly.

'We were feeling so terrible about leaving you alone and going off to see the festivities. Oh, you should have been there, Thakurpo! We wait for the entire year for these few days when the goddess will leave her husband and visit her natal home. Don't you love the idea of celebrating Uma's return to her parents' house after a year! Every time Durga Puja approaches, I can just visualize Uma's mother weeping inconsolably because she has not seen her daughter for so long. And then, she gets the news that her daughter will be arriving soon with all her grandchildren in tow! Can you imagine the joy of being reunited with one's child? Perhaps it's something only mothers can feel! That pull of the umbilical cord.'

Saroja paused with a breathy exhalation, and her expression suggested she might have been thinking of her own mother. But she brightened up when Dhananjoy asked her for a description of the Rajbari celebrations. The next hour was spent talking about the elaborately designed *chaalchitra*, *arati*, the magnificent *beloyari* chandelier, the sindoor-slathered *chalkumro* as a stand-in for the sacrificial goat and the grand feast where people always ate till they were full to bursting.

'Why the pumpkin sacrifice? Why not a goat?'

'Oh, that's because our Thakurani is a Boishnob. Her father had become a Boishnob when she wasn't even born. In fact, that's why he named her Radharani. Three years ago, after her husband's accident, when she took over the running of the estate, she stopped the animal sacrifice during Puja. Some people did grumble, but I think they soon realized that she wasn't about to cave in.'

Bansidhar had entered the room a few minutes earlier and stood listening to his wife while darting anxious glances at his friend. Feelings of guilt and anger had been gnawing at his insides ever since he saw Joy bleeding and helpless. Dhananjoy saw the lines of concern etched on his friend's face and felt a powerful rush of affection for him. Underneath the changed exterior was the same boy who had put worms inside the schoolbag of one of their classmates who had dared to shove Dhananjoy into a pile of cow dung.

'Arre, Bansi, come and sit here. Sit next to me. Stop worrying, will you? Thanks to Saroja boudi's stern-eyed ministrations, I am feeling so much better. She is the kind of cook who can make even a plain *khichuri* taste like manna from heaven. And now, after hearing her descriptions of the Puja celebrations, I am feeling even more energized. Your wife sure has a way with words. Everything came to life as she described it. A grand cook and a raconteur! Where did you find this gem, Bansi?'

'*Thhak! Thhak!* Stop! Enough flattery. You are a worse liar than your friend, Thakurpo! I know you are saying all this simply because you are raring to get back to the investigation,' Saroja said with mock anger even as she blushed with pleasure at her Thakurpo's compliments.

On Dashami, the tenth and final day of the Durga Puja, after the festivities were over and everyone looked exhausted and fulfilled at the same time, Dhananjoy drew Bansidhar aside and said, 'Bansi, we have wasted enough time. If you want this investigation to be done properly, we have to begin questioning the people of the Rajbari. We can't afford any further delays. I usually like interviewing people at a time when their responses are unsullied by too much thinking.'

Bansidhar nodded solemnly and agreed that they would have to visit the Rajbari the very next day. 'I have made enquiries in the village, and it seems Sarala Dasi spent most of her time at the estate. She would visit her house in the village once a week, at best. I think the Rajbari is where we will be able to find answers to the mystery of her murder.'

'In a way that's good, isn't it? Our circle of suspects will be a limited one. Not the entire village.'

Bansi released a long breath through his teeth. 'Yes, but let's see how willing they will be to talk to us. Baap re! Am I glad to have a Calcutta detective inspector going there with me. It would have been the devil's own work to get those high and mighty people to take a local daroga seriously. Besides, my greatest fear is that my mind will go blank and my tongue will turn leaden when faced with the inhabitants of that estate.'

'Don't go down that road, Bansi. We are out to get justice for a poor young woman whose life was cut short by a vicious blow to her head. The coward who did this to her hit her from the back. We will ask questions because we want to find out the truth and because we are acting on behalf of that murdered girl. The world might judge her in different ways, but for us, she is the victim of a ruthless murder, that's all. As police officers, that's what we need to bear in mind. The victim of a murder deserves justice and that's the reason we have to ask uncomfortable questions. The social status of the witnesses and suspects is of no interest to us. Let's clear our heads of everything else and give our full attention to the task ahead.'

Bansidhar squared his shoulders, straightened his uniform and felt somewhat reassured after hearing these words. There was nothing for it but to move on. At the same time, he couldn't quite shake off his sense of relief at the thought of having Dhananjoy by his side while visiting the grand estate.

5

THE RAJBARI

As the two friends walked towards the Rajbari the next day, Dhananjoy asked Bansidhar about Thakurani, the zamindar's wife, whom they were going to meet. It was not usual for a woman to be running a large estate. How did Zamindar Ballabh Ray become confined to his bed?

Bansidhar was silent for a few minutes before he began. 'Radharani debi or Thakurani, as she is to most of us, has had quite a chequered life, you know. She was very young when she was married to Ballabh Ray. Couldn't have been more than ten. She came to live here only after she turned fifteen, though. She was the apple of her father's eye, and he didn't want her to leave his house before she was fifteen. Anyway, everyone thought she would have the perfect life of a queen, for she had married a man who was as rich as Kuber, the god of wealth. Well, I don't know about Kuber, but Ballabh Ray was a real brute who revelled in humiliating and inflicting pain on the people around him. Had every vice that you can think of and he didn't believe in hiding his philandering ways either. From what I have heard, Thakurani's life turned into a living hell once she started living with him. Those who saw her at the time would say that she looked like a pale ghost walking about listlessly in the immense household. No traces of joy on the face of the woman whose wedding had aroused such envy!'

'But didn't her doting father know any of this about the man his daughter was getting married to? How could he have pushed her into the arms of such a brute? Simply because of his wealth?'

'I'm not completely sure. The groom and bride's fathers were very good friends, of course. That's how the match happened. Maybe at the time of the wedding, Ballabh Ray hadn't quite turned into the full-fledged brute that he did once his father died. Dhurjoti Ray knew how to keep his son on a leash. Unfortunately, he died within two years of the wedding, and after that the son didn't take long to turn into a wilful beast. We assume happiness follows inevitably on the heels of wealth, but that's not always the case, is it?'

Bansidhar sighed heavily as he contemplated the weightiness of his own observation about the vagaries of life. The expression on his friend's face remained unreadable.

'And then what happened?' Dhananjoy prodded.

'Well, this was the state of affairs for some years. Then came the fateful day, around three years ago, that changed everything. Ballabh Ray was thrown off his old horse while attempting a brazen leap over a fallen tree and suffered such severe spinal injuries that all the doctors who came to see him shook their heads in despair. In fact, that was when Thakurani called her cousin, Annada Charan, to come and take a look at her husband. Later, once she started managing the estate, she asked Annada babu to move to Rajapur and open a dispensary for the people here. She knew he wasn't happy working in Mymensingh. That his boss was a nasty piece of work.

'At any rate, nothing bore fruit as far as Ballabh Ray's damaged spine was concerned. Thakurani even got an English doctor to come and see him but all in vain. Maybe this was some kind of divine justice. The man who had trampled ruthlessly on everyone was finally laid up in bed, completely immobilized.'

Bansidhar was beginning to feel a little short of breath, and even Dhananjoy thought wistfully of the horse-drawn *ekka gari*s of Calcutta. They had walked for nearly a mile, and there was still some way to go before reaching the Rajbari. The rays of the sun were beating down on their heads, and not a single cloud was to be seen in the clear October skies. A slightly fetid though not entirely unpleasant smell arose from the brackish waters of the dighi. Both men had begun to sweat and decided to rest inside a copse next to the path they were walking on.

After a while, Dhananjoy leaned back on the sturdy trunk of the aged tree he was sitting next to and urged Bansidhar to carry on with his tale.

'Well, after the accident, everyone assumed that Thakurani would leave the managing of the estate to their steward, the dewanji, and spend the rest of her life peacefully. But that is not quite how it turned out. Once it became clear that Ballabh Ray was never going to lead a normal life again, Thakurani began to take a great deal of interest in the running of the estate. Everyone was in for a surprise. It was as though with each passing day she grew more self-assured and less like the wraith that people had seen earlier. Before long, she also managed to figure out that the dewanji had been doctoring ledgers. That he had been pulling the wool over their eyes for several years. Ballabh Ray had been a lavish spender and never taken much interest in what the dewanji was doing behind his back. Thakurani was different. She had been educated by her father, you see. Rumour has it, her father had got an Englishwoman to come and teach her English and maths. Well, she definitely understood numbers and much else. Better than many. A woman of formidable intellect, I'm told. Didn't take her long to get wind of the dewanji's conspiracy. She found out he was plotting with some members of the John Stuart Company to secretly give away a lot of the estate land as *patta* to them.

'She summoned him and asked him some tough questions. It would have been a difficult talk, but she held her own even though the dewanji tried desperately to make her see things differently. Finally, he left the estate in high dudgeon, shouting imprecations. Thakurani, it seems, didn't turn a hair. Simply gave her faithful bodyguard Ramhari and his men instructions to the effect that the dewanji was not to be allowed anywhere near the Rajbari ever again.'

Dhananjoy sat up and embraced one of his knees. 'Interesting,' he said. 'Your Thakurani sounds like an exceptional woman, Bansi. So, in a way, Ballabh Ray did her a favour, don't you think? She would never have come out of her shell otherwise.'

'Yes, or have saved the estate from complete ruin. She introduced a few austerity measures and tightened the belt. The estate has less than half the staff that it had when Ballabh Ray was at the helm of affairs. She knew the measures would be begrudged by many, but she stood her ground. From what I have heard, Ballabh Ray, who rode roughshod over his wife earlier, is now completely dependent on her mercies. But despite all that he has done, she makes sure that he is well looked after.'

'So has anyone replaced the dewanji?'

'Yes, her brother-in-law Rakhal. I had mentioned him earlier, do you remember? He was the one who left the estate for the city the afternoon of the day of the murder. Rakhal babu's wife, Sushila Sundari, is Thakurani's cousin, her mashi's daughter. Sushila's mother died when Sushila was fairly young, and her father then married a girl around the same age as his daughter. Sushila grew up in her maternal aunt's house – Thakurani's parents' house, that is.

'Sushila and Rakhal came to the Rajbari once the dewanji was shown the door. Rakhal babu used to work as a clerk in another taluqdar's *kachhari*. When they moved here, he began helping Thakurani with the management and records of the estate. But Thakurani herself is very hands-on. Once bitten, twice shy. Some people in the village even refer to her as Rani Rashmoni of Rajapur.'

After musing for a bit, Dhananjoy said in a low, thoughtful voice. 'You know, Bansi, I wonder why we invariably use words like formidable or redoubtable for a woman who is intelligent and assertive. Do such words express admiration, or do they smack of something else? Take your Thakurani for instance. Try putting yourself in her place. People around her waiting for her to fail. And yet she waded right into the deep waters and held her own. That would have taken a great deal of gumption. And resilience.'

Bansidhar scratched his chin and nodded thoughtfully. A stray thought swam in the back of Dhananjoy's mind, and he asked, 'Any idea where the old dewanji might have gone?'

'I have heard that he has been employed by the John Stuart Company. Wait, what are you thinking? Do you feel that the murder might have had something to do with his ire against Thakurani? Something he engineered to cast a slur on the Rajbari?'

'Let's not discount any possibility. Is there anyone else in the household that I should know of?'

'Around a decade ago, Ballabh Ray's nephew, Sukanta, and his niece, Usha, came to live with them. They are Ballabh Ray's sister's children. She died of typhoid when the children were fairly young, and their father married an English girl. I think she used to be their governess while the mother was alive. The children couldn't accept her as the stepmother, and seeing how miserable they were, their mama, Ballabh Ray, brought them to their *mamabari* here. He was always quite fond of them, and Thakurani has been like a mother to them. Sukanta was around eleven when they came here. He's a strapping young man now. Strikingly handsome and charismatic to boot. Has become a Swadeshi activist, and his speeches have caused quite a stir amongst the village youth. Usha is probably three or four years younger than her brother. She is old enough to be married. But the girl refuses to get married, I hear. Has her nose inside books all day! Completely absurd behaviour, if you ask me.'

'Phew, Bansi, that's quite a cast of characters.'

Bansidhar smiled and said, 'Patience, my child. There's more.' His hand raised like a swami poised to give blessings, he continued, 'Just a couple more that you might want to know about. Ballabh Ray has a spiritual guru, Swami Brahmanand, who has been visiting the mansion since Dhurjoti Ray's time. Earlier, when Ballabh Ray was hale and hearty, he didn't pay much heed to Brahmanand and his pearls of wisdom. But since his fall, he wants to see Gurudeb almost every two months. Ballabh Ray cleaves to him like a helpless child, I am told, when he is around. Hopes for some miracle, no doubt.'

'And if I am not mistaken, gurus rarely travel without their entourage.'

'Yes, yes, I was coming to that. Swami Brahmanand, or Gurudeb as he is called, used to come with at least five or six of his acolytes earlier on. Lately, unless there's a puja that he has to preside over, he travels with just two disciples. One is an old man whose name I forget. Ramanand, I think. The other is a sombre and silent young man called Nityanand.'

'I see. And these men were around on the day of Sarala's death?'

'Well, when I went to collect information, or the *suratehaal*, I was told that Gurudeb had left with Ramanand a few days back. Travelled back to his ashram in Natore.'

'But the strong and silent yogi maharaj was still around?'

'It seems he has been in the Rajbari since the rains began. It was Gurudeb who asked Nityanand to stay on at the zamindar's house for a few months since he was helping Ballabh Ray with some special medication and exercises that Swami Brahmanand had recommended. I was told the zamindar had been able to wriggle his toes a little bit one day, and Thakurani became convinced it was because of Nityanand and his guru's special potions.'

'What about the servants in the household?'

'I was coming to them. In the kitchen, Kamini and Puti are the only cooks who are permanent employees at the moment. Sarala was the other one. There's a floating population of hired hands that comes in to help with the cooking and cleaning when there are special occasions. The estate also, of course, has lathiyals and a couple of palki bearers, but not too many of them venture near the kitchen. Only Thakurani's old faithful Ramhari lathiyal, who often guards the dokhin dorja, goes everywhere.'

'That's a fine cast of suspects you have just given me, Bansidhar babu. Wonderful! You did say that all their alibis have been checked, right?'

Stretching his back, Bansi clasped his neck and said, 'Well, to the extent that I could. Rakhal babu was the only one who had left the house that day. My men talked to witnesses. Puti had seen him walking to the station at four in the afternoon. And Ahir, the station master, told me he had seen Rakhal babu get on the five-thirty train for Calcutta. As for the others, they were all at home that day, and Ramhari insists he didn't see anyone leave.'

'He would, wouldn't he? An old, faithful servant like that. Anyway, should we make a move now? I'm eager to talk to all of them. Let's find out what they have to say.' Dhananjoy sprang to his feet with a sudden burst of energy and scared a pair of squirrels that had settled down near him into scurrying for shelter. So infectious was his excitement that even Bansidhar forgot his anxieties about visiting the mansion and spent the rest of the journey trying to match strides with his long-legged friend.

~

The mansion, when it loomed before them, was a majestic, compelling piece of architecture, and Dhananjoy wondered why he had no memory of the place. Perhaps because his parents had had no reason to bring him here. Or was it just another instance of his mind having erased most things associated with the village? He stood for a few moments, taking in the beauty of the estate that sprawled in several directions. With the sun behind it, the lines and form of the building stood out with dazzling clarity. Parts of it looked grubby and weather-beaten, but despite the slight jadedness, there was no denying the grandeur of the place. And yet, somewhere at the heart of all this beauty was a canker, and they were there to find it.

The young maid, Puti, led the two detectives through a long, shadowy corridor on one of the upper floors, where every thud of their footsteps echoed. What must it be like to live in such a vast and eerily quiet place, wondered Bansidhar. To be surrounded by so many expensive things that had been cleaned to within an inch of their lives! The constant dread one would feel about leaving a smudge somewhere on the pristine surfaces! His pace must have slackened as he stared at the large stuffed heads of bison and tigers hanging on the walls, for he felt Dhananjoy's admonitory hand tugging his elbow and urging him to hurry up. Bansi felt a little abashed at behaving like a gawking simpleton, but he made a mental note to ask his friend later what he felt about the terrifying trophies adorning the Rajbari's walls. Intimidating though they were, Bansi couldn't help feeling a surge of pity for the magnificent beasts that had been killed by the ruthless landlords to alleviate their boredom. But now was not the time to think of such things. Daroga Bansidhar clenched his fists and gave all his attention to what lay ahead.

At the end of the corridor, the men found themselves in a lofty and well-proportioned room with a screen positioned on one side, close to the door. The reason for it was explained when Thakurani joined them after a while and sat down quietly behind the screen. The two friends were given large brass tumblers full of lime sherbet, and the cold liquid felt exceedingly refreshing as it went down their parched throats. While drinking his sherbet, Dhananjoy looked around the room with interest. The windows of the room had heavy velvet curtains that were pulled back so that the light could stream in, catching the dust motes dancing in the air. A huge oil painting of a hunting scene hung behind their chairs. Was it a scene from *Sakuntala*, Dhananjoy wondered idly. He had never been an avid reader of classical works, but the figures of the deer, the king poised to hunt it with his bow and arrow and a demure maiden seemed to stir some memory of Mamu talking to him about Kalidasa's play. Of how it had sparked the imagination of Western artists and scholars. Most of the chairs and sofas in the room were covered with slightly faded brocade. On the way to this room, Dhananjoy had also noticed several oil paintings of unsmiling, pompous men with bristling moustaches. Ballabh Ray's ancestors no doubt. Similar portraits were hanging in this room as well, the subjects uniformly sour-looking. And yet, despite those glum faces and all the formidably expensive furniture, the room was pleasantly comfortable. It used to be the *sadar khana* of the house, used by Ballabh Ray to entertain his close friends. A *baithak khana* downstairs was for meeting other visitors and acquaintances.

Women, who belonged to the inner quarters, the *andarmahal*, were not supposed to step into such rooms. But the zamindar's accident had changed many things, including the rigid division between the *andar* and *sadar*. Thakurani had not entirely abandoned the purdah, but she had come out of the andarmahal to face the challenges of the world that lay outside the protected confines of the inner quarters. At the moment, she sat on the other side of the heavily embroidered screen, a preternaturally still presence, waiting for the men to begin their questions. Dhananjoy, eager to embark on the interview, cleared his throat and signalled Bansidhar to start the process. The daroga mopped his brow, licked his lips and then addressed Thakurani.

'Thakurani, you must have heard of the terrible thing that happened just before the Durga Puja celebrations began.'

When Radharani spoke for the first time, Dhananjoy was a little surprised to hear a voice that was slightly hoarse around the edges. But it was full of a quiet confidence. The words that came from beyond the screen were measured and carefully articulated. What with the story that Dhananjoy had just heard and now the unusual voice, the detective felt quite intrigued by the figure that remained hidden from view.

'Yes, Daroga babu, I know what you are talking about. You are referring to the murder of one of our cooks, Sarala. Am I right?'

'Yes, yes, Thakurani. That is what my friend and I are here to investigate.'

Dhananjoy puckered his forehead at Bansidhar's mildly unctuous tone. They were there to look into a murder, and the unnecessary forelock-tugging would only ruin the chances of a proper investigation. His friend needed to sound more firm and less obsequious. He shifted in his seat, and Bansidhar introduced him to Radharani.

Dhananjoy quickly ploughed in. 'Thakurani, is it all right if I ask you a few questions?'

'Yes, Dhananjoy babu, of course. Please do. But before you begin, may I say something?'

'Of course, Thakurani.'

'Sarala came to work in our household as a cook at the beginning of this year. Or maybe the end of last year. She was brought here by Haridasi Boishnobi who had heard that my head cook, Kamini, needed someone in the kitchen. Sarala looked all right to me, and I was more than willing to help a young, widowed girl. Once she began working here, I would see her now and then, and she seemed like a diligent worker. On days that Kamini felt unwell, she took charge of the kitchen, and none of us had any complaints. Even Sushila, who can be a little pernickety about her food, never said anything. I really can't imagine why anyone would want to kill that poor girl. Blow to the head, I'm told. It just makes no sense. But then, the world is full of unexplained cruelty, isn't it?' She ended with a heavy sigh and then added, 'Well, that's about it really. I don't know if I can add anything more to this.'

Dhananjoy remained silent for a few moments and then said, 'Yes, Thakurani, I do see your point. Your paths wouldn't have crossed that much, I agree. But let me ask you a few things. When did you or the people in this house realize that she had disappeared?'

'Kamini had come to me three days before Panchami and grumbled about Sarala's absence. The Durgotsav celebrations were around the corner and, as you can imagine, all hands were needed on deck.

Kamini had stood with her arms akimbo and said, 'Sarala has yet to return. What should we do? Just when we need all our cooks and then some, Maharani has decided to disappear. These young girls! Who do they think they are? Can you ever trust them with any responsibility?' She muttered many more things after that. Radharani smiled to herself and thought that not even Ma Durga could save Sarala from Kamini's wrath once she returned.

'And then, the next afternoon I got to hear that her body had been found the previous day. That someone had killed her. Daroga babu's men came to make enquiries.'

Dhananjoy was scribbling furiously in his little diary. 'Thakurani, I am given to understand that Sarala had started living here in the Rajbari on most days. Is that correct?'

'Yes, that is so. The thing is, Dhananjoy babu, there are six people in the house – seven if you count Nityanand Maharaj. Besides, we have guests from time to time, and then there are different pujas. Every so often, the amount of work in the kitchen goes up. It just made more sense for Sarala to stay here. In fact, it was she who had come to me with the request. I think that was close to the month of Shravan. She said the rains would be starting soon and that walking to and from her house in the village was going to be quite difficult. She doesn't... well, didn't have any family at home. I saw her point. We have several small rooms downstairs, many of which are used for storing things. So, from the end of that month, she had started spending most of her time in this house.'

'But she went back home on certain days?'

'Yes, I imagine that she did. In fact, wasn't she killed on the path that leads to her house in the village?'

Bansidhar answered her question. 'Yes, she was. In fact, we think...' Before he could finish his sentence, Dhananjoy stopped him with a gentle kick and a quelling glance. The daroga realized that his friend didn't want him to talk about their findings.

From Bansidhar's abruptly halted sentence, Radharani gathered what was going on. With mild laughter she said, 'Bansidhar babu, tread carefully. Your friend from the city doesn't want anything revealed to us suspects.'

While Bansidhar looked a little embarrassed, Dhananjoy chose to ignore the jibe and pressed on. 'Thakurani, when did you yourself last see Sarala Dasi?'

Radharani said after a while, 'A week before she died. I sometimes take a walk in the evening near the pond in our estate, and I had seen the girl from a distance. She greeted me and then walked off towards the gate that leads to the village. She must have been going home.'

'Thakurani, maybe this will sound like a strange question to you, but I would like to beg your indulgence.'

'You have piqued my interest, Dhananjoy babu. What is the question?'

'On that day when you saw her walking away, how would you describe her? I ask this because at times a person's gait – the way they hold their shoulders, whether they move fast or drag their feet – can reveal something about their frame of mind. Perhaps I'm wool-gathering. But what I've learnt is that in our line of work, even the smallest of things can sometimes prove important. And our bodies sometimes have a way of betraying things about our state of mind.'

'Yes, that's true. I can see what you mean. Let me think.' But after a few seconds, she said, 'No, Dhananjoy babu, I don't think I can shed any light on what you have just asked me. I don't want to imagine something and mislead you.'

There were a few minutes of quiet after that. In Dhananjoy's experience, at times when people had a bit of time to think in silence, certain memories rose, unbidden, to the surface of their minds. Radharani spoke after a while.

'You know, Dhananjoy babu, I don't know if this will be of any importance to you, but in the context of what you just said...'

'Please, Thakurani.' Dhananjoy leaned forward, the expression in his eyes like that of an alert bird of prey. The muscles of his neck looked taut. Bansidhar glanced with some concern at the way his friend's chair had become angled in a precarious manner. The Calcutta detective urged Radharani, 'Please don't hesitate, Thakurani. We don't yet know what's important or relevant. Anything that you can possibly remember will help us. Impressions and feelings are important. They'll come in handy as we build a picture of the murdered woman.'

'All right, this is what suddenly came to mind. That was probably the last time she and I exchanged words. It was when Sarala came to talk to me about staying in the house.'

Radharani had looked up from the ledger that she had been studying when a voice had asked for her permission to enter the room. She found Kamini's assistant walking in with a tumbler full of fruit juice. What was the girl's name? Radharani could remember her as having come to her with Haridasi. 'Kamini didi has sent this for you, Thakurani.' But even after she had placed the tumbler on a table, she continued standing there as if waiting to say something. 'Is there something you want to say to me, Sarala?' She had recalled the name just in time. Even as Radharani studied her features, the short-statured girl straightened herself and gazed back at her. 'Yes, Thakurani, I have a request.' How different she seemed from the terrified creature who had walked in all those months ago with Haridasi and stood in this very room looking like a startled fawn poised for flight! The straight-backed posture, the steady gaze, the firmly held chin, the light yet self-assured voice – it was not one thing but everything together that filled Radharani with wonder at the way in which Sarala had metamorphosed in the past few months. The girl, in a grubby white sari, was wearing her composure like an ornament.

Once Radharani stopped talking, Dhananjoy sagged back in his chair, sending it back with a little crash that startled Bansidhar. And just when he had recovered from that noise, the grandfather clock outside the room began striking loudly to announce that it was noon.

6

GIRL, INTERRUPTED

After the clock stopped chiming, Radharani said with a laugh, 'I hope that sound didn't startle you. That clock has been with us ever since a sahib gifted it to my father-in-law, Dhurjoti Ray, nearly half a century ago. It has almost become a part of the family now! Isn't it called a grandfather clock in English? To me, it's like a trusty old grandfatherly figure. Never fails to give the correct time. Daroga babu, Dhananjoy babu, I must now take your leave. I go to see my husband every day at twelve, and I don't want to be late today. So, I'll make this short. The Sarala who had come with Haridasi Boishnobi to ask for the job and the one who came to me a few months ago with her request to be allowed to stay seemed like two different people. The girl who had come with Haridasi could barely get herself to speak. The one who came to see me with her request to stay here laid down her arguments in such a clear and compelling manner that I couldn't say no to her.'

Both men listened with rapt attention. Dhananjoy was also taking notes. They all jumped a little when someone entered the room and addressed Radharani. It was a woman who remained behind the screen and talked to Radharani in a rapid and somewhat petulant manner, 'Didi, don't you need to visit Jamai babu now?'

'Yes, Sushila, don't worry. I'm about to leave. I was talking to these two gentlemen here. They're here to ask us questions about Sarala's murder. Bansidhar babu, Dhananjoy babu, this is my sister, Sushila Sundari. Rakhal, her husband, and Sushila stay with us here at the Rajbari. Rakhal helps me with estate-related work. I don't know how I could have managed things without their help. They have both been extremely kind to me.'

Greetings were exchanged swiftly, and then the men could hear the two women talking to each other in whispers. After a while, Radharani said loudly, 'Sushi, why don't you sit here and talk to the gentlemen? I'll go inside now.'

Sushila's screeched demurral of 'Me? Why me, Didi?' was firmly brushed aside by her sister.

Before leaving, Radharani said, 'Daroga babu, please feel free to come to the Rajbari to conduct your inquiries. Rest assured that we will all cooperate. What has happened is truly terrible. Why would anyone have wanted to snuff out that young girl's life? Why does the world go out of its way to be cruel to women, Daroga babu? I would really like the killer to be caught.' Then she added in a brisker tone, 'But I am afraid I will have to leave now. I would request you not to detain Sushila for too long. She's with child. She needs her rest.'

Both men rose from their seats to bid her farewell and then turned their attention to the figure who had replaced Thakurani on the chair behind the screen.

Sushila Sundari, unlike her predecessor, fidgeted a great deal. They could hear the constant rustle of her sari, the frequent tinkling of her jewellery and the scraping sounds of her chair. There was also a curiously creaking sound that Dhananjoy realized was the *haathpakha*, the handheld palm leaf fan that Sushila Sundari must be fanning herself with. After a while, he broke the silence.

'Sushila debi, we won't keep you for long. Just one or two questions.'

And then, before he could say anything more, there was a rush of words from the other side. The voice was excited, high-pitched and grated on the listeners' ears. There were also sounds that suggested that Sushila was chewing betel leaf as she spoke to them. 'You want to know about Sarala's murder? Well, all you need to do is talk to that Kamini. Our head cook. That woman is simply venomous, I tell you. Nothing but malice inside her. She hates everyone! Well, everyone except Radha didi. For Radha didi, she will lay down her life.'

When the two men remained silent, she carried on. The flapping sounds made by the haathpakha had intensified, reflecting her excited state. 'Do you know what she did one day when I had simply asked her to get me some *muri makha* to my room? After bringing it up herself, out of nothing but spite, she decided to trip on the leg of the table next to my bed and spill all the food on my Banarasi sari. It was my mother's sari, and I had preserved it with such care. And all it took was one hateful woman to ruin it completely. I could have wrung Kamini's neck that day. There was some mumbled apology, but the face expressed no contrition. It was all done deliberately, I'm telling you. I really don't know what Didi sees in her. She is pure poison. I sometimes wonder what I would do if she decided to harm my child. I don't put anything past that witch. If it were up to me, she would have been out on her ear long ago. Lately, she has also been getting the proportion of salt wrong from time to time in her cooking. Bland dal one day and then an awfully salty vegetable dish the next. What's the point of such a cook? But will Didi ever listen to any of us and give that wretch her marching orders? Of course not.'

A derisive snort escaped her after she had listed Kamini's perfidies. And then, before either of the men could stem this tide of words, the voice went on. 'Didi is too easily taken in by people like Kamini. All kinds of waifs and strays land up at her doorstep to take advantage of her kindness, and she can't see through their ruses.'

At last, the flood petered out, and Dhananjoy quickly dived in. 'Sushila debi, we will talk to Kamini. We will be talking to everyone. But just now, listening to you, I get the feeling that you are a wise and observant person. So, if you think Kamini deserves our attention, we are going to take that very seriously. But we need something concrete that we can question her about. Not seasoning the food properly is, unfortunately, not yet considered a crime by the laws of our land. Can you remember anything specific that happened between Kamini and Sarala?'

When Bansidhar and Dhananjoy looked at each other, he saw the appreciative smile on Bansi's face. That bit about Sushila being a wise person was an absolute masterstroke. The flattery had worked. The initial strain of pique in Sushila's voice was all but gone.

'Yes, well, I keep my eyes and ears open unlike the other people in this household. Everyone else seems to be lost in their own world. But I feel one can't be too careful.'

Dhananjoy coughed and then cleared his throat. His fingers were drumming an impatient staccato on his knees. 'Do go on.'

'Yes, yes, you wanted to know if there was something very specific that I could tell you about Kamini's relations with Sarala. I do remember something now. It was last month.'

After her initial resistance to the idea of any kind of physical exercise, Sushila had reluctantly conceded to the midwife Surama dai's suggestion that she walk in the gardens from time to time. It would help, the dai had said, at the time of childbirth.

Sushila normally resented any suggestions that would force her to exert herself in any way, but to her surprise, she had started to enjoy her hour-long constitutional amidst all the trees, flowers and birds. Never before had she found pleasure in the sight of branches swaying in the breeze, clusters of bokul flowers attracting bees or shrieking parrots suddenly spiralling out of the trees... Sometimes, she would even have conversations with the little being that was growing inside her and then laugh to herself. That day, in August, she had bumped into the lathiyal, Ramhari-da. He had come to the Rajbari a few years ago from Radha didi's father's house. He had seen both Radharani and Sushila since they were very young, and felt personally responsible for their welfare. Sushila was quite fond of him, too. After exchanging pleasantries with him, she moved deeper into the gardens.

And that's when she had seen the two women glaring at each other and exchanging angry words. The air between Kamini and Sarala was fizzing with fury. Unfortunately, Sushila couldn't go any further to listen to what they were saying without risking being seen. She had to make do with looking intently at their gesticulations and expressions. Kamini seemed to be doing most of the shouting. But Sarala's defiantly turned chin suggested she was not willing to back down. Sushila was both taken aback and delighted by the unfolding scene. Sadly, it ended soon, with Kamini grabbing the younger woman's arm with a hissed threat of 'Bujhhechish?' ('Have you understood?') and Sarala removing Kamini's hand and walking away after whispering something to her adversary that left her fuming. Sushila sat in her hiding place, pleased at having had her entertainment for the day.

'You should have seen Kamini,' Sushila said. 'Uff! The witch was spewing fire. The butter-won't-melt-in-my-mouth persona that she projects whenever Didi is around was nowhere to be seen. Wouldn't surprise me at all if she turns out to be the one who murdered the young girl.'

Sushila Sundari had worked herself up to quite a state by the end of her monologue and was panting a little.

Dhananjoy looked at Bansidhar with his eyebrows raised, and they silently decided to end the interview. Bansidhar addressed Sushila and said, 'Sushila debi, you have given us valuable information. We are extremely grateful, and we will definitely get in touch when we need to talk again. Let us not detain you any longer today.'

'Before you leave, Dhananjoy babu, can I ask you something? You have come from the city, am I right? Is it true that women of respectable families have started stepping out of the purdah over there? Going to parks and gardens with their faces bare?'

Dhananjoy looked at Bansi with a mischievous smile before answering the lady behind the screen. 'Why parks and gardens? They have even begun to travel on trains and ferries, Sushila debi.' Leaning a little forward, he added in a loud whisper, 'There is a woman called Kadambini debi who recently crossed the seven seas and went to Scotland all by herself to complete her studies. She is a doctor now. Doesn't give a fig about the veil. And would you believe her own husband supported her! Off she went, leaving her children, to disport herself with the sahibs. Imagine that!'

'What!' There was a little shriek from behind the screen. This was followed by a lot of agitated rustling of clothes. Finally, a peevish voice asked, 'A female doctor, did you say? I hope I die before I hear about any more scandalous developments! What is this world coming to? Why? Why do women have to do all this?'

Bansidhar knew that Dhananjoy was winding her up. Controlling his own laughter, Bansi clutched his friend's hand, and when Joy turned to look at him, he shook his head and asked him to stop. Dhananjoy turned to the screen and said, 'Sushila debi, I am sorry if I have upset you. I was merely answering your questions. The world is changing. I suppose we just have to learn to accept some of the changes. And now my friend and I will have to take your leave.'

As the two friends walked back through the corridor, they espied a tall, slim figure in a mendicant's white robe moving in their direction with long, graceful strides. Dhananjoy felt a slight nudge from Bansidhar and heard him whisper, 'That's Nityanand.' Dhananjoy had guessed as much. As they drew close, Nityanand stopped and folded his hands in greeting. The yogi exuded a quiet dignity. There was a curious stillness about him, accentuated by the fact that his eyes seemed almost unblinking as they regarded the two men in front of him. Despite the slight asymmetry of features, the face was an undeniably attractive one. Bansidhar returned his namaskar and said, 'Nityanand Maharaj, this is my friend Dhananjoy. He's a detective in the Calcutta Police Department. He is helping me with my enquiries at the moment. You know about the murder, I'm sure.'

The yogi finally seemed to blink as he turned his attention to Dhananjoy and nodded. His lips parted in a disarming smile, and then, in a voice that was a magnificent baritone, he said, 'Would you like to ask me anything, Daroga sahib? I have given Zamindar babu his medicine, so I'm free for an hour now.'

After they sat down in the baithak khana downstairs, Dhananjoy looked at the young yogi and said, 'Can I ask you something personal, Nityanand babu? If you think it's too intrusive a question, please feel free not to answer it.'

The yogi nodded ever so slightly to indicate his acquiescence.

'I just felt a little curious. Don't you ever miss a normal householder's life? Especially in a place like this, where you are surrounded by people who haven't renounced normal life?'

Bansi tensed a little upon hearing the question and hoped that his friend hadn't offended the yogi maharaj. But then he relaxed when he saw Nityanand smiling.

'Dhananjoy babu, I am sure other people have wanted to ask me this question, but you are the first to come out with it. I don't mind answering it. It is a natural question. And the answer is no. I feel that Gurudeb, Brahmanand Maharaj and the other yogis of my ashram *are* my family. And believe me, if you had known my alcoholic brute of a father, you would understand why I don't miss the family I was born into.' Yogi Nityanand stopped speaking for a while, and in the silence that ensued, Bansidhar missed the sound of that beautiful, velvety voice.

Then, with an audible sigh, he continued, 'Gurudeb had come to our village once, several years ago, and when he left, I managed to run away with his entourage. I can never forget my first encounter with the man who changed the course of my life.'

The scrawny, terrified boy stood before the bearded man, staring at his feet and fearing the worst. Was he going to be punished? He hadn't thought this through, he realized with growing consternation. He had simply decided that day that he had had enough and made a run for it when his father had begun hurling abuses and then picked up a log of wood kept in their courtyard to hit him. His mother, as usual, stood in the shadows, watching helplessly. Terrified of her husband. Terrified of going against him and protecting her only child. The boy had run out of the house and then kept running till he saw the ashram dwellers preparing to leave their village. He had managed to conceal himself in one of the departing carts. But now, he had been caught and produced before the bearded old man. Gurudeb, as everyone called him. And then, just as he braced himself for a dressing-down, or worse, he felt a hand being placed gently on his shoulder. Gurudeb frowned when he saw the boy flinching at his touch. That's when he looked closely and saw with a rising sense of horror the welts, bruises and barely healed scabs on the boy's body. The plea for help in the child's eyes was hard to ignore. With a clenched jaw, he said, 'The child will come with us to the ashram. No one will be able to take him away from the ashram against his wishes. We don't want to know about his past life or name. Henceforth, he shall be called Nityanand.'

Dragging himself back to the present, Nityanand said, 'That sagacious decision of Gurudeb's saved my life. The music I heard in the ashram gave me solace. It still does. To return to your question, Dhananjoy babu, my life has taught me that ties of blood don't always translate into love and security. The good-natured companionship that I share with my mates in the ashram is so much more valuable to me. In the ashram, I can be as solitary as I want to be and also have strong friendships. Doesn't that sound wonderful? Relationships based on a genuine sense of affinity? Not freighted with the expectations that come with familial ties?'

Bansi couldn't contain himself any longer. 'But don't you regret giving up on the possibility of marriage? Of becoming a father?'

The yogi lowered his eyes. 'No, Daroga babu, I don't. I have seen what fatherhood can be like, and who's to say that I won't turn out to be like that monster who was my father. Can you tell me why I should do that to a child?'

While the yogi kept his expression inscrutable, the sheen of sweat on his upper lip gave away the fury and pain he felt.

Bansidhar opened his mouth to argue but fell silent when his friend raised his hand to cut him short.

Dhananjoy said in a gentle voice, 'It's all right, Maharaj. That is none of our business. We shouldn't even have asked you these questions. As you know, what we are here for is the investigation of Sarala Dasi's murder. Can you tell us anything about her? Anything that you think might be important for us?'

Dhananjoy thought he saw the young mendicant's eyes fill with a certain expression. It had gone before he could decide what it was, and the yogi's face assumed its usual impassiveness. The light in the baithak khana where they sat was not as bright as it was in the room upstairs. The dark drapes covering a large part of the windows made the room cool but also pitched it into an atmosphere of gloom. Despite the jaundiced light of the room, Dhananjoy felt he had noticed a slight change in the yogi's eyes.

'Not much. I've seen her around, but other than that... Well, once, some months ago, I had caught her standing outside Zamindar babu's room, listening to me sing. I sing prayer songs sometimes for Zamindar babu.'

Nityanand had noticed the slender girl in the white sari for the first time that day. He had got up to shut some of the windows in Ballabh Ray's room and was startled when his eye caught a reflection in one of the mirrors. A young woman was standing with her head bowed, and when she looked up and saw that she had been noticed, her eyes became round with shock. She had brought food for Zamindar babu and then found herself unable to move once the singing began. Nityanand placed a finger on his lips, signalling her to be silent, and then pointed to the sleeping zamindar. She nodded mutely, and after keeping the tray on a table near the bed, made to leave.

'She liked my singing and asked me if she could come and sit outside Zamindar babu's room from time to time when I sang prayer songs in the evening. I didn't refuse, and so I saw her once in a while, listening with closed eyes to the songs. That was all, really.'

Dhananjoy looked intently at the yogi's face. Even though the yogi's eyes were opaque, there was a slight flush on his face and throat. That, and the white-knuckled grip with which Nityanand held the sides of the chair on which he sat, convinced Dhananjoy that he had not told them everything.

7

KITCHEN TALES

'So, what do you think, Joy? Do you think we'll be able to solve our case when Kamini is interrogated tomorrow? Sushila debi's statement seemed to suggest that the head cook really had it in for her assistant.'

The two friends were sitting on the daaoa of Bansidhar's house, smoking the cigarettes that Dhananjoy had got for Bansi from Calcutta. There was a fine sheet of rain falling. The moon peeped out now and then from behind brooding, dark clouds, bathing the courtyard in a muted glow. With a hand extended to catch the needles of falling rain, Dhananjoy remembered how Nilu Mama had once pointed out to him all the sound-related words in Bangla that describe the different kinds of rain. *Jhir-jhir, tip-tip, jhom-jhom, tupur-tapur* and so many others. None of which could perhaps make any sense to someone like Smithson. 'Why on earth would you need all these nonsensical words to describe the bloody rain?' The corners of his mouth lifted in a smile as he imagined his boss's bemusement.

Bansidhar's question made him snap out of his dream-like state. He puffed on his cigarette for a bit and said, 'I'm not so sure, Bansi.'

'What do you mean? Don't you believe what Sushila told us about all that she saw happening between the two cooks?'

'I do, Bansi. But did that lead to murder? We don't know. Also, I couldn't help feeling that Sushila debi was a bit too hasty in drawing our attention to Kamini when we asked her what she knew about Sarala's murder. It was almost as though she was prepared for the question and couldn't wait to tell us about Kamini. It made me ask myself if she was trying to divert our attention because she had something to hide.'

Bansidhar turned to look at his friend's silhouette. The moonlight reaching them in filigreed patterns through the mango and coconut trees created a strange chiaroscuro on Dhananjoy's face. He wondered if Joy was deliberately creating problems where there were none. He was too used to the complexities of the city, after all. In a village like Rajapur, things were often more straightforward. Why was Joy not willing to accept the possibility of simple solutions? Why get bogged down by minor details? Was it because he didn't want to ruin the thrill of the chase?

'But, Joy, surely sometimes what is in front of us could very well be the truth! Why chase shadows needlessly?'

'Bansi, you are absolutely right. We don't have to. But our minds should be open to all kinds of possibilities. I am willing to grant that Sushila debi was simply being helpful and forthcoming. That her eagerness to blurt out all those things about Kamini was because she wanted to give us relevant information. But there is no harm in considering other possibilities, different motives. Things are often not what they seem. In fact, we should talk to people and find out if anyone had seen Kamini walking out that evening when the murder took place. Wouldn't Ramhari lathiyal have seen her? Or wouldn't that girl, Puti, have missed Kamini in the kitchen if she had gone missing for half an hour or even more?

I am sure as the head cook, Kamini is not in the habit of wandering off in the midst of hectic kitchen activities.'

Bansidhar sighed and fell silent. After a while, Dhananjoy added in a gentle voice, 'All I am saying, Bansi, is that we shouldn't arrest and punish an innocent person in our haste. Also, remember that the dead girl only has us to act on her behalf. We shouldn't let her down by rushing to convenient conclusions. It would be so much easier to arrest and pin the murder on someone who works in the kitchen than a member of that household. But that won't make it the truth, will it?'

Bansidhar looked a little taken aback by his friend's words.

'You know, Bansi, I can never forget the fact that it was a young woman's murder on a Calcutta street that led to the Detective Department being set up. Her throat had been slit, and she lay there for all the world to see. She was not a lady, but it was felt that her murder should be thoroughly investigated.'

'Is that so? Then that Holmes solved the case?'

Dhananjoy turned to look at his friend with confusion in his eyes. 'Holmes? Who are you talking about, Bansi?'

'Annada babu and you were talking of some great detective called Holmes, weren't you?'

Dhananjoy continued to look baffled, and then, as realization dawned, he laughed loudly. 'Arre, na, na, Bansi, that Holmes is a fictional character. People who read those novels about him assume all detectives are bound to be like him. Personally, I'm not a big fan of that character. I'll tell you about him some other day. The point I was trying to make is simply this. Don't you want to be completely sure of your culprit's guilt when we finally catch them? Will you be able to sleep peacefully if your mind were riddled with doubts and lingering suspicions? We will do what we need to do.

Investigate, examine all the evidence and then and only then will we arrive at conclusions and make arrests.'

'When you put it like that, I do see what you mean.'

Dhananjoy patted his friend's knee and said, 'Don't look so perturbed. Chalo, let's talk of something else. I haven't come to meet my friend after all these years only to discuss this case, have I?'

And so, the two friends sat and chatted about various things. At some point, Dhananjoy began to recount a particularly complicated case he had solved in Calcutta. The maze of clues through which he had had to navigate before reaching the right answers. Even as he recalled all the details, Dhananjoy could feel the adrenalin course through his veins. But when he turned towards his listener excitedly to describe what he thought was a particularly interesting twist in the case, he realized that his friend was snoring softly. His storytelling skills needed some work, Dhananjoy thought and laughed soundlessly.

The next day, the two friends, along with Saroja, were still laughing about this when a messenger came from the thana with a message for Bansidhar. His friend, Daroga Shyamacharan of a village called Bibichini, was asking him for help in nabbing a gang of dacoits, known locally as the *gamchha mora* gang. The members of the gang would ambush lone travellers from behind, cover their heads with a gamchha and suffocate them. Similar cases had occurred last year in Rajapur, and Bansidhar had played a crucial role in getting some of the members arrested. Dhananjoy could see his friend dithering and said, 'You go, Bansi. If you can trust me with the work here, I'll be happy to carry on with the investigation in your absence for a few days.' Bansi hugged his friend and, for the umpteenth time, expressed his gratitude. 'You are a lifesaver, Joy. I'll never forget all that you're doing to help me.' It was good to see Bansidhar looking animated with purpose as he left for Bibichini. The air of haplessness he had carried around him the last few days had disappeared.

~

And so it was that Dhananjoy found himself making his way alone to the Rajbari. Picking up one end of his dhoti and walking gingerly to avoid the puddles, he wondered whether Bansi was right, that he was hell-bent on chasing shadows. Was he fixated on finding problems simply because his brain craved difficult puzzles? Did he want things to be askew even when they were fairly straightforward? He was sure he had heard Smithson talk about Occam's razor, but his own experiences in the field, although not as vast as that of many of his colleagues, had taught him one thing. That the human mind could be a dark, tangled web of sinister secrets and lies. Lies that people even told themselves at times. Investigating a crime like murder wasn't just about finding scraps of cloth or a stray footprint. Dhananjoy was of the view that the clues lay in the human mind. Maybe the world's greatest writers knew something about that. How else could Shakespeare have painted a villain as intriguing as Iago, that genius of manipulation? The human mind fascinated Dhananjoy, and he had read his well-known predecessor Richard Reid's accounts of his investigations as a police officer, in order to learn from his insights. But he couldn't quite agree with Calcutta's first detective chief that the human visage was an 'unerring index of the human heart'. Evil, Dhananjoy had seen, could exist in the most ordinary-seeming guises. It didn't come in the shapes of the demons and spectres that they had read about as children. Ordinariness could simply be constructed as a façade. For all his respect for the writer, Dhananjoy had privately concluded that Reid's theory was not infallible.

Maybe one day he would have the time to pen his own experiences as a kind of counterpart to Reid's memoirs. But if Bansidhar's snores last night were any indication, he had miles to go before finding success in that department. Preoccupied with such thoughts, Dhananjoy missed the stone lying in his path, lost his balance and would have fallen if a hand had not grabbed his elbow and steadied him.

'*Dhanyabaad!*' he said instinctively and then turned to see a well-built man, around his height, standing close to him. A muscular body, tough and leathery face and a lathi in his hand. One really didn't need to be a detective to guess his profession. The man had all the hallmarks of a lathiyal: long hair down to his shoulders, kohl-lined eyes, a *merjai* (waistcoat) on his torso, amulets circling both arms and a metal girdle around his waist. The hand that gripped his arm felt rough and calloused. Well-oiled and thickly corded muscles on his neck and arms rippled and shone in the sun. Dhananjoy carefully considered what he would say to the hulking giant. The question he finally asked was a rhetorical one.

'Are you by any chance the Ramhari-da that Sushila debi mentioned yesterday?'

Subjecting him to a hard stare, the lathiyal nodded and then enquired, 'So you are the babu from the city who's helping our daroga babu solve Sarala's murder?'

'That's right. Namaskar. My name is Dhananjoy Lahiri. And yes, guilty as charged. I am the detective inspector from Calcutta. Helping out my friend.' Dhananjoy folded his hands, and the other man seemed to soften a little at Dhananjoy's respectful demeanour.

He returned the inspector's greetings before replying, 'To answer your question, Inspector babu, I am indeed Ramhari lathiyal. Both Thakurani and Sushila thakurani call me Ramhari-da. I have seen them grow up when I was a *barkandaz* at Thakurani's father's house. I would carry them around on my shoulders and sometimes even join them in their childish games. Feels like yesterday. I came here two years ago when one of the lathiyals here died in a skirmish. Those men from the John Stuart Company are absolute pigs. Forever looking for ways to trouble our Thakurani. See this scar?' Ramhari pointed to a thick scar that ran across his forearm.

'This was the token of their love the last time we met. But you should have seen the state of those men after I was done with them. They won't be coming back here in a hurry.' Ramhari grinned as he remembered the scenes of violent combat, and Dhananjoy felt a little uncomfortable. The man clearly enjoyed beating up people.

'I see. So, you have known both Radharani debi and Sushila debi as little girls. You must be extremely fond of them.'

'Yes. I will lay down my life for those two girls. In my heart, I think of them as my daughters. I can close my eyes and recall their endless giggling as they used to run around and play hide-and-seek in Pratap babu's estate. Their little plaits flying.' Ramhari's gaze had softened as he replayed those memories of little Radha and Sushila in his mind, but Dhananjoy wondered if there was a veiled threat for him hidden in all of this. Was the lathiyal trying to give him some message? Telling the detective to steer clear of the Rajbari? Or was his imagination running wild again?

'Thakurani-ma has told me that you were to be welcomed into the house whenever you arrive. Is there anyone in particular you wanted to meet?'

'I was hoping to have a chat with Kamini.'

'In that case, Babu, I'll take you to the kitchen.'

Kamini was inspecting the *chholar* dal that Puti had made when she heard the crunch of approaching footsteps and turned around to see Ramhari walking towards the kitchen with a babu. Eyes narrowed to slits, she watched the two advancing figures. Wasn't it the same babu who had come to meet Thakurani earlier with Daroga Bansidhar? Was this about that wretched Sarala?

Puti had also stopped midway while adding bits of ginger to the dal, which was bubbling away on a massive bronze *kadai*. She sat and stared at Dhananjoy with large, petrified eyes. It was not unusual for Dhananjoy to see that kind of terror in people's eyes when they saw a police officer, but he always found their fear deeply disconcerting. Three years of experience as a policeman had taught him that there was no point in taking it personally, yet it never failed to unsettle him. Of course, he had enough colleagues who got a sadistic thrill when they detected fear in the eyes of people like Puti. Men who felt that policing had given them the right to administer kicks and blows at will. He loathed such bullies. They were the ones who had helped create this terrifying image of the police.

Dhananjoy thanked Ramhari in a low voice, and the latter bowed his head and left. The detective then turned to the middle-aged woman with striking features and muscular arms and said, 'Namaskar. Are you Kamini debi?'

'Hain. Yes, Babu, I am Kamini. Who's asking?'

After introducing himself, Dhananjoy informed her that he needed to ask her a few questions related to Sarala's death. She strode out of the kitchen and stood in front of him, arms akimbo, eyes flashing. Her face and arms were slick with sweat, and her brows were knitted in a heavy frown. Turmeric-stained fingers had left a trail of yellow on her forehead.

'*Kaino*, Babu?' Kamini fumed. 'Why me? Do you suspect me of something? Based on what, may I ask? Just because we work in the kitchen, are you going to arrest us for something we haven't done? I know all about the ways the police work. You can't put one over on Kamini. Two years ago, in one of the neighbouring villages, there was a woman called Promoda who was framed for her husband's murder by the daroga there. And why do you think that happened? Because the daroga had found enough evidence against the young son of Barin Ghosh to hang him for murder. Barin Ghosh, who has money to bribe and silence the entire police force. So before one knew it, that poor girl Promoda found herself being intimidated and punished for a crime she didn't commit. Everyone knows that's how you people operate.'

After presenting this incontrovertible proof of police corruption, Kamini stood casting a gimlet eye at the detective. Dhananjoy looked quite unruffled at this outburst. He decided to sit on the daaoa to make himself seem less threatening. Then he said gently, 'Na, Kamini-di, you are wrong. There's no talk of arrest. I can understand why you are angry. I admit, in our country, the police often harass the poor, but believe me, I simply want to talk to you for some time. And I assure you, I'll not rush to conclusions about anything. Which is why I want to do this properly. Let me put it this way. Don't you have to go through several steps before you are completely satisfied with something you cook? It is the same when we are investigating a crime. Just like you begin with lots of ingredients and then arrive at that one dish, I have to sift through a whole lot of information before I arrive at the truth.'

Kamini gave him a hard look before relenting with a harrumphing sound. 'All right, Babu, you have addressed me as Didi, so I won't refuse. Let me get you a cup of tea first. I know that people who live in Calcutta drink lots of tea. Wait, I'll ask Puti to get it.' Then she turned to the wide-eyed Puti and said, 'Puti, stop gaping and make some tea for this babu.

And bring it to the bench in the garden. Remember we have to make some *lauchingri* for Sukanta dadababu's lunch today. He had said to me once, "Kamini-di, all you have to do to win over your enemies is to feed them some of your *lauchingri*." That boy really knows how to flatter.' Kamini was smiling by the end of it, and even Puti was giggling a little, her mouth covered with the end of her sari. Sukanta's blandishments seemed to have had their necessary effect on these ladies in the kitchen, Dhananjoy thought.

As she led him to a bench inside the verdant garden, Kamini wiped her face and blew out her cheeks. 'It's nice to be able to take a little time off from kitchen duties and breathe some fresh air. We are a little short-handed in the kitchen at the moment. Khemi was never a regular, and now, after having her baby, she comes once in a blue moon. With Sarala gone, it's a bit of a struggle for Puti and me. I will have to start looking for someone soon. Maybe even two.'

Dhananjoy sat on the bench and wriggled his back till he found a comfortable position. There were bits of moss covering some parts of the bench, which he took care to avoid. Kamini settled down on the protruding root of a tree, fanning herself with the end of her sari, the stiffness of her back relaying her reluctance to speak.

From the bench where he sat, the detective could see a different side of the mansion. Besides several rooms with shuttered windows, a large terrace could be seen. He turned his attention back to the woman sitting at an angle from him. The outline of her clenched jaw was clearly visible. Dhananjoy decided he needed to do some ice-thawing before bringing up the subject of Sarala. Mentioning Sarala immediately would raise the head cook's hackles and lead to perfunctory answers. He lit a cigarette after having a few sips of the tea that Puti brought. For some reason that he had never been able to fathom, both tea and cigarettes tasted so much better when he had them together. Feeling relaxed, Dhananjoy leaned back on the bench with a sigh and said to Kamini with a smile, 'Thank you for the tea. I really needed it. Achha, Kamini-di, can you tell me a little about yourself? How did you land up here? Are you from the village?'

There was a minute of silence before Kamini said, 'Na, Babu, I am not from this village. It's a long story.'

'Well, I like long stories. I am in no rush to go anywhere.'

Kamini stared at the ground and wondered where the beginning of her story lay. Was it when she ran away from home with her cousin Mukul, who lived in their neighbourhood or when, as a thirteen-year-old girl, she heard her parents planning to marry her off to a fifty-year-old Kulin brahmin?

Kamini had just returned home after visiting Mukul. He had talked incessantly about his burning desire to go to Calcutta and join a theatre company. Mukul was fixated with the idea of becoming an actor after seeing the jatra-palas *that came to their village. He was certain that his future lay in Calcutta and that all he had to do was meet famous playwrights like Girish Ghosh. They were bound to notice his talent. Kamini's parents had not heard her come back. She could hear their voices. 'Do we have a choice?' her father was saying. 'No one will want to marry her if she gets any older. It is with great difficulty that I have found this groom.'*

'But he is fifty years old and has ten other wives,' her mother protested plaintively. And then she heard her father crush her mother's voice.

'He is allowed to have twenty more wives. As long as he can rescue our daughter from the stigma of being unmarried despite crossing puberty, he is a good son-in-law.'

'Rescue?' Kamini had rarely heard her mother raise her voice like that in her husband's presence. 'You said that during Girija's wedding as well. And we know how that turned out.' Her voice cracked and she started weeping. Girija! Kamini's

Giri didi! That name was rarely spoken in the house ever since Giri didi drowned herself in the village pond some years ago. Whenever she recalled that day, Kamini would feel rage pushing against her throat. Rage at Giri didi for choosing to walk into the dark, algae-filled waters of the pond, at her parents for failing her sister and at the crowd that had gathered that day on the ghat, like beady-eyed vultures salivating to make a meal of their grief.

All little Kamini had known was that Giri didi had been married to a man much older than her – a cadaverous, heavy-lidded Kulin brahmin – and that when he had come to spend a few days in their house, her plump, ever-smiling sister had cried incessantly. Even after he had left, Giri didi had refused to smile or eat. Only once had Kamini overheard her whispering in an unrecognizable voice to Ma, 'You don't know, Ma, what he did to me at night. You can't even imagine. Ma, I can't, just can't put it out of my mind...' Ma had stroked her head and hushed her up even as Kamini strained her ears.

'Na, na, shona, my precious girl, don't think about it. Everything will be all right. Believe me, it will be.'

Didi had continued in a voice that sounded like it was being wrenched out of her, 'I'll die if I have to spend time with him again.'

'Arre, you mad girl, why are you thinking of something that's likely to happen only once in a blue moon? Your husband has several wives. He has to visit them all. What makes you think he'll be here any time soon?' And yet, she must have failed to convince Girija, for a few days after this conversation, Girija didi drowned herself in the pond near their house. Her mother had held Giri's lifeless body, caressed her hair entangled with weeds and screamed as though someone were running a knife through her.

Dhananjoy listened very quietly to Kamini's account of her past, stirring his tea with his gaze fixed on the middle distance. The cook's face was stiff with all the pain and rage she could still feel while recollecting some of the things she had gone through. She was cracking some twigs between her fingers as she spoke. 'You can guess some of the rest, can't you, Babu? I ran away from home with Mukul once I realized that that useless baap of mine was all set to sacrifice another daughter at the altar of Kulin honour. And Babu, even after all these years, I have not forgotten my Giri didi. She was not even fifteen when she decided that life wasn't worth living.'

'What brought you to Rajapur?'

She sighed heavily and said, 'I used to stay in Mathaghasha Lane in Calcutta. Babu must have heard of the place. Not exactly one of the salubrious neighbourhoods of Calcutta. Mukul and I shared a tiny apartment and were harassed everyday by our *bariwaali*. She would behave as though, along with the house, she pretty much owned us as well. Sometimes when I think about it, all of it seems to have happened in some other lifetime. At any rate, Mukul's plans of becoming an actor weren't succeeding and he was becoming an intolerable drunk. One day, I decided to gulp down all my tears and look for work in the city. Well, I'm sure you know that for a girl like me, there wouldn't exactly have been a glut of choices.'

Dhananjoy knew that like Kamini, there were many women who escaped to Calcutta in the hope of a better or a different life from the one they had in their villages. Most ended up becoming domestic workers. Others were forced to sell their bodies for survival.

8

THE CANTANKEROUS COOK

'Before long, I began working as a maid in a babu's house in a neighbourhood in Calcutta,' Kamini said. 'And in time, the babu's wife realized I was a fairly decent cook. Thakurani happened to be her distant aunt. After a few years, when she told me that there was an opening for a cook in the Rajbari kitchen here, I threw my meagre belongings into a cloth bundle and bid farewell to the city.'

'How long ago was that?'

Kamini thought for a while and said, 'I think I have celebrated seven or eight Durga Pujas here, but it might be more. Never been able to keep track of time. Rakhal babu once showed me his watch and tried explaining how it worked, but those contraptions are useless to me. The movements of the sun, the cycles of seasons, what fruits and vegetables are available – these are the only markers of time I know.'

'Have you ever regretted leaving Calcutta and coming here?'

Kamini shook her head, and finally, her face broke into a smile. 'No, Babu. Not for a minute. Once I came here and met Thakurani, I knew this was where I was meant to be.'

Kamini could recall the day she had met Thakurani like it was yesterday. When she had gone to the room in the antahpur, where the mistress of the household had summoned her, she had prepared herself for a brief and impersonal encounter. Instead, the meeting had opened up a crack in the protective carapace that Kamini had created around herself, and left her feeling shaken. When Thakurani raised her large eyes and gazed at her, the floor under her feet had tilted ever so slightly. For Kamini could see in those eyes the same world of pain that she had seen all those years ago in the eyes of her Giri didi. The pain of a woman tied to a bestial husband, she had later understood. She had gripped her own arms and stood there waiting for the rising tide of emotions within her to subside. Was life giving her an opportunity to make reparation for the sin of failing her Giri didi?

Now that Kamini had begun to speak, the words just seemed to pour out of her. The creases of irritation that had been etched on her forehead when Dhananjoy stood outside the kitchen were gone. Dhananjoy got up from the bench, went behind it and stood holding its back and leaning on it. He paid close attention to all that Kamini had to say. Then he asked her, 'And what about Zamindar babu? You must have met him when he was hale and hearty.'

Kamini's expression became shuttered when Ballabh Ray was mentioned. 'I don't really wish to talk about Zamindar babu, if you don't mind, Babu. All I'll say is our Thakurani deserved a better husband than him.'

Ballabh Ray, Kamini had soon realized, was an obnoxious man, and having watched his irascibility from a distance, Kamini could not bear to think of all that Thakurani must have to endure as his wife. Her heart swelled with sympathy for the woman trapped in a gilded cage with a beast that tormented her for its pleasure.

Kamini found herself drawn irresistibly to her sad and lonely mistress. All those years ago, she had failed her Giri didi, but now she was determined to alleviate her Thakurani's pain. One day, taking her courage in both hands, and after discussing some mundane kitchen matters with her, she asked Thakurani about the books in her room. 'What are all these books, Thakurani?' And when her question was rewarded with a broad smile that lit up Radharani's face, Kamini felt deeply rewarded.

'They are my friends, Kamini, my only true friends in this whole wide world. Have you heard of novels, Kamini? Let me tell you about them. They are truly wonderful things. Stories of people like you and me. People who don't really exist, and yet you feel you might meet them some day. You can step into their lives, think their thoughts. Escape your own life for a while. Some of these are foreign novels, but do you know which ones are my favourites? The ones by Bankim Chatterjee. So many of them are about women like you and me. Do you really want to hear some of them? Let's begin with one of Bankim's tomorrow. We can sit after lunch when all your work in the kitchen is over.' Thakurani's eyes were sparkling, and right in front of Kamini, she transformed from her listless and laconic self into an animated woman who couldn't stop talking.

Thakurani was right. Every afternoon, Kamini would feel a pang of disappointment when Thakurani stopped reading. Bankim's stories left her hungering for more, and Kamini often wondered how a man – a deputy magistrate at that – could have understood an ordinary woman's heart so well. Thakurani also read out novels written by women like Nirupama Debi and Swarnalata Debi. But it was to Bankim that they always returned for memorable characters and ingenious plots. Kamini noticed that quite a few women ended up dying in Bankim babu's novels. Strong, passionate women who had stood up for what they wanted. Like Giri didi, they had to die.

Besides books, Kamini's talks with her mistress also meandered to other subjects. With her chin placed on her fist, Thakurani would listen bemusedly to Kamini's accounts of Calcutta and its mosaic of diverse neighbourhoods. And once, when Thakurani had asked her if she had ever seen the famous Bagbazar Reading Library (after explaining to her what a library was), Kamini could not bear to disappoint her. So, she lied and said, 'Oh, yes, I would pass that building quite often, although I never realized that it had books in it.'

After Zamindar babu's accident, when Thakurani began to run the estate, Kamini suggested that she start applying oil on her head and abundant tresses in the afternoons. She had seen Thakurani droop with exhaustion by the time her day was over. Ballabh Ray's wife had surprised everyone with her skills and efficiency in running the estate. But Kamini, watching her like a hawk, could not help but notice the strain that was beginning to show on her face. She had convinced Thakurani that she needed an hour away from the ledgers to ensure she didn't fall ill. In those moments when she caressingly massaged Thakurani's scalp and her stalk-like neck, she experienced a kind of joy she had never felt before. Time would stand still, and she could feel frissons of delight that brought a smile to her face, which no one could see. And on some afternoons, as Kamini would massage Radharani's scalp, the latter would reminisce about her happy childhood and of the special bond she had had with her father. In those moments, her fingers trembling with all the feelings of love churning inside her, Kamini vowed to herself that there was nothing she would not do to protect her Thakurani from all kinds of possible harm. Anyone who dared to trouble her would first have to deal with Kamini.

Kamini stopped when she realized that she had talked a great deal to the babu. He had a way of being still and listening with utmost attention to what was being said. It was flattering to have one's words paid such attention to. Maybe that's why she had unburdened so much of her past. But not everything. Even so, more than what she could recall doing to anyone else.

In a hurry to leave the place, Kamini tried to hoist herself precipitously, lost her balance and fell back again. Embarrassed, she made a second attempt, and this time, managed to stand up successfully. Adjusting her sari, she said, 'Babu, I am sure you want another cup of tea. Let me get it for you. That silly girl Puti will never do anything unless I give her clear instructions.'

Dhananjoy sensed Kamini's growing restlessness and said in a light voice, 'Don't worry, Kamini-di, I won't detain you much longer. I'll have that tea in a bit. Truth be told, I'm not that fond of tea. Could you stay for a while longer? Please sit down. Tell me, has everyone in the household been equally kind to you?'

Sensing the unasked question, Kamini bit her lip and looked away. When she met his eyes again, she sniffed and said, 'I know what you are getting at, Babu. You want me to blab about Sushila didi. Well, there's no point hiding that she and I have never got along. The lady has had it in for me from the beginning. She simply couldn't stomach the fact that her Radha didi enjoyed reading her books to me.'

Sushila and her husband, Rakhal, had come to the zamindar bari a few months after Ballabh Ray's accident, and Kamini soon realized that Thakurani's cousin had no intention of ever going back to her marital home in Badalgram. She had prevailed upon that husband of hers, who was far too gentle to resist her machinations, and also persuaded Thakurani to employ Rakhal babu. To Kamini's shrewd gaze, it appeared that even though Sushila fawned and simpered in Thakurani's presence, and never failed to invoke memories of their shared childhood, she was there to exploit her sister's generosity. Kamini gnashed her teeth with exasperation at the way Sushila would barge into the room in the afternoons when Thakurani and she sat together. The interruptions seemed deliberate, but there was little that Kamini could do. 'What are you up to, Didi?' she would say in her sing-song voice as she swanned into the room and pretended not to see that they were reading or discussing a novel. With Sushila in the room, babbling away, Kamini would soon have to leave. Was it her imagination or would she see a triumphant gleam in Sushila's eyes when this happened? Could Thakurani not see what was going on and put that scheming sister of hers in place? In the rare moments when Kamini allowed herself the luxury of self-pity, she wondered with bitterness why so many of her cherished relationships in life had left her feeling abandoned.

Tears had begun to well up in Kamini's eyes, but she controlled her emotions. Holding her knees tightly to prevent them from shaking as all those moments of being slighted and humiliated by the vile woman came rushing into her mind, she said evenly, 'But so what if she hates me? I don't have anything to worry about as long as Thakurani trusts me. And I can walk through fire for her. Besides, everyone else in the household – Sukanta-da, Rakhal babu, Usha didi – is fond of me. I've never heard a single harsh word from any of them. Rakhal babu has even apologized once or twice for his wife's uncouth behaviour. Everyone assumes I am a widow, and I have let them believe what they want. What is the point of telling them that I never got married? It's just better this way.'

'Tell me, Kamini-di, was everyone home in the evening on the day Sarala died? I'll ask Ramhari, of course, but I just thought of asking you as well.'

Kamini gave a short laugh, which turned into a snort. 'Ramhari-da? You will ask that opium addict whether he remembers about people leaving the house that evening? Ask away! Truth is, once the sun sets, he sits and nods, lost in a world of dreams. The only reason he hasn't been thrown out of his job is because Thakurani has known him since she was a child. He used to work for her father. Both Sushila-di and Thakurani have a soft spot for him.'

'Well, in that case, can you confirm everyone was at home?'

Kamini's answer, which came in the form of a perfunctory nod, was accompanied by a refusal to meet his eyes. Dhananjoy could feel she wasn't being entirely honest but decided not to press her. Instead, in a mild voice, he deftly segued to a different question.

'And what about Sarala? What did you think of her?'

There was a change in Kamini's expression when she heard the question, but she quickly arranged her features back into blank coldness.

'What is there to say? We worked in the same kitchen, and that's about it.'

'Did you like your assistant?'

'There was no need to like or dislike her. We did not have to be friends. We both understood cooking, and that's all that mattered. She kept her head down and knew her place. At least in the initial days.'

Soon after the young girl had started work, Kamini had made sure that Sarala knew her place in the kitchen. She conveyed to her in no uncertain terms that any attempts to undermine her authority would not be tolerated. And Sarala had seemed to understand what was expected of her. She kept her head down and did as she was told. In time, Kamini realized that the girl was a good cook and knew how to use her instincts in the kitchen. When she had first seen the frail sixteen-year-old girl, she had mentally dismissed her as yet another brainless novice like Puti. But the girl had proved her wrong. It was good to have her by her side. It was after a few months, however, that she began to notice changes in her behaviour. The quiet deference seemed to have been replaced by an understated insolence. Soon she began to express her opinions about how she felt certain dishes could be improved. Kamini had wanted to wring the whippersnapper's neck, but she controlled her fury and told her through gritted teeth to keep her ideas to herself. The sly creature had even gone behind her back and talked to Thakurani and wrangled a room for herself in the Rajbari. And after that, things between them began to go downhill and were never the same again.

'Babu, let me tell you this. I should not speak ill of the dead, but that girl was trouble. Not initially, no. Not when she had just arrived and would look terrified of everything in this house. But gradually, she gained confidence and grew into something quite different. And once that happened, Babu, everything in the Rajbari seemed to change.'

'What do you mean by that, Kamini-di? Everything changed? How?'

'Well, it's hard to put a finger on it. Let me put it this way. It was very similar to what happens when a breeze enters a kitchen full of things. Even though things don't always move or crash down from their places, they seem disturbed, askew. It was like that. As if the equilibrium of this place was thrown off-kilter. Sushila-di became more crotchety, Rakhal babu more preoccupied, Usha didi looked distracted and even Puti seemed to become restless. Nityanand Maharaj began his excessive fasting.'

'Excessive fasting, did you say, Kamini-di?'

'Yes, you heard right. He began to eat almost half of what he usually did. When I asked him, he simply said in that calm voice of his that gluttony was a sin and that he was teaching his body not to crave such pleasures. Told me that he knew of many sadhus who could go without food for days. It was all about self-discipline, he said. Well, if you ask me, Babu, god has given us this body, and hunger and thirst are part of it. Why punish the body in that manner?'

Perhaps because there was something he felt guilty about, Dhananjoy thought. He stood with his hands clasped behind his back.

Kamini got up and looked determined to end the questioning. 'Babu, I have already spent too much time chatting with you. God knows, if I stay here any longer, Puti might burn the kitchen down. Or sit and daydream so that everything will get delayed. All I can tell you is this. Working here had really turned that girl's head. She was pliant and obedient when she first came here with that Boishnobi, but she definitely did not stay that way. Forgot her place in the kitchen and needed a few sharp reminders.'

'Kamini-di, let me ask you a straightforward question. Did you ever have fights with her?'

Kamini tilted her head and demanded in a voice laced with acid, 'Who's been tattling to you? Bring them here to me and then ask them what they have heard. My mother used to say that if you keep two or more brass utensils in one place, they are bound to clang against each other and create a lot of noise. We were two good cooks working in a single kitchen. Scraps and squabbles were inevitable. In our heads, we probably dreamt about killing each other every day. But that was all it was. Everyone does it. Kill people in their minds. That's not the same as actual murder, is it? Anyway, I have to return to the kitchen now. So please forgive me.'

Dhananjoy realized that it would be pointless to press Kamini any further. Not wanting to antagonize her, he didn't demur when she made to leave. They walked back in a silence that remained unbroken till Kamini tripped and stumbled twice on the uneven ground of the garden and muttered angrily to herself, *Will my troubles with that girl never end?* Kamini stopped to pull out a thorn that had pierced her heel. *The wretched girl was like this thorn,* she thought. *Despite being removed, it will continue to itch and hurt. Why did the witch have to step into the Rajbari?* After a hurried namaskar to the babu, Kamini began marching back towards her fiefdom, the kitchen.

Dhananjoy called her back with one last question.

'Kamini-di, are there any dhatura plants growing in this estate? Would you know where they are?'

With a nonplussed expression, Kamini said, 'Dhatura, did you say, Babu? I have no idea! I am only interested in plants and herbs that I can use in my cooking. Dhatura? No, don't know about that. But the gardens are large, and all kinds of things grow here. I can ask the gardener if you are interested. Yogi Maharaj is also interested in plants. You might want to ask him.'

With that, she turned and walked back into the kitchen, and within a few minutes, her voice could be heard admonishing Puti for her carelessness and then cursing her own fate for being saddled with the world's greatest fool as a kitchen hand.

9

THREE MEN AND A GOAT

Wending his way to the gates of the Rajbari, to return to the village, Dhananjoy stopped to pull out a tiny piece of stone that had somehow lodged itself in his shoe. When he looked up after throwing it away, he caught sight of a thin, bespectacled man walking towards the kitchen hurriedly with what looked like ledgers under his arm. His face was long and gentle, with a vaguely anxious expression, and ears that stuck out. A straggly moustache struggled to make its presence felt on his upper lip. When their eyes met, he stopped in his tracks and cast an enquiring glance at the detective. A tentative smile hovered on his lips. Dhananjoy walked towards him and introduced himself. The man, he noticed, had perspiration beading on his hairline. A faint stench of sweat wafted from him. He also seemed to have a problem making eye contact. After greeting Dhananjoy with folded hands, he said, 'Dhananjoy babu, I'm Rakhal, Rakhal Bagchi. I work for Thakurani didi in the kachhari.'

'Namaskar! You are also her brother-in-law, am I right?'

'Yes, yes, that too. Sushila, my wife, is the daughter of Thakurani's maternal aunt, her mashi. But I would like to believe that she has retained me because of my skills. I heard from Sushila that you met her yesterday.'

Dhananjoy nodded and then waited for the other man to speak.

Rakhal finally filled the silence. The words came out unsteadily, in fits and starts. 'You are here about the murder, right? Why don't we sit down tomorrow and talk? I know you're questioning everyone. I'm free in the afternoon tomorrow. Today I have to go and sit with Kamini and get some *hisheb* of the foodstuff and other things that arrived for the Durga Puja. It's enough to drive anyone crazy. But I don't mind. I like working with numbers. You get what you see.'

With a smile, Dhananjoy said, 'Rakhal babu, what you said just now reminded me that in my childhood, I would often hear my father say similar things about numbers. He was a teacher of maths in the village pathshala.'

'He did, did he?' Rakhal's face lit up, and he finally looked the detective in the eye and gave a high-pitched laugh. 'I can't agree more. Yes, numbers never let you down. Even when this world is over, numbers will stay.' He nodded after saying all of this in a rush.

'Dhananjoy babu, now that you have told me about your father teaching maths, about his love of numbers, I feel much better. I... I have this problem. I don't make a good first impression. Strangers make me nervous. My heart races, I become tongue-tied, sometimes I stutter. As it is, I am afraid of my own shadow. It only gets worse when I meet anyone new. I don't know how to explain it. You might think it's ridiculous.'

Rakhal babu stopped to see how Dhananjoy would react to his confession. With his slightly protruding ears and receding chin, he looked, for all the world, like an earnest student waiting for the teacher's verdict.

'No, Rakhal babu, I don't find it ridiculous.'

'Most people do, Dhananjoy babu. Ballabh dada would often make fun of me. Ask me to be more of a man. Anyway, that's how it is. Thankfully, my work is with ledgers. They don't make me nervous like people do.'

Just then they noticed Puti scurrying out of the kitchen with tears coursing down her cheeks. Turning his attention to the girl, Rakhal asked her, '*Ki re*, Puti? Have you got on the wrong side of Kamini again?'

Puti came and stood near them with her head bowed. Dhananjoy could see the girl was not more than fifteen or sixteen. Another child widow, Dhananjoy thought with a sigh. Her front teeth protruded and overlapped slightly, and she worried her lips frequently as Rakhal tried to comfort her. The policeman's presence was making Puti uncomfortable, and every so often, she darted nervous glances in his direction. Dhananjoy was reminded of a rabbit he had once seen outside his house as a child. Frozen with fear, it had stood with its nose twitching and, despite Dhananjoy's desperate attempts to appear as friendly as possible, had bolted after a while, as if pursued by all the demons in hell. Puti's plump cheeks were drenched with tears, which she kept wiping with her hand. Rakhal asked affectionately, 'What is it, Puti? Has Kamini scolded you for something?'

Sniffling loudly, Puti said in a voice thick with tears, 'I'm never able to do anything that makes her happy, Rakhal dadababu. She just flies off the handle over trivial things. You should have seen the ruckus she created when I told her I couldn't find the stored coconuts in the kitchen last week. Tell me, is that my fault? Am I here to cook or to keep track of coconuts! Ever since Sarala didi's death, she seems to be in a worse mood than usual. You would imagine she would be happy, given how much she hated her! But no. And who do you think gets the brunt of all the surliness?' Puti stared at her feet and looked extremely miserable.

'Arre, you know Kamini, don't you? Her bark is much worse than her bite. Come, silly girl, stop crying. I'll take you back to the kitchen. Let's see if we can find a way to improve her mood.'

And then, as they turned to leave, Rakhal tripped on a stone and his notebooks tumbled out of his hands. Rakhal slapped his head and laughed at his own clumsiness. Dhananjoy helped him pick the notebooks up, dusting them before returning them to their owner. After Rakhal had collected all his notebooks and thanked him profusely, Dhananjoy stood and watched him walk towards the kitchen along with a teary-eyed Puti.

~

'Dhananjoy babu!'

Dhananjoy turned sharply to see who was calling him and found the yogi, Nityanand, walking towards him. He was carrying a small woven basket full of flowers and leaves in his hand.

'Namaskar, Maharaj! Is there anything you want to say to me? Should we go and sit in the baithak khana?'

After they had both settled down in the baithak khana, Dhananjoy turned to look questioningly at the yogi. The thin, red veins visible in the young mendicant's eyes and the puffed skin underneath, spoke of disturbed nights and a troubled mind. Remembering Kamini's words about his excessive fasting, Dhananjoy paid closer attention to the man sitting in front of him. He felt that his face looked gaunt and more sharply chiselled than before. The pronounced angularity and tautly stretched skin of the face seemed to have enhanced the yogi's good looks. But the pallor wasn't healthy.

'Dhananjoy babu, I wanted to know if I could leave for the ashram in the next few days. I feel a great need to see Gurudeb. I've never been away from him for so long.'

'Na, Maharaj, that, I'm afraid, won't be possible. At this stage of the investigation, we need everyone to be present. Is there something in particular that's bothering you?'

'I... I... no, no, nothing in particular. You were right when you asked me whether I felt any disquiet amidst all these householders. I have been feeling very restless lately. What am I doing amongst all these people and their petty everyday concerns? I ask myself. I have renounced this world, haven't I? I don't want to be here. I feel stifled. And now this horrible death. I need to breathe the ashram air. Be close to my gurudeb.'

'But won't Zamindar babu be needing you any more?'

'If you agree to let me go from here, I can talk to Thakurani. Zamindar babu's recovery will take time. I don't think I can be here waiting endlessly for him to get better. I'm keen to be back at the ashram. At least for a while.'

Dhananjoy could see the yogi getting increasingly agitated. Sweat was beginning to sheen his face. In a sympathetic voice, the detective said, 'I can understand why you are feeling so perturbed. But you'll have to be patient for some time. Why don't you give it another week? Or ten days? If Bansi and I haven't had any breakthrough by then, I will talk to Bansidhar and see if we can arrange for you to be at the ashram for some time. Give us a bit of time. We've just about started the investigation. And surely you would want the perpetrator of this heinous crime to be caught, wouldn't you?'

The yogi nodded gravely and then got up from his chair. He had regained his composure and bowed his head in a dignified namaskar. As he made to leave, Dhananjoy asked him, 'Maharaj, one question before you go. Would you know anything about dhatura leaves? Is there a dhatura plant somewhere on this estate?'

Nityanand became absolutely still, and then, after a few seconds, turned to look at his interlocutor.

'Dhatura did you say? Why do you ask about that poisonous plant, Dhananjoy babu?'

'Why don't you answer *my* question, Maharaj?'

'Yes, I do know what dhatura looks like. There are several types of dhatura plants, and we even grow them in our ashram since some of the varieties have medicinal properties. I am interested in medicinal herbs. I go around collecting them to make concoctions. I saw you looking at the cuts and scratches on my hands a few minutes ago. Those are the hazards I face when I go looking for rare herbs. Anyway, Gurudeb had noticed my interest and encouraged me to pursue it. I felt deeply gratified when one of my concoctions helped the zamindar feel a bit of sensation in his toes. But getting back to your question, yes, if I'm not mistaken, I have seen them in this estate as well. Near the pukur, in fact. Those are the venomous varieties of dhatura. If taken in large amounts, they can be lethal. I hope that answers your question?'

'Yes, it does. Thank you, Maharaj. And now, we both need to be on our way.'

~

On the way back, Dhananjoy decided to take a break in a shaded copse when he felt his hamstring burning with the exertion of having walked for a long time. Was that a blister he could feel under his heel? Maybe he could just sit and make some notes based on all that he had heard and seen that day. Dhananjoy had developed this habit of noting down every single detail – even the seemingly insignificant ones – when he went out to gather accounts from witnesses. He encouraged them to speak about themselves to make them comfortable, and then, once the ice was thawed, most people were happy to talk – what they remembered about the victim and various other things around the time of the murder. Some needed gentle nudges, even extravagant compliments about their perspicacity, whereas others were only too excited at the prospect of having a captive audience for their outpourings. The scribbles and squiggles in Dhananjoy's diary would probably make no sense to anyone else, but they made perfect sense to him when he studied them later. Secreted away in those cryptic notes and observations were the connections and clues – the little keys – that patiently awaited discovery so they could help him unlock a difficult mystery.

Searching for a place to sit, Dhananjoy noticed that the roots of some of the trees formed a complex pattern and created an indentation in the ground. It looked like a comfortable place to settle down in. He was also quite famished and regretted having refused Saroja's offer to pack some *khoii-murki* for the road. A broad grin split his face when he spotted a guava tree. A memory from his childhood, of clambering up such trees with his long legs and then throwing down the gathered loot to the patiently waiting Bansi underneath, flashed before his eyes. He was sure he could do it again without damaging his bones. A few minutes later, having created a little pile of guavas next to him, he sat down to make a record of all the information that had been gathered at the Rajbari.

Deeply immersed in his notes, Dhananjoy missed the friendly shout of '*Ki go*, Babu? What are you doing here under the trees?' It was only when he felt something wet and rough tickling his outstretched foot that a startled Dhananjoy looked up with a little cry of surprise. What he saw made him gape incredulously for a few seconds. A goat was licking his foot while gazing at him with beady, impassive eyes. In a burst of panic, Dhananjoy folded his leg and made some shooing noises at the animal. Animals made him nervous, and the instinct to clamber up a tree or flee from the spot was suppressed with some difficulty. It was just a goat, he told himself. There was no need to get all worked up. But where had the creature come from all of a sudden? The mystery was quickly solved when he noticed the lungi-clad, sunken-cheeked man whom Bansi and he had seen fishing the other day at the dighi, squatting at some distance and staring at him with eyes full of curiosity and mild amusement. Quite a few of his teeth seemed missing when he opened his mouth to grin reassuringly at the detective. Dhananjoy remembered Bansidhar's warning about the man's garrulity, but there was no escaping him and his goat now. Stifling a groan, he waited for Hakim chacha to speak.

'Babu, don't worry about Pyaari. She seems to like you. Like all of us villagers, she's only a little curious, that's all. I normally don't take her out for feeding. My nephew, Alam, does it. But Alam is sick today, so here I am. I'd have preferred to go to my favourite spot near the dighi with my fishing rod. But didn't have a choice today. Pyaari here needs her outing.' After thumping Pyaari's rear for a bit, he asked, 'So, what are you doing sitting here?'

'Nothing important, Chacha. Just finishing some work.'

Without getting up, Chacha advanced towards him slightly by sliding his feet left to right. His voice was accompanied by a pronounced wheeze every time he spoke. 'Aren't you Dhirendra Lahiri's son? You went away all those years ago when the epidemic devastated our village, isn't that right? Like you, I lost two of my loved ones at that terrible time. I call myself a hakim, and yet, I could do nothing to save them. They went on losing weight and becoming pale shadows of themselves right in front of my eyes.' He wiped his eyes with the corner of a gamchha hanging on his shoulder. 'I lost my wife and my son. Sijad's father. You've met my grandson Sijad, haven't you? Sijad was just a toddler at the time. Not even two years old. I would probably have killed myself when my wife and son died, but the thought of raising that little one kept me alive. How could my poor daughter-in-law have done it all on her own? Who knows why Allah makes us suffer in the ways that he sometimes does.' After being silent for a while, he looked at Dhananjoy with narrowed eyes.

'So you thought of visiting your ancestral village after all these years?' With that, he hawked loudly, spat out some phlegm and wiped his mouth.

Dhananjoy simply nodded in response. Pyaari, to his great relief, had lost interest in his feet and, after being chastised loudly for trying to chew his dhoti, had wandered off calmly to investigate some of the plants and shrubs nearby.

But Pyaari's owner was hard to shake off. If Dhananjoy thought his terse replies would dissuade Chacha from talking, he was deeply mistaken. Hakim chacha had no intention of leaving him alone. After fifteen minutes of listening to his continuous monologue, Dhananjoy was fairly certain there could not be anything more to be learnt about the hakim's daily routine. Or that of his neighbours and relatives. Finally, the old man ran out of steam. After massaging his joints for some time, he got up and flashed his gap-toothed smile at the detective.

'This is where your roots are, Babu.' Dhananjoy was a bit confused at that abrupt assertion, especially since the hakim was pointing with a bony finger at the tangled roots on which he was sitting. By now, Pyaari had joined them again, her jaws moving rhythmically. Both the goat and its owner stared at him in unison with sombre expressions that looked remarkably similar. Chacha then went on, 'Don't forget that. Your roots are here. Don't become a stranger to this place once you return to that city. Achha, I'll be off now. I know I have talked your ear off. Nobody wants to hear an old man burbling, but what to do? I love to talk. When my wife was alive, she would often wonder how a talkative man like me could remain so silent while fishing.' With a cackle, he continued, 'I used to tell her that's one of god's greatest mysteries. Anyway, I'm glad you are helping our daroga. Not the cleverest of boys, that one, despite his good heart. He could use all the help he can get. Sijad told me that he met you at the doctor's house the other day. He couldn't stop talking about the fact that you've come from Calcutta.'

Dhananjoy kept his diary aside with a sigh. This was going to take some time, he realized. After coughing for a few minutes, Chacha went on.

'That grandson of mine is completely enamoured of the city. Somehow, he has got it into his head that that's where he wants to spend his life. You know, catching fish in that dighi is one of my greatest passions. But I have to beg and cajole him to learn how to do it. The boy is just so impatient and restless. The last time we were at the dighi, he sat and fidgeted, and I could see he wanted to make a run for it. I tried telling him that the things he would learn while fishing would help him in his life. But it's useless talking to young boys about the importance of patience, isn't it? He was beginning to doze off at some point. You should have seen his relief when Rakhal babu placed his hand on my shoulder and startled us both. I knew then that boy was not cut out for fishing. Rakhal babu's too kind and well-mannered to have ignored us and walked off to the station. The people of the Rajbari are kind. Thakurani, after hearing about Sijad's ambition to become a doctor, has promised to help with his fees at the medical college.

'Nothing can now stop that boy from dreaming about his future in the city. That day, as soon as he heard that Rakhal babu was going there, my grandson asked him if he could order a coat from a tailoring house in Calcutta. Ganguli Brothers! That was the name of the shop. He had read about them in some advertisement and wanted to gift one to Annada daktar. When Rakhal babu agreed, you should have seen the boy's delight. As if money grows on trees!'

Even as the old man made scoffing noises, Dhananjoy could see that Sijad was the light of his life. But the detective wanted to get on with his work. Some of his increasing restlessness must have become hard to ignore for the hakim finally took the hint and made to leave. 'Please give Sijad your blessings, Babu. The poor boy lost his father when he was nothing more than a baby. He just has his mother and me now. All I want is for him to become a well-established daktar. Achha, I'll get going. We'll meet again, I'm sure.'

Then he made some clicking sounds with his tongue to beckon his goat. 'Let's go, Pyaari. I'm sure you've had your fill, you greedy girl. Get a move on, now. The babu has to work.'

After Hakim chacha left, Dhananjoy leaned his head back on the crook of the tree that was closest to him. He mulled over all that Hakim chacha had said and even made some notes. The puzzle this murder presented was far from being solved. But in that moment, he wanted to enjoy the peace and quiet around him. Inhaling the fragrant breeze, he thought how different this was from the city with all its unpleasant odours. He wondered about the tall trees around him. So many of them would have been there far longer than most men and women of the village. If only they could talk, what stories they would have to tell. He had read about a scientist called Jagadish Bose who had proved that plants and trees were living beings. Could that be true? He had often seen Nilu Mama talking to the plants in their garden. When Dhananjoy had laughed at what seemed like craziness to him, Mamu had talked about there being more things on heaven and earth than humans could claim knowledge of. He informed his sceptical nephew with a contemptuous sniff that his roses bloomed much better when he conversed with them.

His thoughts had begun to ramble, Dhananjoy realized. He kept his diary and pencil in the pocket of his kurta and closed his eyes. The surroundings gave him an unaccustomed sense of well-being. Maybe Smithson had been right in insisting on a holiday. For all his initial resentment, he could feel the advantages of what his boss had talked about. The air of Rajapur had done wonders for him. He slept well, ate far more than he had in a long time and his tremors and palpitations had become a thing of the past. He felt like a different man altogether. A pleasantly relaxing, self-forgetting feeling went through him. There was something important that he thought he needed to make a note of, but it would have to wait. The urge to simply close his eyes for a little while was becoming hard to resist. Before he could control it, his mouth opened in a wide yawn. No harm in resting for a while, he thought. And that was his last thought before his chin dropped on his chest, his spectacles slipped down his nose and the soft sound of his snores became a part of the melange of noises in the woods.

10

SAUDAMINI'S CURSE

It was the snapping of a twig and the subconscious feeling of being watched that made Dhananjoy wake up with a start. Even after putting on his spectacles and sitting up properly, he had to blink several times before it registered that a woman he had never seen before was gazing at him steadily. First the goat, and now this! *What is going on?* Dhananjoy wondered. Had he entered some magical part of the grove? Was he having out-of-body experiences that included encounters with friendly goats and wood nymphs? He shook his head a little to clear his mind of such absurd ideas.

Clad in a white sari with a dark border, the woman in front of him had two straight white lines applied on her forehead that ran down to just below the bridge of her nose. Her hair was parted on one side, and she was holding the musical instrument popularly known as the *khanjani*. Other than a white flower stuck next to her left ear, there were no ornaments on her body. When she saw him sit up and blink, she put the khanjani in the cloth bundle that was slung over her shoulder and then turned back to look at him.

'*Jai Radhe*! You must be the babu from the city who is helping in the investigation of Sarala's murder.'

Dhananjoy rubbed his face vigorously to get rid of all traces of sleep. How was everyone in this place able to recognize him unerringly as the visitor from the city? It was almost as though he wore an invisible placard around his neck announcing that he was new to these parts. By now, the fog in his brain had cleared and he was fairly certain he knew the person who stood before him. 'And you, I presume, are Haridasi Boishnobi? Am I right? How are you here?'

'Oh, Babu, don't look so bewildered,' said Haridasi with a laugh. Now that he was fully awake and seeing her properly, Dhananjoy could see that the Boishnobi had a charming face and a beguiling smile. When she pointed her finger at a patch of grass nearby, and raised her eyebrow to ask if she could sit down, he nodded. Taking out a piece of cloth from her bundle, she spread it on the grass and then collapsed on it. An *ooof* sound of exhaustion escaped from her mouth once she had settled down.

'I wander all over the place, Babu. There's a babaji's *aakhada* in the village of Shimuli where I sometimes spend long periods of time. It's a half day's walk from here. But other than that, I'm an inveterate wanderer. There's hardly any village in the vicinity that I haven't visited. My little cloth bundle here has all that I need.'

'Where are you off to now?'

'I'm on my way to the Rajbari today to meet Thakurani. She's a Boishnob as well. While I'm there, I also sing and dance and entertain whoever gathers there to listen to me. They take care of my meals. They also give me some foodstuff that I can carry on my next journey.' After wiping her brow with the end of her sari, she continued, 'I have been walking for several kilometres today, and my legs aren't what they used to be. Like you, I had the bright idea of resting here for a while. I heard the villagers talking about the Calcutta detective who has been asking questions of those who knew

Sarala. Aren't you glad we have met like this, Babu?' She gave him an enigmatic smile. 'I can be quite hard to pin down. I am sure you have questions for me.'

Dhananjoy had never met a Boishnobi in his life, only heard about them. And not very flattering things either. They weren't looked upon kindly for their unconventional ways. Wandering, taking lovers without bothering to marry, singing and dancing to earn a livelihood – Boishnobi women didn't quite fit in with the usual notions of good femininity. But the woman in front of him seemed so self-possessed and articulate. Her movements so lithe and graceful. Realizing that he was gaping, the detective gathered his wits and then ran his fingers through his unkempt hair.

'Yes, yes, this is quite unexpected. A real piece of luck. I have heard that you were Sarala's friend and confidante. And that you helped her get the job at the Rajbari. Is there anything you can tell me to help with the investigation?'

Hand cupping her chin, she reflected for a while before saying, 'Can't think of anything very significant, Babu. As far as I knew, Sarala was just doing her job. Making ends meet by working in that kitchen. Why would anyone want to kill her like that? But then, nothing much about human beings surprises me any more. That's one thing that my travels have taught me. Humans really are the oddest of creatures.'

Changing tack, Dhananjoy asked, 'How did she become your friend, Haridasi? Weren't you her husband's—?'

When the detective stopped, Haridasi completed the sentence with a piquant smile. 'Mistress? Is that the word you are looking for? Yes, strange, isn't it? That Nobin's wife and his mistress became friends?'

'So, how did it happen?'

Haridasi cast a shrewd glance at him. 'I hope you're not trying to make me say something inadvertently, which you can then twist and manipulate and get me into trouble? Policemen are quite well-known for doing such things.'

There it was again! The distrust of the police. The inevitable viewing of them as liars and deceivers. The sound that escaped Dhananjoy's mouth expressed his frustration and disquiet. The Boishnobi hastened to reassure him.

'Oh, no, Babu. I didn't mean to upset you. I wasn't being serious. Just pulling your leg. I am sure you are not that kind of a policeman. I'll tell you all that I can recall about Sarala. I met her when she came to Rajapur as Nobin's wife. She was probably ten or maybe eleven at that time. Rail thin with large, staring eyes. That's what she looked like when I first saw her. I know that Nobin gave her a rough time. I noticed bruises and marks on her frail limbs when I visited their house, but there wasn't much I could do. He was her husband, after all. And to be honest, I didn't really want to get involved. I might even have been a little miffed about his marrying her.'

'How long had you known Nobin?'

'Long before he got married. We had met in Nabadwip, and after our first encounter, we knew that we would keep meeting. I feel he shouldn't have got married, but he told me there was a lot of pressure from the village elders. It was an unhappy marriage for both of them. Nobin must have been chagrined at having his hand forced in that manner by the village elders and took it out on that poor girl. And she had nowhere to go. Sarala, I think, was more than a little relieved when he died in an accident. Can't blame her either. I never got to see the side of him that she did.'

Haridasi fell silent for a while and then continued. 'Why I bothered to go back and check on her, I don't know. When Nobin was alive, she and I rarely talked to each other. I used to find those bulging eyes, staring out of that pale face, extremely annoying. And yet, after his death, when I wandered into Rajapur, I couldn't contain my curiosity. I wanted to find out how Nobin's widow was faring, and it was a good thing that I knocked on her door. The poor girl was at her wits' end and needed help. Everyone, including her parents, had pretty much turned their backs on her. Her neighbours left her alone, although I'm certain they watched her like a hawk to see if she would break any of the rules that bind a widow like a twine made of the toughest of ropes. They would have salivated at the prospect of punishing her had they caught the slightest whiff of a scandal. How I hate that word, scandal! If you ask me, it's just a word invented to sniff at love that people don't understand. Tell me, Babu, unless you are hurting someone, how can love be bad? But so much of suffering, so much pain, so many lives ruined simply because people won't accept this. They want to judge and punish. You have heard of Saudamini's curse, haven't you, Babu? Linked to the Rajbari?'

'No, what's that? Although now that you mention it, I did hear a gentleman referring to the Rajbari being cursed.' Dhananjoy recalled the station master's cousin's comment on the day he had arrived. It felt like a lifetime ago, although only a bit more than a week had elapsed.

'Yes, he must have been talking about Saudamini's curse.'

'Who was she? I'm intrigued.'

Haridasi settled into a more comfortable position and laughed sadly. 'She was Dhurjoti Ray's elder sister. Ballabh Ray's aunt. A lot older than Dhurjoti Ray. A gap of fifteen years at least. Saudamini was a child widow who came back to live in her natal home. At the Rajbari. She couldn't have been more than eleven or twelve when she was widowed. She was more like a mother than a sister to Dhurjoti when he was born. Around the time she was seventeen or eighteen, she made the mistake of falling in love with one of the *gomashtas*, Rajshekhar. Rajshekhar was an abandoned orphan brought up by Dhurjoti's parents. Saudamini and he used to play together as children. But when she returned as a widow, they were no longer children. You can imagine the rest, can't you, Babu?

'They were caught one day when Rajshekhar had climbed into Saudamini's room for an assignation. He managed to jump out of the window and disappear into the night. Poor Saudamini bore the brunt of her father's wrath. Ballabh Ray's grandfather punished her in all sorts of ways for her transgressions and then bundled her off unceremoniously to Kashi. That hell on earth for widows. The story goes that on the day she was meant to leave the Rajbari, she fell at her parents' feet, howling like an animal in pain. Begged them not to exile their only daughter. Told them she was willing to take any other punishment but not that. Even the servants had tears in their eyes when they saw her plight. But her father remained firm, and her mother didn't oppose him. Maybe they also felt a little helpless. Fear of that dreaded word "scandal"! Whatever it was, her screams fell on deaf ears. And then, after all her tears had dried and she was being dragged to the palki that would take her on her final journey, she cursed the house she was born in. Eyes blazing, she cried out that the men of the Rajbari would never ever have peace.'

Haridasi had narrated the tale in a dramatic manner, complete with voice modulation, finely timed pauses and dextrously used words and gestures. After she stopped, there was complete silence, except for a slight susurration of leaves from a bamboo grove nearby. It felt as though even the trees around them were listening to Saudamini's sad tale with bated breath. Dhananjoy could feel goosebumps on his arms.

Looking at the detective's creased brow, the Boishnobi smiled as if to comfort him. 'Who knows how much of it is true, Babu. Besides, what would a zamindar mansion be without its share of buried secrets and skeletons? It's only some that come to light and become local legends. Tales that keep getting embellished and spiced up with every retelling. So many of them about women silenced forcibly. In this case, the curse seems to have had some effect. It's not just Ballabh Ray who met with an accident. His grandfather also met with a grisly accident while on a hunt, and his father died of an undiagnosed disease. No wonder the legend of the curse has gathered strength over the years and got handed down from one generation to the next.'

Haridasi rolled her neck, shifted on her seat to find a more comfortable position and continued. 'But you are here for Sarala, not Saudamini. Where was I? Yes, I remember. When I told Sarala she had no choice but to look for work, she agreed. From then on, I would visit her house now and then, and we would sit and talk. There was never any jealousy or malice. Strange business, given she had been Nobin's wife and I his mistress. But we really hit it off once he died. She was happy to have someone in her life who didn't frown at her for not being miserable. Who didn't expect her to sit around moping because of her widowhood. Someone who made her laugh. Brought news and gossip from the world outside the village. After a few days, when I asked her if she would be interested in the Rajbari job, she all but jumped at the opportunity.'

'What about her parents?'

'Her mother died of some disease a year after Nobin's death, and from what I know, her father then moved to the city in search of work. She didn't really like talking about them. I could see the restrained rage on her face when she once told me that even birds took better care of their young.'

She stopped to draw breath, and then, pulling out a tiny bundle of cloth from the one she was carrying on her shoulder, she poured out some dry-roasted gram, *chhatu*, on her hand and ate it. Having dusted her hands and flicked off some stray bits that had fallen on her lap, she said, 'You know, Babu, she once told me that while Nobin had been a hateful husband, there was one thing she owed him gratitude for. It was because of his tantrums that she had become a good cook. A well-cooked meal put him in a good mood and saved her from being thrashed or humiliated, and so she poured all her energy into mastering that skill.'

'Tell me, Haridasi, did your friend confide in you? Anything that you feel might be important in untangling the mystery of her murder? Anything at all?'

'Truth be told, Babu, we didn't meet that often once she started living at the Rajbari. Every time I walked past her house in the village, I would find it locked. But yes, there's one small thing that I do remember, now that you ask me. During our last meeting, maybe a week before she died, she had said to me that she was thinking about moving to the city. She had clasped my hand and begged me not to tell anyone. She wanted to be in a place where no one would recognize her, she said, and she could begin life afresh. She was fairly confident that with her cooking skills she could get work anywhere. She had had enough of Rajapur. Well, I didn't know what to say, Babu. Who knows where the impetus for that kind of change had come from. I have no idea. It could simply have been a reaction to a skirmish in the kitchen with Kamini. But even if she were planning something of that sort, surely that couldn't have got her killed?'

Dhananjoy was scratching his chin, and after Haridasi stopped speaking, he made a few notes in his diary. She hummed a song under her breath while he wrote. When he looked up after a few minutes, he noticed what seemed to him like a venomous centipede moving at a stately pace on her sari. Following the detective's troubled gaze and seeing the object of his agitation, Haridasi raised her palm as though to say, 'There's no need to worry.' Then she placed the creature on a leaf carefully, stretched her arm as far as possible and put it on a low-hanging branch of a tree.

Suddenly, Dhananjoy sat up straighter as he remembered something.

'Haridasi, I have thought of something important I needed to ask you. Did your friend tell you that she was pregnant?'

'What did you say?' The Boishnobi's jaw fell, and it was clear that she hadn't known anything about this. After a while, her brow cleared and she said, 'Aah, so that must be the reason why she seemed so keen to move from here. From what I could gather about her life, Babu, that girl had never known much love. Now I think I understand. So, the murder was punishment for her audacity, wasn't it? I wonder why the world is so dead set against women finding love on their own.'

A faint sound like the distant rumble of thunder was heard, and the Boishnobi got up hurriedly from her perch. 'Babu, I'll be on my way now. If I tarry any longer, I'll get caught in the rain. I would suggest you go back home as well. These village roads can be quite treacherous. Tear off a big leaf and carry it so you can take shelter in case there's a sudden downpour. *Jai Radhe*!'

When she had moved some distance, Dhananjoy shouted after her, 'Aren't you going the wrong way, Haridasi?'

The Boishnobi turned around, and with a twinkle in her eye, said, 'There's no such thing, Babu. They all ultimately lead to the Lord's door. Don't worry about me. I'll be fine. I hope you can find your way back home.'

~

When Bansidhar returned home the next evening, his face clearly expressed his quiet satisfaction at the successful nabbing of the bandits in Bibichini. And yet, when he sat down to tell Dhananjoy about the events, he began to look somewhat dispirited. Quick to pick up on the sadness, Dhananjoy asked, 'What is it, Bansi? Is something wrong? Why the long face?'

'No, no, nothing's wrong. We did manage to catch the culprits and yet...' and here he stopped to draw a ragged breath. 'And yet, when I saw those so-called dakats, Joy, I felt a pang of pity in my heart. I have caught thieves before this, but never have I felt this way. Those bandits looked like they hadn't eaten in days. Their ribs poking out of their meagre chests and eyes that looked flat and lifeless, like that of dead fish. Most of them told us they used to be cultivators who were forced to turn to a life of looting because of debt and hunger. Many had lost their *lakheraj*, or freehold lands either to the greedy zamindar or to the whims of the river. We sat and heard their stories, but what could we do? They will now languish in prisons, and nothing will change.'

Dhananjoy placed his hand on his friend's shoulder.

'I'm glad I have a friend like you, Bansi. Not many of us in the police are able to think about criminals in that manner.'

'I got the impression that they really are nothing but peasants who had been tested to their limits by the burden of unpaid debts. I get very confused, Joy. At times I feel this sarkar has rescued us from lawlessness and rampant banditry, and then, when I see all this, I am not so sure. Haven't they also caused so much of the misery that has led to this kind of banditry? Maybe the young men talking of Swadeshi *andolan* are right, after all.'

The two friends sat in pensive silence for a while, and then Bansi asked Dhananjoy to fill him in on what he had learnt from Kamini. Before telling him about his exchange with Kamini, Dhananjoy also told him about his chance encounter with Haridasi.

Bansi heard him out and then pulled at his moustache with a thoughtful look. 'That's interesting. So, Sarala was thinking about leaving this place.' Turning towards his friend, he asked with a creased brow, 'Why, though? To avoid scandal? To get an abortion in the city? I got my men to ask the local midwives, and none of them claimed any knowledge of her being pregnant.' When Dhananjoy silently raised his palms heavenwards, as if to say, 'Who knows!', Bansi turned his attention back to Kamini.

'So, what do we do next? How do we get her to spill the beans about that fight? Should we pull her in?'

'I think we have a problem on our hands, Bansi. There seems to be no way of getting the women to talk freely to us. I would, for instance, like to talk to that Puti, but I know the poor girl will feel so intimidated that she'll be paralysed with fear and retreat into a shell. Sarala might have confided in her, or she may have noticed something, but I doubt she will talk. As for Kamini, that woman is also a tough nut to crack. What should we do?'

11

A FEMALE DETECTIVE

The two policemen sat for a while in despondent silence, watching the smoke of their cigarettes curl upwards in a spiral. Dhananjoy took off his spectacles to rub the bridge of his nose and then put them back on again. And just then, Bansidhar felt his spine tingle with excitement. He gaped at Joy as suddenly, from some deep recess of his mind, an idea came thundering. Brimming with excitement, he grabbed Dhananjoy's arm and shouted, 'Joy I have thought of something. We can get a *meye goyenda*, a girl detective, to find out a few things for us from the Rajbari women!'

Then he elaborated on what he meant when he saw the flummoxed expression on Dhananjoy's face. It was Daroga Shyamacharan who had explained the strange phenomenon of a girl detective to Bansidhar yesterday.

Their torsos were gleaming from all the oil that Shyamacharan and Bansi had applied liberally before taking a bath in the pukur as preparation to join the celebration at the thana. Shyamacharan was deeply grateful to his friend for having arrived promptly and helped in the arrests. Just then, a jamadar had come and asked Shyamacharan if he should pay Bama the amount that they had promised her. 'Yes, yes, pay her what we had promised. Her help was invaluable.' After the jamadar left, Bansidhar turned to his friend with a questioning look. Shyamacharan explained, 'A few thanas have started employing girl detectives to help crack cases. Our meye goyenda is a poor young widow called Bama. About twenty years old and very easy on the eye. When we began suspecting Chhidam and Dinu of being the leaders of the gang, we had no way of confirming our suspicions. That's when Bama stepped in to help us. She befriended Dinu, convinced him that she was a lonely widow looking for love and, within a fortnight, had wormed out most of the gang's secrets from him.' Bansidhar couldn't believe his ears! 'Meye goyenda!' Girl detective!

'What do you think, Joy? Didn't you say Kamini is looking for a new assistant in the kitchen? If we can get Bama and train her for a day or two, she can be the kitchen hand that Kamini is looking for, and while she's working there, not only can she talk to Puti, she can also be our eyes and ears. She can report to us anything that might help our case.'

Dhananjoy was staring at his friend as though Bansi had just offered a pot full of amrit to him. 'That's a brilliant idea, Bansi! A stroke of genius! Absolute genius!' He clapped his friend's shoulders energetically.

Bansi finally understood what it meant to be over the moon. He waggled his toes from sheer delight. He knew he could never match Joy's quick-wittedness. But never before this case had he felt that he might be utterly inadequate, incompetent. And that his friend might consider him a cumbersome millstone around his neck. That fear, which had sat like a leaden weight in his mind, was now allayed by the beaming expression on Joy's face. Even if he could never be as quick on the uptake as Joy, he was not a write-off. Daroga Bansidhar Gupta was capable of coming up with good ideas.

With a loud, gusty sigh, Bansidhar said, 'And now we need to give our full attention to the ilish that I have brought from Bibichini. I can guarantee that you've never eaten ilish like this anywhere in that city of yours. Can you smell the aroma wafting from the kitchen? Wait till you taste it! It'll feel like magic on the tongue.'

~

The very next day, a letter was sent to Shyamacharan. Dhananjoy had urged Bansi to tell his friend that there was no time to lose. Bama, the meye goyenda that Bansi had talked about, came to their house the following evening. Dhananjoy was taken aback when he saw her. But then he reproached himself for feeling surprised. What was he expecting? He wasn't quite sure. The very notion of a meye goyenda, in fact, had boggled his mind. He had tried imagining what she might look like and failed. And then, when he saw Bama, he was struck by the fact that he would have walked past the thin, bright-eyed girl on the road without ever being able to guess that she worked as a goyenda. But that was a good thing, wasn't it, he chided himself. It meant she could blend in wherever she needed to. As they explained everything to her, the young woman tilted her chin and listened to them with the utmost attention.

Finally, she nodded. '*Thhik aachhe*, Bansidhar babu. I'll go there tomorrow and tell Kamini I have heard she's been looking for someone to help her in the kitchen. I should have a convincing story ready about how I landed up here. Maybe I could pretend to be a distant cousin of Saroja boudi. Fallen on bad days and looking for work. Now that Lakshmi Puja is almost upon us, I'm sure Kamini will be only too glad to have an extra pair of hands. I doubt there'll be too many questions asked, given that I'm the right caste for a kitchen hand. And, most importantly, my chopping and grinding skills are excellent.'

A few days later, when Dhananjoy and Bansidhar went to the Rajbari, they saw Bama and Puti sitting and giggling together while slicing mounds of vegetables. Even though neither looked at the boti, their hands moved in a deft and rhythmic manner as evenly chopped vegetables rose in colourful piles. When Puti saw the two men, she whispered something to her companion, and then the two fell silent. It was quite obvious that Bama was playing her role very convincingly. Puti looked genuinely happy at having found a new friend. The two inspectors were headed upstairs, and this time it was Ramhari who escorted them.

The grandfather clock had just stopped announcing that it was two p.m. when they sat down to talk to Rakhal. Clad in a starched white kurta and dhoti with neatly combed, well-oiled hair and a serious expression, Rakhal looked even more like an earnest student wanting to impress the new headmaster. His pasty complexion made it quite obvious that he spent most of his time indoors, working on ledgers. Every so often, he pressed the back of his neck as though troubled by a niggling pain. Despite his efforts to appear relaxed and smiling, Dhananjoy could see that Sushila debi's husband was prone to involuntary twitches. Finally, with a hoarse-sounding laugh, he announced that he might need a cigarette to calm his nerves.

After all of them had lit and inhaled their cigarettes in a satisfied manner, Dhananjoy began with his tried-and-tested conversational gambit which invariably put people at ease by inviting them to talk about themselves. 'Rakhal babu, can I ask you how long you've been working for Thakurani?'

'Not more than three years. Sushila and I came here soon after Ballabh dada, my jamai babu, had his accident and became confined to his bed. Actually, it was my wife, Sushila, who persuaded me to stay on and help Thakurani didi. I don't think the few times that Jamai babu had met me before he fell from his horse, he thought much of me. I remember him punching my shoulder once and saying with a wink, "What kind of a man are you, Rakhal? You don't seem interested in drinking or in visiting *baiji*s! I know a few ladies in Calcutta who can help you get rid of all your nervousness. All you have to do is ask."'

Rakhal had a sad smile on his face as he recalled the conversation.

'You know, Daroga babu, you'll probably find this hard to believe, but my father used to work as a barkandaz in the household of a taluqdar in a small village called Badalgram. That's where I grew up. And it was my father who insisted that I spend time in the pathshala. He would keep reminding me, "*Lekhapora kore je, gari ghhora chorhe shey* (He who studies hard, travels on horses and in carriages)." I don't blame him. Unlike our Ramhari-da, he wasn't happy being a lathiyal. He would often have nightmares about the villages he had helped burn down, families he had uprooted, men whose heads he had split open with his lathi, women and children whose cries he had ignored. That is why he made sure I spent my time solving difficult sums and learning how to read and write. As soon as I was old enough to work, he got me the job of a gomashta in his taluqdar's kachhari. The fact that I could spend my days doing calculations in the ledgers gave him an immense sense of peace. Ironical, don't you think? The man universally admired for his martial skills was determined that his son should become a pen-pusher, cooped up in a room all day. He felt immensely proud when I became one. But he didn't live long after that. Died in an accident.'

Dhananjoy and Bansidhar could see that Rakhal's face was a picture of desolation as he spoke of his father. His hands were clasped tightly between his knees. Dhananjoy prodded him gently.

'So, why did you leave Badalgram?'

'I... I was miserable there once my father died, even though the taluqdar himself tried to help me. He got me a place in a different part of the village so that I could move away from the house that reminded me of my father. He arranged my marriage with Pratap babu's niece. But even Sushila could see I would never be happy in that village. She never fails to remind me that the reason I'm in better spirits now is because of her timely decision. And she is right. I felt overworked and underappreciated in that kachhari. My back and neck hurt all the time. Sushila was also tired of a husband who spent most of his time sunk in gloom. I could read pity in her eyes at times.' And then he added after a slight pause, 'I'm glad our circumstances changed before her pity could curdle into contempt.'

'So, being in Rajapur has worked out well for you, would you say?'

'Yes, no doubt about that. So many good things have happened here. I have always loved working with numbers, but in Badalgram, my meticulousness, my ability to control the chaos in those ledgers, wasn't appreciated by the dewan. But Thakurani didi is very different. She notices everything and makes a point to give praise where it's due. For instance, when I told her that I make rough drafts of important papers so that the final sheet is without any errors, she smiled appreciatively and then said she wished everyone would do that. What's more, she insisted that Annada babu suggest something for my chronic backache, and when he said that standing and writing would ease my backache, she got a special desk designed for me. The pain has improved a lot, I must say.

'Also, I have a friend in Sukanta. He has opened my eyes to so many things happening in the world around us. Sushila is happier here. She grew up on a zamindar's estate. She missed her old life in Badalgram. This house, servants at her beck and call, she likes all that. Most importantly, I'm going to be a father in a few months! I still find that hard to believe sometimes. Someone who will call me Baba. That has to be the best feeling in the world, don't you think?'

By now Rakhal babu's hands were no longer fidgeting. The twitches had also gone. Nor was he struggling to make eye contact. He met their gaze as he spoke.

Bansidhar interjected, 'Rakhal babu, what did you mean when you said that Sukanta opened your eyes to many things?'

For the first time, Rakhal babu's face broke into a smile.

'Aah, yes, let me explain. He really is like a force of nature. I can still clearly remember the first day I met young Sukanta.'

When Thakurani didi had first introduced her young nephew to Rakhal, he had felt a jolt of envy. The younger man seemed to be everything that he was not. Sukanta moved with the inherent grace and assurance of someone who would never be thrown off his stride by life's challenges. On their first meeting, he had gripped and shaken Rakhal's hand with gusto and laughed. 'Arre, Dada, don't look so alarmed. This is how sahibs greet each other.'

After a few months, Sukanta invited him to his room one day in the evening. As they were finishing their meal, he turned to him and said, 'Rakhal-da, why don't you come up to my room for a while? Let's have a proper adda. We live in the same house, and yet, we have barely had a proper conversation. We both need an ally in this place where we are outnumbered by the womenfolk, don't you think?' While everyone was laughing at what he said, Sukanta smiled impishly and addressed Sushila. 'Ki, Sushila-di? Is it all right if I steal your husband for some time today?'

Even though Rakhal was older than Sukanta, he was in awe of the young man. In fact, it never failed to surprise Rakhal that Sukanta had even bothered to befriend a rustic and diffident fellow like him. The first day when he had stepped into Sukanta's room, Rakhal had been utterly amazed by the number of books, journals and pamphlets strewn all over his bed and even on the floor. Sukanta had guffawed at the stricken expression on his face.

'Don't look so dazed, Rakhal-da. This is how I study. You should go to Usha's room if you want to see a reader who can sit still for hours and read. I just can't be like that. Usha says I must have been a sparrow in my earlier birth. Never in one place for long.' And then followed that disarming smile, which put Rakhal at ease. After that day, they would meet for adda quite regularly. It was Sukanta who did most of the talking, and Rakhal didn't mind sitting and listening to him. The younger man knew so much more about things of all kinds. He studied in Calcutta and talked at length about the city. His eloquence was fascinating. Sukanta had once quoted some lines by an English poet called Cunningham and said, 'Do we really want to be remembered in that manner, Rakhal-da? Don't you think we should use this life of ours to make a difference?' The lines had been: 'That he was born, cannot be denied. He ate, drank, slept, talked politics and died.'

'Once you talk to Sukanta, you'll understand, Daroga babu. He has read so much. Met so many writers, thinkers, philosophers. I had never really given any proper thought to the way the sarkar has been draining our wealth, humiliating us in so many ways, preventing us from entering certain carriages in trains or walking freely in parks. The more he talked, the more I felt ashamed that I had never spent any time reflecting on such things. He has been telling me about how we need to be wary of Viceroy Curzon and the things he has up his sleeve.'

Deciding that it was time to steer the conversation to the murder, Dhananjoy said, 'Rakhal babu, tell us what you can remember about the murdered girl. Is there anything in particular that you can recollect about her?'

Rakhal stared intently at a table with intricate inlay work placed next to him and, after tracing his finger on the floral design for a few minutes, said, 'Since I knew you were going to ask me about Sarala today, I spent some time after you left yesterday thinking about what might be important. I'm not very good at thinking on my feet. I get all flustered. Unless, of course, it's a maths problem. But since I had time... there's actually one thing that I recalled. This happened close to a month ago.'

Rakhal had stepped out for a smoke and decided to go downstairs and walk for a bit. Sushila had never liked what she called the 'stench' of cigarettes, and once she discovered she was pregnant, she began to claim that the smoke made her nauseous. It was peaceful outside. And then Rakhal began to hear voices floating out of somewhere close to the coconut trees. Once his eyes had adjusted to the dark, he could make out two shapes, a man and a woman. Rakhal knew it was a private conversation and he had no business eavesdropping. If Sushila had told him that she had done the same thing, he would have berated her. And yet there he was, rooted to the spot with curiosity.

The woman was saying, 'I really can't take this any longer. How long do I have to keep pretending? Aren't we ever going to make a decision?'

The voice was undoubtedly that of Sarala, the kitchen help.

And then a male voice that Rakhal couldn't hear clearly. Was it Sukanta's? The male voice had still been speaking when Sarala interrupted it somewhat loudly.

'But wait for how long? Don't you see I can't wait much longer? Everyone will know, will begin to suspect...' It was clear that Sarala had begun sobbing quietly and her male companion was making comforting sounds.

And just then, Rakhal's cigarette had scorched his fingers and a noise escaped his lips, after which the voices had fallen completely silent. Rakhal stood there feeling a little disoriented. What was that he had heard? Should he tell someone? But he really wasn't interested in poking his nose in other people's business.

'I would see Sarala off and on, especially once she started living here. To be honest, that's the only time I heard her speak so fiercely. A couple of times, I had seen her standing in the corridor outside Jamai babu's room and listening to Nityanand singing. She seemed mesmerized. Can't blame her, though. Yogi Maharaj sings like Tansen himself.'

Dhananjoy rose from his chair, and Rakhal was a little taken aback by the abruptness of his move.

'All right, Rakhal babu, you have been a big help. We have disturbed you on a day that you are taking a break from your work at the kachhari. We'll leave you now to enjoy the rest of your day. But before we take your leave, can I request you for one last thing?'

'Of course, Dhananjoy babu, anything you need. I... I don't really like gossiping, you know... it's because you asked me...'

Dhananjoy smiled reassuringly. 'I know, Rakhal babu. But what to do? What everyone thinks of as gossip is often crucial information for us. Can you also give me the address of the place where you stayed in Calcutta?'

Bansidhar saw Rakhal becoming slack-jawed at the sudden change of tack and chimed in, 'Rakhal babu, don't worry. This is just routine procedure. I'm sure you understand that we have to check every little thing. Nothing personal.'

Rakhal regained his composure. 'Yes, yes, of course. Please note down the address of the guest house where I stayed. In fact, I'm glad Dhananjoy babu has reminded me of that day's visit. While walking to the station that day, I had encountered Sijad, and he asked me to look for a long coat in Calcutta. He wants to gift it to Annada Charan. I need to tell him that I have placed an order for one. He will get it when I visit the city next time.'

And then, just as they got up to leave, Rakhal said, 'You know, Dhananjoy babu, this death, this murder of that poor girl has affected us all. Everyone's on edge. Quite often, poor Puti gets the brunt of it. Sushila keeps imagining she sees dust everywhere and shouts at Puti for not cleaning properly. If I try to reassure her, she says that she wants the house to be spotless for our child when it arrives. I really don't know what to say. Lately, she has also started imagining she can hear the sound of footsteps coming from upstairs after we lie down to sleep. I'm a heavy sleeper, especially after a long day at the kachhari. But Sushila claims she can hear someone pacing!'

With a sigh, Rakhal stopped talking. Dhananjoy looked at him thoughtfully and said, 'Rakhal babu, the truth, when it comes out after our investigation, could be an ugly one. But however unwholesome, it needs to be dragged out from the dark.'

Before Rakhal could respond to Dhananjoy's words, a woman's voice could be heard calling him. 'Rakhal-da, o Rakhal-da.'

12

A HOLMES FAN

A plump young woman with a thick plait flung carelessly over one shoulder marched into the room and then froze in her tracks when she saw the two strangers. She was not pretty in the conventional sense, thought Dhananjoy as he looked at her, and yet he felt that one couldn't help wanting to look at her twice. Never before had he seen a more arresting pair of eyes. Large, shaped like almonds and ringed with a thick fan of lashes. But what made them compellingly attractive was the fearlessness with which they held his gaze.

After doing a brief namaskar, she turned to Rakhal and said, 'Rakhal-da, Sukanta dada has been running a fever since last night. When I went to meet him today in his room, his eyes looked bloodshot and his forehead felt quite warm to the touch. Of course, he told me not to make a fuss, but I am beginning to get a little worried. I've rarely seen him lying in bed like this. He's not eating much either. Shouldn't we do something? Call Annada mama?'

Rakhal looked dismayed at her words. 'Sukanta has fever, did you say? Let me see what I can do. Don't worry, I'll send someone to fetch Annada Charan. It's probably nothing, but why take a chance? I'll take care of this, Usha. Don't you worry.'

He made to rush out of the room and then stopped and said sheepishly, 'What's wrong with me? Where are my manners? I have not even introduced these gentlemen to you. Dhananjoy babu, Daroga babu, this is our Usha. Sukanta's sister, as you must have gathered. Our niece, even though both Sukanta and she call my wife Sushila-di and me Rakhal-da.' The last line was said with an indulgent smile.

After the exchange of greetings, Usha looked at the two inspectors and said, 'I guessed as much. Sushila didi has been talking about the two detectives who questioned her. She bragged to me that she had given the police some very valuable information. Well, let's see if I can match what she has told you. Would you like to ask me any questions?'

Rakhal babu asked her to sit in the chair he had vacated and then began to hasten out of the room. Dhananjoy suddenly said, 'One minute, Rakhal babu. How did you injure your hand? I think I saw a bandage on it yesterday.'

'Oh, that? On my way to Calcutta, I hurt my hand on the train. Kept it on a surface where there was a piece of glass. That's all really. It had bled quite a bit at the time, but it's more or less healed now.' He extended his hand to show the two policemen, and the signs of a healed gash were clearly visible.

'Thanks for clearing that up for us, Rakhal babu. We won't trouble you now.'

Once Rakhal had left, Dhananjoy turned to Usha and caught a glint of amusement in her eyes. The girl looked perfectly poised as she sat with her arms folded and waited for the detectives to speak. After a while, she cocked an eyebrow slightly and said, 'Dhananjoy babu, I'm sure you have seen women like me in Calcutta. Women of respectable households who have stepped out of the purdah. My father is a Brahmo.* From what I've heard, he wasn't too keen to marry Ballabh Ray's sister but was forced by my grandfather. Anyway, my father made sure I was taught to read and write, and he urged me to forfeit the purdah. That made my mother quite unhappy, but, of course, it was his word that prevailed. I was torn since I loved them both equally, but after a while I decided not to spend my life behind a screen. I have never had cause to regret that decision.'

Dhananjoy cleared his throat and shot her a searching glance. 'Usha debi, you use the present tense while talking about your father. So how is it then that...?' He left the question hanging in the air.

Usha's face clouded a little upon hearing the question. As he looked at her downcast expression, Dhananjoy suddenly remembered that Bansi had mentioned something about a stepmother whom Usha and Sukanta didn't get along with. He would have done anything to retract his question, but it was too late to backpedal now.

Those remarkable eyes stayed lowered, but after a while they looked up at the two men with admirable calm. With a dry smile, Usha said, 'You don't miss much, do you, Dhananjoy babu? Yes, you are right. Baba is very much alive and living in our Beltala house in Calcutta. With his second wife. My mother died when both Dada and I were fairly young. After two years, Baba married Miss Matheson, my English tutor.'

She stopped at this point to draw in a long breath and then went on after a while, her fingers pressed into the edge of her chair. 'I wish I could cast aspersions on the lady and blame her for luring our father, but that would be lying. Miss Matheson and he were in love. I don't think my baba and ma

---

* Brahmos were members of the Brahmo Samaj that was established in 1828 in Calcutta at the initiative of the well-known reformer Raja Rammohun Roy and some of his distinguished friends. It grew out of Roy's passionately held ideas related to monotheism.

had a happy marriage. I was quite young when my mother died, but I rarely saw my parents sitting together for a chat or laughing together. Ma kept busy in her puja *ghar*, and Baba had his own life. Part of me can't blame him for loving Miss Matheson. I loved her, too, when she was my governess. I was very close to her, in fact. She taught me some valuable lessons in life. Things that perhaps the British appreciate far more than we do. The importance of punctuality, for instance. She was also an avid reader of detective novels, and what do you know? Those novels are my best companions today! Nevertheless, Dada and I couldn't bear to see her take Ma's place. But don't feel sorry for us. We've got used to being in our mamabari now. I can't imagine being anywhere else. And I know this will sound terribly ungrateful, but things have become so much better after my mama, Ballabh Ray, became paralysed. I adore my aunt, Thakurani-ma. I feel she runs the estate with such aplomb. But the strange thing is, despite all that she has had to go through as Mama's wife, she still believes in the importance of marriage. Every now and then, she asks me when she should start looking for a husband for me.'

With a grimace, she went on, 'Well, I am perfectly happy with the way things are. I have Dada, and I have my books. Baba comes to visit us every now and then. I go to the Beltala house once a year when Miss Matheson sails off to Brighton to visit her folks. Other than that, I am quite happy being at the Rajbari. There you have it. That, in a nutshell, is the story of my life.'

She moved her sharp chin defiantly to gauge the reactions of the two men. Bansidhar examined his toes to avoid her eyes, and while the girl's candour had stirred his heart, Dhananjoy managed to look inscrutable. Usha's carefully projected indifference and ironic tone had not really deceived him. He could sense a deep hurt that lay under the well-cultivated poise.

After being silent for a few seconds, he said, 'We appreciate your honesty, Usha debi, but believe me, I did not mean to pry. We are here to get information that would be relevant to the case.'

'Yes, I know that, Dhananjoy babu. But it's better that you hear about my family and my life from me. Well, now, let's hear what other questions you have for me. As I said, I am a great admirer of detective novels.' Then, with a broad smile, she added, 'My secret ambition is to write detective novels someday. I want to create a detective like Holmes, who will appear in all my novels. Perhaps a female detective?' When the men remained silent, she continued in an amused voice, 'Someone who won't be able to travel like her male counterparts but will use her wisdom and knowledge of human nature to solve cases. Maybe I'll give her a male assistant who can do all the running around on her behalf. What do you think? Won't that be interesting? To be honest, a part of me can't help feeling thrilled to be in the midst of this investigation. It's like I have entered the plot of a book that I've been reading.'

Usha's eyes were sparkling with merriment, but Dhananjoy refused to be drawn into a discussion about detective novels. He wanted to tell her that real-life investigations were rarely about thrills and chases.

Instead, in a crisp voice he asked her, 'What can you tell us about Sarala Dasi, Usha debi? Why would anyone have wanted to kill her?'

'I've been thinking about that for some days now. What did I think of the young widowed girl who helped Kamini didi in the kitchen? Hmm... Nothing much really, except that she seemed efficient and less prone to unnecessary attacks of panic than Puti. Well, there's one thing...'

Dhananjoy could see that Usha had more to say, but the decision to share the information was causing her some internal struggle. He waited quietly while she gripped her own hand and reflected on how to proceed. Her brow was furrowed with fretfulness, and she was biting her thumb.

'Yes?' Bansi encouraged her gently.

Her mind made up, she looked at them and said, 'This is not going to be easy for me. What I'm about to tell you involves two people whom I regard as family. I don't even know if this information is significant. I know from my reading of detective novels that people like you need to piece all kinds of information together to solve a case. But wouldn't I be betraying my loved ones when I talk about them behind their backs? Not that what I'm going to say proves their guilt, but it still feels like treachery of sorts.'

It was all that Dhananjoy could do not to reach out and pat Usha's hand to reassure her that she was doing the right thing. Surprised at how tempted he felt to shed his habitual reserve, he rose from his chair and walked up to one of the windows in order to put some distance between them.

Bansidhar said, 'Usha debi, we understand. Take your time. We'll wait till you feel ready to talk.'

After a few minutes, Usha made a clicking noise with her tongue, fidgeted with one of her plaits and then said, 'All right, let me get it off my chest before I start getting cold feet. Please bear in mind that this was just something that I happened to observe. Maybe it meant nothing. I'll leave that for you to work out.'

Both men nodded solemnly and waited for her to continue.

'What I'm about to describe took place a few months ago. I think Sarala was more or less living in this house at the time. That was the day I noticed the young girl.'

The skies had looked threatening since the morning, but it was only close to the evening that peals of thunder could be heard. Usha had stepped out on the veranda outside her room on the second floor as the storm broke and a few drops of rain fell, making sounds like the tapping of tiny bird feet. She had just finished reading a novel by Panchkari Dey, and while she had liked the twisty plot, it had also left her feeling annoyed. Why, she wondered, must words like mayabi, mayabini, kaalnagini be used for women who wanted things on their own terms? Why did they always have to be seen as wily enchantresses or deceitful serpents? When she wrote her detective novels, she would do things very differently. But what if her publishers insisted that she toe the line? Well, she would just have to convince them of her point of view. And it was while a stormy exchange with her imaginary publishers was raging in her head that she looked down and saw a curious scene unfold.

The whole thing was over in minutes, and yet it left her with a sense of disquiet as though she had witnessed something private and forbidden. Rakhal-da was standing at the bottom of a staircase, well hidden from the kitchen, his gaze trained on a young woman sitting outside the kitchen and chopping vegetables. Usha had not really paid much attention to the new kitchen hand before that day, but she looked at her carefully now. The girl's skin looked like burnished copper, and the gracefulness of her slender limbs, accentuated by the rain-dampened sari, made even the mundane act of vegetable-chopping seem enchanting. And then she noticed another person staring at this tableau from the first-floor veranda. Sushila-di must also have come out of her room to look at the rain and become transfixed by what she could see. She must have been busy braiding her hair in her favourite jilipi style of complicated knots as she stepped out. Only half her hair was tied, while the other half remained untended as her hands gripped the edge of the balcony and her eyes stared at the scene below.

The object of their attention, however, was completely oblivious as she worked on the boti with fierce concentration. Even when she stopped to arch her aching back and press her neck, Sarala remained as unaware of the man watching her with keen interest as that of the woman whose eyes smouldered with visceral hatred and jealousy. And just then, Sukanta emerged from one of the rooms near the kitchen with a book in his hand, and upon seeing him, Rakhal darted upstairs. Sushila-di also retreated to her room.

'That's all I needed to tell you. Don't you want to write all this down in your diary?'

Dhananjoy smiled wryly and said, 'Don't worry about it. There are some things that we can remember without noting them down.' Just then, they heard the grandfather clock strike four times. Usha looked a little agitated and said, 'Achha, I have to take your leave now. I need to go and see if Dada wants anything. I can't bear to see him feeling poorly. It's so unlike him. He's always up and about, brimming with energy. And today when I saw him, he... You will have to excuse me. I'm sure I'll see you again while this case remains unsolved, am I right?'

Before she could leave, they heard tentative footsteps outside the room, and Puti entered bearing a tray with cups of tea and sweets on it. Usha looked at her and smiled approvingly. 'The clock chimes four and Puti enters! Well done, Puti! Your punctuality would please even the sahibs. Place the tea and sweets here for the babus. I'll take care of the rest.' Usha looked at Puti's retreating back and said, 'The poor girl was quite shaken by Sarala's murder. Besides, she's also had to take on quite a bit of what Sarala used to do. For some reason, I have this bee in my bonnet about having tea at this time. Picked it up from Miss Matheson, and even though I have tried to shake the habit off, my throat betrays me and begins to crave tea just when it's close to four.'

Usha gripped the bars of the window of her room and stood watching the two police officers walk out of the Rajbari. She was glad she had been able to give them something to gnaw on. But did she do the right thing in throwing Sushila-di and Rakhal-da to the wolves? It was true that the hatred she had seen in Sushila's eyes that day had been real and intense, but should she have spoken about it to the detectives?

As a detective novel aficionado, she knew that every bit of information was important, and it was her duty to tell the police everything she could think of. But she hadn't been able to tell them everything, had she? She couldn't, for instance, bring herself to tell them that even after Rakhal and Sushila had left, she had continued to stand on the veranda. And had seen the way Sukanta, her Dada, had stood and chatted in a familiar way with the attractive young cook. There were more things that she couldn't have talked about. No, she couldn't have told them everything. She could not have brought herself to utter a word that could get Dada into trouble. Truth be told, she was glad that young woman was dead. What business did she have batting her eyelashes at Dada or talking and laughing as though they were friends, she thought as she bit her lip and clutched her fists to her sides. The girl was an overreacher. She really had it coming.

Ever since Usha had been a lonely and confused child, stunned by her mother's death and then what had seemed like her father's treachery, Dada was everything to her. The very possibility of losing him made her feel ill. She had a great deal of affection for Rakhal-da and felt sorry for him for being saddled with that busybody of a wife. But Dada was her bulwark, her world. When she was tiny, her mother used to tell her about her own brave grandfather, a wild game hunter, who had met his nemesis in a tigress. The tigress had seen him as a threat to her cubs and mauled him to death.

Usha felt like that tigress, ready to go to any lengths to protect her dada.

Had she really succeeded in throwing the tall and lanky detective from Calcutta off the scent? Her pulse had quickened as she sat talking to him and covertly scrutinized the face with its pronounced jawline, aquiline nose and untidy hair. He had such a forceful gaze. His eyes looked like they could pierce through all evasions and prevarications and zero in on the truth. Even as she had put up a steely front while talking to them, her heart had been banging against her ribs and her nails had been digging painfully into her palms. It was a good thing her chair was angled away from him and he couldn't really see her hands. Usha drew a deep breath, sat down heavily on a nearby chair and stared at the ceiling. All her reading about crime and detection had convinced her that the line between right and wrong was a clear and unmistakable one. And that she would always know where it lay. Like the man she hero-worshipped – Holmes – she had assumed she could remain unflinchingly objective and neutral in all circumstances. And yet here she was, drowning in ethical dilemmas and indecision. Holmes, very conveniently, didn't have to face such problems. No one could make him feel vulnerable and conflict-torn. Hadn't she vowed to herself that she would not be the kind of woman who let her emotions get the better of her? But the urge to cry was becoming stronger by the minute as Usha recalled some of the shameful things she had done. It was to protect her dada. But was such a rationale actually enough? If only there was someone she could turn to for answers. She had often gone to Thakurani-ma with her problems, but that wasn't going to be possible this time. After a while, Usha sniffed loudly and let the tears flow out of her eyes.

13

THE LEAVES OF DHATURA

'What did you make of what you heard today, Joy?' Bansidhar asked his friend in the evening. Dhananjoy was sipping hot tea from a brass tumbler while Bansidhar sat with a hookah, looking deeply relaxed as the smoke travelled to his lungs. Without planning it, the sitting together at the end of the day to discuss their investigation had become a kind of daily ritual. Both men cherished and looked forward to it.

After carefully cleaning his spectacles with the side of his kurta before putting them on, Dhananjoy said, 'I'm still not sure, Bansi. I want to sit down tonight and study all the notes that I've made. There are too many questions whirling around in my head. Questions with no convincing answers. Why was Kamini threatening her kitchen hand? Who was Sarala's paramour? The father of her unborn child? What was it that had made her change into a confident woman? Was more than one man interested in her? Who all had found out that she was pregnant? Why did she have those dhatura leaves in her stomach on the day she was killed when she died due to a blow to her head? Were there two killers? Only one of whom succeeded? Do you remember Annada babu had talked of Sarala having visited him after hurting her foot? Was that injury simply an accident? What's the yogi maharaj hiding from us? Had Sarala confided in him and was the secret becoming too much of a burden to hold on to? Why are there coconuts missing from the Rajbari kitchen? As I said, too many questions. Just too many bloody questions!' The vexed frown between Dhananjoy's eyebrows kept deepening with each question.

'Hold on! What did you say? Really? Are you serious? Missing coconuts are part of the list of questions related to Sarala's death? Are you having me on?'

The corners of Dhananjoy's lips lifted slightly. 'It might not be important at all. But I just don't like unsolved puzzles. My thoughts keep snagging on things like this. So, I have included it in my list.'

Bansidhar shook his head as though to say that he would never fully understand his friend's quirks but was willing to humour him. 'Well,' he said, 'I can think of another important question. Who was it that threw the stone at you that evening? Maybe Bama can fill some of the gaps when she brings us news.'

'Hmm... or what she tells us might muddy the waters even further. We also need to meet the young man Sukanta. I didn't insist on seeing him today since it sounded like he was unwell. But he's also an important player in all this. Quite the charmer, too. Even the ill-tempered Kamini smiled fondly while talking about him.'

Bansi's head swivelled towards his friend. 'Do you think Sarala's pregnancy...?'

'It has to be somebody belonging to the Rajbari, don't you think?'

Just then, they saw a woman open the gate of the house and slip in silently. Bansidhar jumped a little upon seeing the shadowy figure, but once she unveiled her face, he realized it was Bama. She was a little winded by the walk from the Rajbari, and Bansidhar went in to get some water for her. After a while, when she had had water along with some sweets, she settled down to tell them what she had learnt about Sarala during her last few days of working as a kitchen hand.

'Bansidhar babu, I have learnt a few things from my chats with Puti. My work actually became quite easy since the girl is a chatterbox. Not averse to eavesdropping either, from what I could gather. Puti and Sarala were quite thick. Maybe it was an alliance formed of necessity. She told me whenever the two of them sat down together for a chat, they griped about Kamini. No surprises there! Kamini is a hard taskmaster and quite pernickety about how things are to be done in the kitchen. I have seen that myself. But Puti also told me that lately, Sarala had been saying to her that if she were to reveal a certain truth about Kamini, the head cook could lose her precious job. That she had better watch out.'

The two men exchanged glances, and then Bansidhar asked, 'But what Sarala knew was kept a secret, right?'

'Yes, she never told Puti what it was. But the young girl could feel a great deal of tension in the air whenever Kamini and Sarala were in the kitchen together. In fact, Puti said that at times the anger between them was so potent that even without their uttering a single word to each other, she felt like there was an argument raging in the kitchen. It was all she could do not to run away from the kitchen whenever those two were in it.'

'That bad, huh?'

'Yes. But other than that, there are two other things that I thought might interest you. One was an incident involving Usha didi.'

Upon hearing that name, Dhananjoy looked closely at Bama and shifted in his chair.

'What was the incident, Bama?'

'Puti said it happened last month.'

Puti was sitting outside the kitchen, waiting for Sarala to return from upstairs after giving Usha didi the cup of warm milk that she liked to drink before going to sleep. Kamini didi had already gone to her room. Sarala and Puti were given charge of taking care of the little things that needed to be done before closing the kitchen for the day. That day, an exhausted Puti was waiting for her friend to return from Usha didi's room so they could have their daily chat without any fear of interruptions. It was taking Sarala too long, and after a while, Puti began to make her way upstairs to see where her friend had gone. And that was when she heard the sound of glass shattering, which seemed to come from Usha didi's room. And then she saw Sarala hurrying down with broken bits of glass in her hand. Puti quickly went back to where she was sitting, and from there, she could see that Sarala was crying. Going up to her, Puti asked tentatively, 'Sarala didi, what is it? Are you hurt?'

Sarala turned to look at her with tear-filled eyes and said, 'Yes, Puti, more than you can imagine. And I don't mean my hand.' When Puti held her hand to console and comfort her, she whispered, 'Do we not have the right to be happy, Puti? Just because our husbands died, are we not to have even the slightest bit of joy in life? What have we done to deserve this punishment, bol toh?'

After finishing this account of what Puti had told her, Bama added, 'I wasn't sure whether this incident is important. After all, in grand households like the Rajbari, it's par for the course for maids and cooks to be shouted at, isn't it, Daroga babu? Who cares about their feelings or dignity after all? And yet, in the days that I have worked in the Rajbari, I have noticed that people are not unkind to the domestics. Puti told me she'd heard that things were different in Ballabh Ray's time. He did not hesitate to beat or kick his servants when he lost his temper. But with Thakurani, things are very different. Sushila didi is the only one who might throw a tantrum or two. I saw her spitting fire one day because she had discovered a handkerchief belonging to Sukanta babu in her room and was certain it was because of Puti's carelessness. She called her a slow-witted moron for getting things mixed up and reduced her to tears. And she's also obsessed with the floors being spick and span. Woe betide poor Puti if her broom and mop miss anything. But other than that... I can't think of anyone else who treats the servants badly. That's the reason I found it strange that Usha didi had flung a glass and uttered words that were harsh enough to make Sarala cry.'

The two men silently absorbed what Bama had just told them. Bansidhar cast a few sideways glances at his friend and saw that his jaw had hardened. Earlier in the morning, Bansi had sensed a shift in the air when Usha had stepped into the room and Dhananjoy and she began speaking to each other. His friend was drawn to the girl and not just as someone who could give them potential leads for the case. And yet, what Bama was saying meant that Usha had had some kind of falling out with the murdered girl. She had not been entirely honest with them. Why though? What could she be hiding?

'What else did Puti tell you?' Dhananjoy's voice sounded a little gruff.

'Yes, I felt this might be the most important thing for the case.'

'Go on. We are listening.'

'Puti said that she had once heard Sushila-di talking to Ramhari and pleading with him to take care of something. Puti said it was probably a fortnight before Durga Puja, on a day that Sarala had gone back to her house in the village.'

Puti had been feeling quite miserable that day. Those three days of the month, when her stomach would hurt and the bleeding would leave her feeling exhausted, were almost upon her. It was inauspicious to go anywhere near the kitchen on those days, and so she would be in her room, writhing in pain and calling out to her mother. She had heard from other women that labour pangs were far worse, but Puti could not even begin to imagine what that might be like. In any case, a widow at ten, it was pointless for her to think about childbirth. And unlike Sarala, she didn't really mind it either. She didn't know what to say when Sarala told her how she would give anything in the world to be held by a man and loved. To give birth to a child and love it to bits. Puti would listen to Sarala rail against the injustices that bound a widow's life and nod. But inwardly, she felt if it was their fate, then why fight it? Sarala had started talking in this manner ever since she had heard Sukanta dadababu hold forth about a man called Vidyasagar and what he had tried to do for widowed women. Once, Sukanta dadababu had even teased Kamini-di. 'Ki go, Kamini debi? What do you say? Widow marriage has been legalized by the sarkar. Should we fix the date? I'm ready if you are.'

And Kamini-di had smiled and said, 'Yes, Sukanta dadababu, you are the only one I am willing to marry. Set a date and let me know.' After that, they had all burst out laughing. That was Sukanta dadababu. He could make everyone laugh. But Sarala must have taken all the talk about widow marriage seriously. Na, Baba, Puti wasn't interested in marrying again. She was happy to have enough food to fill her stomach every day and a roof over her head in the Rajbari.

Her thoughts were suddenly disturbed by whispers that she could hear. Puti could never resist listening in on other people's conversations. She kept very still and paid close attention.

Wasn't that Sushila didi speaking? Why was she whispering? Puti was more used to her loud tirades. In a low voice, she was saying, 'Ramhari-da, you have to do something about this. Who else can I turn to? Do you want that slip of a girl to wreck my marriage?'

Lathiyal Ramhari tried to calm her down. 'Who's been filling your head with all this, Sushila didi? Rakhal babu is too decent a man for the kind of things you're imagining. Have you ever seen him being interested in anything other than his work? Only lately has he started showing interest in some of the things that Sukanta dadababu talks about. But this? No way. No, you are wrong.'

'Believe me, Ramhari-da, I'm not imagining it. That new girl has cast a spell on my husband. The father of my unborn child.' Puti could hear Sushila whimpering and sniffling.

'What do you want me to do, Sushila didi? Why don't you talk to Thakurani about this?'

'Radha didi would just laugh at my worries and call them imaginary. But I'm telling you...'

The voices dropped and became too low for Puti, and she couldn't really hear anything much after that.

Dhananjoy's attention had begun to drift a little bit, but he sat up straight when he heard Bama say, 'Daroga babu, Puti then said that she thought she had heard something about dhatura leaves being mentioned by Sushila-di. She couldn't hear exactly what was said but Puti was sure she had heard Sushila-di say something about those leaves.'

'Did you say dhatura leaves?'

'Yes, that's right.'

Bansidhar, too, stopped smoking the hookah, and his eyes widened. Had they finally found the lead they needed?

'Bama, you have been a great help. We are truly indebted to you for all that you have done, for the information that you have gathered. Let's hope we can crack the case soon. Till then, please bear with us and continue to work in the Rajbari kitchen.'

Bama nodded. 'That's all right. I don't mind working there, Dhananjoy babu. Kamini-di shouts from time to time, but it's not that bad. And I like Puti's company. There's no malice in her. Quite a scaredy-cat as well. Tells me that Sarala might have been bumped off by a ghost. Claims that in the week before Sarala died, she would hear some curious thwacking noises in the night, which apparently stopped after the murder. Bansidhar babu, I have a request. Is it okay if I spend the night here today and go back to the Rajbari early in the morning? It's just that I've told Kamini-di I needed to visit my didi in the village.'

Saroja, who was coming out at that moment to ask them about their nighttime meal, heard the last part of Bama's speech and said, 'You were absolutely right in saying that, Bama. You do have a didi staying in the village. And you don't have to ask Daroga babu if you can spend the night here. This is your didi's house, too. You will come and stay here whenever you please. Come, let's finish up the work in the kitchen, and then we can all eat.'

Bama had a broad smile as she got up to accompany Saroja. Before she went in, she turned to the two detectives and said, 'One last thing, Daroga babu. Puti told me that on that last day when she bid farewell to Sarala, she had looked very happy. She said that Sarala was often given to brooding, but that day, her face was lit up with smiles. She had hugged Puti on an impulse and said that she felt certain her life was about to turn a corner and that nothing would remain the same. That was her last memory of her friend, Puti said.'

At night, after both Saroja and Bama had gone to sleep, Dhananjoy and Bansi sat to discuss the case and what they should do next. Bama had told them that Thakurani had left for her parents' house after receiving news that her mother was unwell and that she would return in a few days. Ramhari had gone with her but was expected to be back soon. Everyone else was in the Rajbari.

Bansidhar sat and leaned his head back against the wall while Dhananjoy lay on the madoor with his arms folded under his head. The silence around them was interrupted intermittently by the piercing cries of chatak birds announcing the arrival of rain sometime soon.

'Joy, you were right. The questions seem to be just piling up. We are no closer to making sense of the things we hear than we were when we began. I am beginning to feel like Abhimanyu caught in that maze. What do you think?'

Dhananjoy mused for a while. 'Yes, you are right. I am also getting tired of these half-truths and lies that we come back with. Maybe not everything that's being held back from us is relevant to our case. But we won't know what to eliminate till we find out what they are hiding. The time has come to rattle their cages a little bit.' After scratching his chin for a while, he went on. 'All right, here's what we can do. Since Kamini needs to be questioned, you talk to her and try to find out what made her hate Sarala so much. I get the feeling that Sarala had something on her that was upsetting the balance of power in that kitchen. But what exactly was it that Sarala knew?'

'Do you think I would need to take her to the thana?'

Dhananjoy remained silent as he considered Bansidhar's question while stubbing out his cigarette. Then he adjusted his spectacles and said, 'I have a feeling the threat of being pulled in will do the trick. If you go along with two jamadars in the morning and tell her that you will have to arrest her if she doesn't cough up the truth about what was going on between Sarala and her, she will realize that you mean business. Let's take advantage of Thakurani's absence. With her not there, Kamini will be easier to pressurize.'

'What's your gut telling you? Could she have killed Sarala?'

'She is definitely a strong woman, used to hard physical labour in the kitchen. A few years ago, in Calcutta, there was a woman called Trailokya who killed quite a few prostitutes. She was given the death sentence once she was caught. And that day, Annada babu also said it wouldn't have been impossible for a woman to bring that brick down on Sarala's head with the required force. If Puti is to be believed, Kamini despised Sarala. Sushila debi also talked of having witnessed that altercation between them. From my chat with Kamini, it is clear that she can do anything for her Thakurani.'

'Could she have found out about Sarala's pregnancy and felt enraged at how it would add to Thakurani's troubles? As it is, there was no love lost between the two cooks. That might just have been the last straw.'

'Kamini was evasive about certain things when I questioned her, but I think you'll have to extract the truth from her. One way or the other, we need to know. If she's innocent, she should just tell us the truth and clear her name.'

'What about Ramhari? He could have had something to do with the dhatura leaves that Sarala took, don't you think? Based on what Bama told us about what Puti had overheard, he might have been acting at Sushila's behest. Given the lathiyal's soft spot for Thakurani and Sushila, it wouldn't have been hard for her to manipulate him with her tears. But we'll need to question him as well, right? Also, he's a lathiyal, and Sarala was killed with one well-aimed blow. Surely Ramhari could be our man.'

'Yes, that's right. Both Kamini and Ramhari need to be pinned down and asked a few tough questions. Talk to Ramhari as soon as he returns. Arrest him if necessary. I doubt he'll admit that he was doing it for his Sushila didi, but at least let's find out if those leaves came from him.'

'What do you plan to do?'

Dhananjoy pointed to his notes and said, 'I have a couple of things planned. I want to go through my notes again and see what we have missed. Somehow, every time I try to construct a picture of the killer in my mind from the information that we have, the image seems to escape through my fingers like smoke. I want to give it another shot.'

'You know, Joy, in all honesty, I can't bring myself to imagine any of the people that we have talked to as a cold-blooded killer.'

'And yet, one of them is. Hard as it is to imagine, someone in that household was driven by desperation or jealousy or anger or hatred to take that drastic step. The thing is, Bansi, we assume killers look a certain way. Maybe like a Ravan or a Mahishasur? But murderers aren't always born killers. They have been driven by something, something that has pushed them to cross the line. To act in a manner we consider inhuman. Something that they can justify to themselves.'

Bansidhar looked crestfallen. 'Yes, yes, you are right. Not a Mahishasur but someone who looks as ordinary as you and me. And that makes it even more frightening, doesn't it?'

'Yes, and our task of finding them even harder.'

'What's the other thing you are planning to do? You said you have a couple of things planned.'

'Why don't I tell you tomorrow? It's simply something that will keep niggling my mind till I find a satisfactory answer for it. It could very well be a wild goose chase.'

'Like the mystery of the missing coconuts?'

With a smile, Dhananjoy said, 'Yes. Something like that.'

14

AN UNEXPECTED VISITOR

Next evening when the two detectives met, having parted ways in the morning, Bansi looked a little deflated. Dhananjoy could see that things had not quite turned out the way the daroga had expected them to.

'How did it go, Bansi?'

'Not exactly the result I was expecting.' Bansi sounded gloomy.

'I think I've worked out what Kamini's big secret might have been. The one that Sarala had cottoned on to and become insolent about.'

'What! You have? Why didn't you tell me in the morning when I was leaving for the Rajbari?'

'I wasn't entirely sure. It was just something I pieced together from my notes when I studied them later at night. Why don't you tell me what happened when you went to question Kamini, and then I'll tell you what my conclusions are.'

'As expected, when I went to the Rajbari in the morning, Kamini began by squawking and putting up quite a fight.'

Kamini's eyes had flashed with a ferocity that made Bansidhar a little nervous. If he had to force himself to imagine a female killer, the figure in front of him with her blazing eyes and belligerent air certainly came close to the one in his imagination. But despite the flutter in his heart, he stood his ground.

'Kamini, we know that you have not been telling us everything. There was definitely something that was causing enormous tension between Sarala and you. She had threatened to expose some secret, and you hated her for holding that over you. I have two jamadars positioned outside the dokhin dorja, and they are waiting for my signal. If you continue to play fast and loose with us, I'll have no choice but to summon them and have them drag you to the thana. I'm sure you don't want that.'

'What else can you people do but harass poor people like me?'

In a firm voice, Bansi said, 'Look, Kamini, you know very well that's not what this is about. You have met my friend, Dhananjoy, too. Do we strike you as being the kind of police officers who like persecuting the poor for no reason? We've been talking to people in this household, and it is based on information we have that I have come here.'

'What information exactly? If it's Puti who's been gabbling behind my back, I'll...' Kamini stopped when she realized that issuing threats against her kitchen hand would only land her in bigger trouble.

'If you must know, someone from the family saw you squabbling with Sarala in the gardens and then grabbing her hand and shouting threats. Things are not looking very good for you, Kamini. So, if you want to tell me everything here and now, this is your last chance. Else I'll have to call my jamadars.'

Kamini's shoulders had slumped, and after looking behind her to make sure that Puti and Bama were out of earshot, she said, 'It's all right, I'll tell you what was going on, Daroga babu. But you'll have to believe me. I hated that girl's guts, and I really wanted to wring her neck, but that was just all in my mind. I admit I'm short-tempered, but I could never kill another human being. Never!'

'And then she took you aside and told you that her eyesight has been failing – a major disaster for the head cook of a kitchen – and that Sarala had found out about it, am I right?'

Bansi's jaw dropped, and after trying and failing to talk for a few seconds, he finally managed to say, 'What! How did you do that, Joy? I can't believe you knew that!'

'Arre, it was no great feat. It occurred to me while I was looking through my notes. I'll tell you in a bit. First, tell me what Kamini had to say.'

'She was reluctant at first. But then, she realized, like you said she would, that it would be better to tell me everything than visiting the thana.'

Around the time of the monsoons, Kamini noticed that her eyesight had begun to fail, and she walked around with a hard ball of anxiety and frustration lodged in her gut. She would have died rather than reveal to anyone that she was unable to distinguish between the seeds of cumin and fennel when tempering or between the white and black mustard seeds when cooking fish. Accidents had been narrowly averted because her sense of smell remained as strong as ever. Little did the other cooks in the kitchen know that behind the grim expression on her face lay suppressed panic. Panic that tampered with her memory and led to accidents like over-salting or under-salting the food. Panic at the thought that her life as a Rajbari cook could just crumble to pieces and that she might have to leave Thakurani. She had nothing to fear from that ninny, Puti, but Sarala was nobody's fool.

And then, one day, Kamini had heard a sharp intake of breath while she was peering closely at the spices in her hand, her eyes screwed up in concentration. She realized her fears had come true. Sarala had found out her weakness. Kamini remained silent, and surprisingly, so had Sarala. But then the little acts of rebelliousness began, and Kamini knew that she had to confront the girl and have it out with her. She had also begun to notice the young widow's excessive friendliness with Sukanta dadababu. What was the wretch up to? And so, one day, when she saw Sarala wiping her hands in an effort to remove the residual smells and stains of all that had been cooked that day and preparing to leave the kitchen, she had asked her to walk with her to the garden. Once inside the garden, she had squared up to her.

'Listen, Sarala, this behaviour has to stop immediately. And don't try to play the innocent with me because you know very well what I'm talking about.'

Sarala had looked at her with an unnervingly calm face and said coldly, 'Let go of my arm, and don't take that tone with me. You don't scare me. And nothing is going to stop because you say so. I've had enough of your bullying.'

Kamini could feel rage course through every vein of her body. Eyes narrowed into slits, she hissed, 'What did you say, you she-devil? Do you know who you are talking to?'

Quick was the unruffled reply. 'Yes, to a blind old cook who can barely see what spices are going into the pot on the stove. Or even figure out the right amount of salt for a dish.'

Restraining an overwhelming urge to throw the girl on the ground and stamp on her impudent face, Kamini shouted, 'I am still the head cook here, do you understand? Do you? Bujhhechish? Nothing will change that.'

'Joy, Kamini kept insisting that that was as far as it went. Just threats shouted in a moment of anger. Besides, she said that because of her eyesight problem, she rarely goes anywhere after dark. There was no way she could have followed Sarala that day and killed her. After listening to her, I found it hard to disbelieve her. She's desperate to hold on to her job. That position as head cook means a lot to her. But I doubt she killed for it.'

'Hmm, I believe that too. Besides, as she says, given the state of her eyesight, it would have been physically impossible for her to follow Sarala in the evening, take the right aim with the brick and then return in the dark. But at least we now know why those two were at loggerheads. Kamini is a proud woman; she could barely admit to herself that her skills as a cook might diminish because of her eyesight problems. No way could she allow the world to find out about it. A lot of nervous desperation lies behind all that bluster. She's not our killer. We can strike her off our list of suspects.'

'Yes, that's why when she held my hand with desperate urgency and begged me not to disclose her secret to anyone, I didn't refuse. But, Joy, you still haven't told me how you worked it out.'

'Believe me, it was no big deal! Remember how Sushila told us about the mistakes Kamini had started making in the proportions of salt? Or how she had tripped and spilt food on her? I had myself seen her stumbling on the root of a tree twice even though it was fairly hard to miss. Once I settled down with my notes, it wasn't very difficult to connect the dots.'

'If you say so. I could never have figured that out by myself in a hundred years. What next? Ramhari will be returning the day after tomorrow. I'd thought of sending two men to Gobindapur. That is Thakurani's natal village. But then I decided it would be far easier to arrest him when he returns. Over there, Pratap Ray Chaudhuri, Thakurani's father, might create problems. Once the lathiyal is here, it'll be that much simpler to grab him. I'll post two men outside the Rajbari to keep an eye out for his return.'

'That sounds like a good plan.'

'But, Joy, what do we do about Sushila? If it was she who forced Ramhari's hand, should she be allowed to evade punishment completely?'

'What *can* you do, Bansi? I admit it'll be a grossly unfair thing, but as I said, Ramhari will die before giving her up as a co-conspirator or the prime mover of the plan. His loyalty is blind and unshakeable. Especially since she's pregnant, he'll want to protect her with his life.'

'And without his saying anything, we won't have a speck of evidence against her.'

'We won't. Even if Puti were to be convinced to give testimony against a member of the mighty Rajbari – which I very much doubt is likely to happen – it won't be strong enough to help us put Sushila behind bars. You know, Bansi, we really need to find out who the father of Sarala's child was. Given that she barely left the Rajbari, it has to be either Rakhal or Sukanta, don't you think?'

'Rakhal babu, it seems, was attracted to her. Or so Sushila believed. What Usha debi told us that day also seems to suggest it. But would Sarala have wanted a relationship with him? A married man? Also, would Rakhal have had the gumption to commit adultery at a time when his wife was pregnant? I'm not so sure. He doesn't look the type. But stranger things have happened. And he could well have concocted that overheard conversation with another man to throw us off the scent.

'Sukanta, on the other hand, seems to be popular with the ladies. It could very well be that he had got her pregnant and was then shocked when she dug her heels in and refused to end the affair. If Sarala told Haridasi she would be going away to Calcutta, it could either mean that she was extracting money from her lover or that her lover had promised her they would elope together to the city.

'Let's just ask some blunt, straightforward questions and see what answers we get. Shake the tree and see what falls.'

Bansi looked a bit uncertain about the efficacy of the tree-shaking method, but he trusted his friend too much to demur. And then, just as their discussions of the day's events were getting over, both the men heard something that made them sit up alertly. The gate to the house was being opened, and this time, it was not Bama who was walking towards them with faltering footsteps but Sijad.

~

'Sijad! What brings you here at this time of the night?'

The shy young man looked quite flustered when addressed in this direct manner, so Dhananjoy decided to give him some time to overcome his skittishness. Placing a gentle hand on Sijad's shoulder, he guided the frightened-looking young man to the madoor and, asking Bansi to stay with him, went inside to get some water. After a while, feeling restored enough to talk, Sijad gripped his hands together and said, 'Dhananjoy babu, Daroga babu, both of you know that I adore and admire Annada babu.'

Bansi and Dhananjoy reassured Sijad that not just they but everyone else in the village knew that.

The young man's eyes filled with tears, and he curled into a foetal position, his distress palpable. After gulping a few times, he began. 'I have been wondering for some time now whether to tell you this or not. I just didn't want to do anything that might harm Daktar babu. And yet, ever since that woman died, this memory has been like a constant dull ache inside me.' The young man broke into sobs.

After a few minutes, Dhananjoy held his shoulders and said, 'Look here, Sijad. Murder is a nasty business and, unfortunately, it then becomes the job of officers like us to go probing into areas of darkness. A lot of the stuff that we dredge up is irrelevant, but some of it ends up helping us solve the mystery. The thing is, Sijad, that while everyone has the right to their secrets, when a murder happens those considerations have to be cast aside. Believe me when I say that whatever you tell us here will be in the strictest confidence. Relieve yourself of this painful burden you seem to have been carrying on your young shoulders. Let us deal with it.'

Dhananjoy's steady, reassuring voice had the necessary effect and, after a few minutes of biting his knuckles, Sijad began to tell them what he had accidentally seen and heard one evening.

Sijad had been reading one of the medical books that Annada Charan had given him when he stumbled upon a problem that he felt warranted an immediate discussion with his mentor. It was late afternoon, and he enjoyed walking to the doctor's dispensary. Helping Daktar babu treat his patients had given Sijad a great deal of practical understanding of what it meant to be a doctor. From snakebites to various stomach ailments, he had seen it all as Annada Charan's informal assistant. As he walked, Sijad thought idly that it would be close to evening by the time he reached the dispensary. The last of Daktar babu's patients would have left, and the two of them would have all the time in the world to discuss Sijad's question. It was almost evening when he reached the dispensary. But as Sijad was about to march in, he heard raised voices emanating from inside. The young man froze in his tracks. It was a woman that Daktar babu seemed to be arguing with.

'I need to talk to Radharani about this. I can't keep this a secret from her, Sarala.'

The woman's voice sounded full of desperation. 'No, Daktar babu, you can't do this to me. I came to you and didn't go to a dai because I see you as a decent person who will help a poor widow and not sully her reputation. I haven't even told Haridasi Boishnobi about this. I need to keep on working for a while before I sort out things. I beseech you, don't bring Thakurani into this.'

'No, no, Sarala, you are putting me in an impossible position. Radhu needs to be informed. If something were to happen and she were to find out later that I knew and kept her in the dark, I would never be able to look her in the eye again.'

The sounds that followed suggested that Sarala was trying to use tears to convince Daktar babu as she begged and pleaded. But after a while, when Annada Charan refused to give in, the mood in the room shifted. The pleas fell silent, and when Sarala spoke, it was in a voice that was hard and cold. 'So that's all that you care about? Losing your precious Radharani's trust? A poor widow's ordeal means nothing to you, is it? Well, don't think I'll give up so easily. If you're going to be stubborn, I'll have no choice but to spread rumours about Thakurani and you. I've seen the way you look at her. And believe me, this is not an empty threat. You know how it is in the village. All I need to do is drop a hint here and there. She, for all practical purposes, is leading a widow's life, and here you are, a cousin she has brought from somewhere. Is the setting up of a dispensary just a smokescreen for other goings-on? The rest will be left to people's imagination. And you know how the people of Rajapur love nothing more than juicy bits of gossip. What do you say now? You have left me no choice.'

The sound of the flat of a hand being slammed with great force on a table made Sijad jump with fear. Daktar babu must have been sitting, for as he rose, his chair fell back with a crashing sound. 'What? What did you say, you foul-mouthed creature? Have you gone completely mad? How can you even say something like that about the woman who took you in and gave you your means of livelihood? Have you forgotten everything already? Don't you feel?'

Sarala's loud, strident voice interrupted him. 'Feel what? Gratitude? Yes! Of course! Because that's what I have to keep feeling all my life, right? My entire life has been about the need to be grateful, hasn't it? Grateful to my parents for letting me survive, grateful to that husband of mine for marrying me, grateful to the people of the Rajbari for employing me. I'm tired of being grateful. Do you hear, Daktar babu? Tired of being a supplicant, begging for crumbs that the world deems fit to throw in my direction. I want to lead my life differently. I really want my child to live. I hope it's a girl and that she can learn how to read and write. Is that a crime? Well, you might think what you want, but I'm going to try my utmost to make it happen. And for that, if I need to spread vile rumours about Thakurani and you, I'll do that. The world loves nothing better than to tear a woman's reputation to pieces and bring her down from the pedestal they had placed her on. Go ahead and chew on that.'

'What a despicable mind you have! I wish I could tear that tongue out right now. I...' Sijad had never heard the doctor lose self-control and shriek in that manner. Even in a crisis, he kept his calm. Where had this angry shouting man emerged from? After a while, he heard Sarala storming out and quickly hid himself. She was hissing, 'Remember my words, Daktar babu,' as she strode out. And in a voice that made Sijad's blood run cold, he heard the doctor say, 'Remember that I'm a doctor, Sarala. Until now, I have used my medical knowledge to save lives. Today, you have reminded me that I have the skill to destroy a life as well.' Even after the angry scene was over, Sijad kept sitting there, hidden from view. His heart was pounding. Could rage make people this unrecognizable? Was that really the gentle, compassionate man he admired? That evening, Sijad had simply stayed hidden for a while to recover his wits and then walked back without meeting the man he idolized. Later, he told himself he would try to pretend that the entire thing had been nothing but a bad dream.

After hearing what Sijad told them, Dhananjoy said, 'Believe me, you have done the right thing by coming to us. Go home and leave the rest to us. And if possible, try to put that exchange out of your head. You can trust us with this information.'

After Sijad left them to walk back home, his shoulders sagging, the two detectives sat silently, digesting all that they had heard. Finally, Bansi said, 'Surely, we can't include Annada babu in our list of suspects, Joy! That is surely ridiculous.'

Dhananjoy had the bridge of his nose pinched between his fingers. All he said finally in response to Bansi's exclamation was a soft, 'Is it?'

15

THE NATIONALIST CAUSE

Over the next few days, incessant rain put a damper on all plans of the investigating officers to go anywhere. Trapped indoors, Dhananjoy spent long hours hunched over his notes, going over them again and again in a feverish manner. Every so often, he would lift his head to stare at the rain with unseeing eyes and think about what he had read. At times, his jaw would harden. Or he would mutter indistinctly to himself and rub his forehead. Saroja felt more and more concerned for her Thakurpo. Once or twice, she marched into the room where he sat with his notes, like a monk in a solitary cell, determined to admonish him for neglecting his health, but the heated words died on her lips when she realized that nothing she said would make a jot of difference. Bansi had become quite used to his friend's eccentric style of working by now, so he held Saroja's wrist and gently drew her out of the room and told her not to disturb him. Nor did he flinch when he heard his friend slam his fist on the ground and shout, 'I knew it!' Only once did Dhananjoy step out, saying distractedly that he needed to clear his head and see how Sijad was doing.

After three days, the heavy curtain of dark clouds finally parted, allowing the sun to peep out. By noon, only a few white puffs remained in the rain-washed cerulean skies. The two men decided to brave the slush-filled road leading to the Rajbari. Bansi grinned when he saw the exaggerated care with which his friend was placing his feet to avoid his dhoti being splashed with mud. Dhananjoy, meanwhile, was thinking about the two people he wanted to pin down and question, once they reached the Rajbari. Sukanta, of course, but he was hoping to see Usha, too. The girl had not told them everything. Oh yes! She had definitely not told them everything. Besides the spat with Sarala that Bama had reported, he had discovered something else from his notes.

As he had replayed the scenes of their earlier exchange with Usha in his mind, he felt like kicking himself. How could he have allowed himself to be taken in by those enchanting eyes and unselfconscious manner? The next interview with her, he swore to himself, would be very different. She was about to find out that Dhananjoy Lahiri was made of far sterner stuff than she had imagined. And yet, if he were to be completely honest with himself, was he not thinking of her when he had chosen to wear the crisp blue shirt over his dhoti? Bansi had arched a mischievous eyebrow when he saw his friend and then began humming a folk song about Radha and Krishna's secret rendezvous. A reproachful glare from Dhananjoy made him hum even louder. And the accompanying grin became broader. Finally, with a huff of exasperation, the Calcutta detective had marched to the kitchen in search of Saroja boudi and a cup of tea.

As they drew close to the dighi, the two police officers suddenly espied Annada babu walking purposefully towards the village with rapid steps. His hair was askew, and his clothes looked like they had been thrown on in a tearing hurry. His jawline looked grim. It was a beautiful day with a slight breeze riffling their clothes and feathering their face, but Daktar babu was clearly not out for a walk. Even when the two greeted him, the hard lines of his face didn't soften. Dhananjoy couldn't help asking him what had happened.

'Annada babu, is something wrong?'

The doctor's eyes seemed to blaze with anger. 'The two of you will understand my mood when I tell you. Poor Sijad has been attacked and injured by some young ruffians.'

'Sijad? What! But why? I can't imagine that courteous young fellow getting on the wrong side of anyone!' cried Bansi.

'These are all young men being exhorted and trained by that nephew of mine, Sukanta. Well, we are not really related, but since he's Radharani's nephew, I've also looked upon him as family. Anyway, these are men who have become his acolytes. They work themselves into a state by chanting "Bande Mataram" and then expect others to join in. That's their way to resist Curzon's evil plans to divide and rule. I have a great deal of affection for Sukanta, but I don't think he realizes the extent of the havoc he is about to wreak. Of course, for some of the young boys, the training in martial arts is a good way of channelizing all the restless energy. But there's also this beastliness that has been let loose. Thanks to their self-styled leader's rabble-rousing speeches, the ne'er-do-well youngsters are turning into louts who think they can go around terrorizing people in the name of Swadesh and *jatiyatabodh* (an awareness of ideas related to the nation).'

'I see. Now I understand why they would have attacked poor Sijad.'

'Yes, they came upon him as he was returning from Calcutta, and began shouting "Bande Mataram" loudly. When he became confused and hesitated to join in, they thrashed the poor boy within an inch of his life. Called him a *desher shatru*! An enemy of the nation! Imagine! Threw his skull cap on the ground and trampled on it. Other abuses were hurled as well, which I don't wish to repeat. There were four of them, and they behaved like animals.'

As he finished his speech, Daktar babu's fists clenched. 'All that poor boy has ever wanted is to study in the medical college and become a doctor in the city. I...'

Bansi was also looking extremely upset. He placed a comforting hand on the doctor's shoulder and said, 'Come, Daktar babu, I'll go with you. Dhananjoy, won't you be able to carry on with the interrogation in the Rajbari today? I want to see how Sijad is doing, and if he can give a statement about his attackers, I'll see what can be done. I can't bear to think what poor Chacha is going through. We won't allow this kind of hooliganism in our Rajapur.'

~

Kamini was making sure that all the utensils were kept in their right places in the kitchen when she saw the taller of the two policemen walking in through the dokhin dorja. This time, however, there were no abrasive words poised on her lips when she saw him. Instead of bristling with indignation in her usual way, she bowed her head and did a brief namaskar. Dhananjoy felt glad that he had managed to change her view that all police officers were tarred with the brush of corruption. When he returned her greeting, she came out and asked whom he wanted to meet. Kamini then turned to Puti, who was crouched over a stove and fanning the kindling inside it, and said something in a low voice and sent her off to inform Sukanta that Dhananjoy babu wanted to talk to him. After Puti left, Kamini looked distinctly uncomfortable as she addressed the detective in a contrite voice.

'Dhananjoy babu, I just told Puti to take her time and walk slowly since I need to talk to you. That day when you had asked me if everyone other than Rakhal babu was at home on the evening that Sarala died, I had said that they were. But I wasn't being truthful.'

Dhananjoy's body tensed when he heard this. He nodded and indicated that she should go on.

She rubbed her eyes and continued to look a little sheepish as she spoke. 'My instinct was to protect Sukanta dadababu. I'm immensely fond of that boy. Perhaps because he showers high praise on my cooking. I know flattery comes easily to him, and maybe those extravagant compliments are meaningless. And yet, I am touched by the fact that he thinks I am worth flattering. That he notices when I make his favourite food and rewards me with profuse expressions of gratitude.'

'Kamini-di, are you saying you saw Sukanta go out that evening?'

'No, not exactly. But that afternoon he had told me not to worry about giving him tea or *jolkhabar* since he was still feeling quite full after a heavy lunch. The meal, he said, had made him drowsy and he wanted to sleep undisturbed so he could study at night. But I made *chinrebhhaja* that evening, and he loves it. So, I decided to check if he was awake and wanted some. I took it up myself for the boy.'

Sensing the detective's growing impatience, she said solemnly, 'Well, when I went up to his room, the door had been bolted from outside. I even waited outside the room for some time, thinking he might have gone for a wander inside the estate, but there was no sign of him.'

'Was it dark when you went up?'

'Close to sunset but not dark. Sarala had definitely left the kitchen by then.'

Controlling the tide of excitement rising within him, Dhananjoy thanked Kamini and made to leave for the sadar khana to meet Sukanta. After taking a few steps, he turned around and said, 'Might I ask why the change of heart, Kamini-di?'

Kamini bit her lip, and then, with an embarrassed smile, she said, 'Well, it had not been sitting well with me, that lie. Besides, the last few days, Thakurani has been reading the words of a saint to me. Someone called Ramakrishna. Some of his devotees also refer to him as the Paramhansa. Have you heard of him, Babu? I think he lives in Calcutta. When Thakurani read the *Kathamrita,* some of his words left a deep impression. Especially what he has said about the importance of truthfulness. That we should cling to the truth like an ant holds on to a sugar granule.'

'I see. So, I should thank that Calcutta saint for this important bit of information. It has come at just the right time, too. Well, let's find out what Sukanta has to say for himself.'

Once Dhananjoy was seated in the sadar khana, it was, however, not Sukanta who entered the room but Usha. She looked somewhat frayed about the edges and refused to meet his eye when she sat down. Gone was that strikingly self-assured manner they had encountered three days ago. She looked worse for the wear and bleary-eyed. Despite himself, Dhananjoy felt a little concerned. But then he shook off the feeling and decided to go on the offensive.

'Is there something you want to tell me, Usha debi? Did you leave out a few things the other day when you talked to us? We have learnt that you had a bit of a run-in with the dead girl. Is that right? Also, as I was going over my notes, I remembered something. Well, two things really. I remembered being told that Sushila debi has lately become obsessed with cleanliness and makes sure that all the surfaces and floors are without a speck of dust. And I remember reading a detective novel, not so long ago, during one of my train journeys. Someone had left it on the train, and I ended up reading it. By an upcoming Bengali novelist. What was it called? *A Well-Planned Death*, was it? You would know surely, wouldn't you?'

'Dhananjoy babu, I...' She stopped and raised those eyes to look at him, and yet again, the detective was thrown off balance by the depth of emotions they conveyed. Her breathing had accelerated, and tears had begun pooling in those expressive eyes. Dhananjoy felt a jolt in his chest as he looked at her. What was wrong with him? Why could he not see her simply as a suspect who had been hiding things? He had seen panic flare in her eyes and knew that he needed to be firm in his interrogation. He averted his gaze from her face and concentrated on a gently swaying cobweb on the wall.

And just then, a young man walked into the room and said in a light-hearted tone, 'Here I am, Dhananjoy babu. The man you have been looking for. Aren't you here to talk to me? Apologies for not being able to meet you earlier.'

Dhananjoy rose from his chair to return the young man's greeting. Once they had sat down again, Usha rose to leave the room.

With her gaze lowered, she said to the detective, 'Please sit and talk to Dada. Let me organize *jolkhabar* for you.'

Dhananjoy turned his attention to Sukanta, but he told himself that Usha's questioning would need to be resumed. For now, though, her brother needed to answer some questions.

Sukanta, meanwhile, was waiting for his questions, an easy-going smile on his face. With slightly drooping eyes, fine strands of hair falling over his forehead and an easy manner, Sukanta's charm was hard to miss. There was a small red birthmark on his temple that resembled an ink stain. As he began to speak, Dhananjoy thought with an irrational sneer, *Here's a young man who invests a lot of energy into his charisma.* His appearance was impeccable – from the artfully combed hair to the freshly pressed clothes. Each word he uttered, each gesture he made, was for studied effect, as though he were on a stage, addressing an adoring audience. Everything about him set Dhananjoy's teeth on edge.

Sukanta said, 'Please ask whatever you need to. I'll try my best to answer your queries. I can't believe Sarala has died. Murdered! Why would anyone do that?' He had got up and ambled towards a nearby mantelpiece. Leaning against it, he turned to look at the detective with a casual air. And yet, for all the attempt to appear nonchalant, his smile seemed a little strained.

The detective drew himself up and folded his arms.

'So, Sukanta babu, you are involved in the Swadeshi movement, are you?'

Sukanta looked slightly thrown by the question but then recovered quickly and drawled, 'Yes, I know you have talked to Rakhal-da and he would have told you about my beliefs and ideals. That's still not considered a crime though, is it? Being a believer in swadeshi?'

'Unless you are making a bomb or planning to assassinate someone, no. At least, not yet. But I'm sure you already knew that. However, I'm sure you have heard about what's happened to young Sijad.'

Sukanta tried to hide his discomfiture by fiddling with the edge of his kurta sleeve and scratching the birthmark on his temple. It was clear that he was trying to compose an answer. When he spoke after clearing his throat several times, he chose to look elsewhere rather than at the other man.

'Well, yes, what's happened is indeed unfortunate, but I would not like to stem the tide of enthusiasm that has arisen amongst the young men of Rajapur. They have got a bit carried away perhaps in this instance, but that's easily rectified. I'll talk to them. Meanwhile, Sijad might want to reflect on his refusal to join in the chanting of "Bande Mataram".'

Dhananjoy's jaw had hardened, but he refrained from saying anything. The man in front of him fancied himself a leader of the village youth, and while his pomposity was aggravating, to say the least, Dhananjoy realized that challenging his views at this point might make him sulk and clam up. Sukanta had regained his stride by now and spoke in a voice he obviously reserved for his followers.

'As far as I am concerned, those who are not bestirred by all that's going on are committing a crime of sorts. Have you read Bankim babu's *Anandamath*, Dhananjoy babu? If you haven't, please do. Everything that he says about the need for the Bangali jaati to retrieve its lost glory is so true, so very true. Why did we become like this, Dhananjoy babu? The butt of everyone's jibes and jokes? Even writers like Kipling haven't spared us! Why are we so listless, so laidback, so accepting of every wrongdoing? Desperate to study a foreign language, our oppressor's language, with all its idiotic and inexplicable rules? Ruining our health in the process? And for what? To become *keraani*s, clerks, in some dark and dank office? That ideal of the *bhaalo chhele,* the good boy, who keeps his head down and follows rules, which every parent tries to instil in their son, has been the main cause of our downfall. As if the meek are ever going to inherit the Earth! When I see all these young men in their tight boots and china coats spouting Shakespeare and Milton... chhah!' He stopped to make a derisive noise and then continued, 'No wonder we have become incapable of raising our voices.'

Despite his decision to remain silent, Dhananjoy found himself protesting, 'That's not true, Sukanta babu! After all, so many young men have begun questioning the excesses of the sarkar. And you are wrong to say that this is the first time we are seeing something like this. There have always been protests and revolts against the British in Bengal. Don't forget the Indigo Rebellion or the Pabna Revolt by our peasants. Or is it that you don't consider such protests worthy of any note since they weren't led by the *bhadralok* like you?'

Sukanta refused to be thrown off his stride. He considered the detective's words with a grave expression. 'Well said, Dhananjoy babu. And you are right. But surely the time has come to rise against whatever Curzon sahib is planning. I hear he is planning a partition of this great land of ours. We can't, we won't allow it. You should have been at the meeting that took place in Town Hall, in Calcutta, earlier this year, Dhananjoy babu. Nobody can stop us now! And if, as a result, some naïve youths like Sijad end up getting the rough end of the stick, they are partly to blame for whatever happens to them. I am sure you will agree. Even though, clearly, you have decided to work for the enemy.'

Dhananjoy thought of young Sijad lying injured for having stood up to bullies, and he couldn't take any more of Sukanta's grandstanding. He knew the Swadeshi activist, for all his idealism, was also trying to get a rise out of him. He needed to keep his anger on a tight leash before the temptation to raise a fist and smash the young man's patrician nose got the better of him. Keeping his voice deliberately devoid of emotion, he said, 'Sukanta babu, let me ask you this. Especially since we are not here to discuss Bengal's politics but to investigate a murder. When was the last time you saw or met the murdered girl?'

Sukanta licked his lips before speaking. 'What? Sarala? Why, I... I can't really recollect when I might have seen her.'

Dhananjoy looked at him solemnly and said, 'I have time. Why don't you think a little and then tell me?'

The young man turned a shrewd gaze on the detective. 'Why do I get the feeling, Dhananjoy babu, that you have taken against me? Do you see me as a rich brat who lives off the fat of the land? Someone who has had an easy life with too much time on his hands? And has suddenly decided to take up swadeshi as his latest pastime, like a bored child excited about a new toy? Let me tell you, both Usha and I have had our fair share of struggles. Do you think it was easy for Usha to find out that that useless man we call our father had decided to make her governess our *notun* ma? Our new mother! Or to be wrenched out of our home and grow up in our mamabari? Every day I had to answer my little sister's questions about whether she had done something wrong and why Baba didn't come to take us back. Did he not love us any more, she would keep asking me. I was a child, but I had to take on the role of a grown-up and assure her that she could always count on her dada's love.'

Dhananjoy could see that as Sukanta became agitated, he scratched his birthmark quite furiously. The feigned nonchalance of the last few minutes was all but gone.

'I know I don't need to tell you any of this, but I don't want you making assumptions about me. Do you know when Baba offered to pay for my college education, I refused to take his money? I told Ballabh mama that I would stay in a hostel in the city, tutor young boys and take care of the fees myself. Those days in Calcutta were the best and worst days of my life.'

What Sukanta had not been able to tell his mama was that the boat trips from Rajapur to the city terrified him. Mama didn't like trains and had insisted that Sukanta go on the boat owned by the Rajbari. Sukanta had grown up in Calcutta, and the aquatic journeys left him jittery. The constant rocking motion of the boat made him feel sick, and every time he looked into the water, his mind would imagine crocodiles or other unnamed creatures lurking in its depths. Besides, quite often when the maajhi malaah sat together to eat gur and chire, their talk would invariably turn to the various dacoit gangs that attacked boats. A young lathiyal sent by his uncle to accompany Sukanta on those rides would sit next to him with an inscrutable face. But the entire thing made him extremely uncomfortable. So, after a while, he had fixed a room in a basha bari in the city, where many other boys of his college stayed, and told Ballabh Ray that he needed to stay near his college and the library. And after that, in the next few months, he went through the most harrowing time of his life. He was teased constantly by the boys in the hostel for his cherubic good looks. They had even come up with a name for him. Chhotobou! The young bride! He was forced to cook for some of them when the hostel's cook didn't turn up, and while the smoke from the stove hurt his eyes, his tormentors would sneer, 'What's going on, Chhotobou?! Why are you taking so much time to cook, huh? You are quite useless.'

He had gritted his teeth and kept quiet. Just as he had gritted his teeth and kept quiet when one night, three of the older boys had entered his room, asked his roommate to leave and then advanced towards him saying, 'Oh, no, our lovely Chhotobou, we can't let you sleep tonight...' He had let his mind wander as the rest of the hour unfolded, and it seemed as though he watched from afar while his body was mauled and torn apart. Later, after they had left and he had gathered his dhoti and sobbed into the pillow, Sukanta had resolved that he would not let this go on. One of the boys had licked his ear and whispered that they would be back again. But he was going to make sure they would not torment him ever again. So, the next time they arrived, he was armed with a knife stolen from the hostel kitchen, and when he leapt out of bed with a savage scream that rang through the corridor, his abusers were stunned and left in a hurry. After that, he had never been troubled again. The incident taught him that the weak would always be preyed on. He was determined never to be one of them. That's why when he had drifted into meetings where speakers talked about the importance of the Bengali youth realizing the value of bahubal or physical prowess, it made a lot of sense.

The area around the birthmark gradually turned scarlet with all the fierce scratching that accompanied the flooding of his mind with those excruciating memories that could not be shared. Not even with the keen-eyed detective. Not anyone. Dhananjoy realized there was a great deal that was troubling Sukanta as his face acquired a haunted expression. But whatever be his private demons, Dhananjoy needed to bring him back to the questions about the murder. Sukanta said, 'I faced many hardships, but it was in college that I met like-minded people, became part of reading clubs and then began to understand the importance of jatiyatabodh.'

He stopped when he saw Dhananjoy raise his hand.

The detective looked at him in a noncommittal manner and said, 'Sukanta babu, I really don't need to know all this. My personal opinion of you is completely irrelevant. I am here to help Daroga Bansidhar solve a murder. So can you please answer my questions about Sarala?'

'What do you want to know? I was simply a well-wisher who sometimes stopped and chatted with her. She was particularly interested in the idea of widow remarriage, which I had once mentioned. So, I would talk to her about Vidyasagar moshai and all that he had tried to do for young brahmin widows. That's all, really.'

'I see. Sukanta babu, I'm going to ask you something without beating around the bush. I'm getting tired of everyone giving evasive replies to our questions. So please, let's not play these games any more. Can you answer this simple question for me? Where were you on the evening that Sarala was killed? For there's a witness who confirms you were not at home at the time. You can answer me here, or Bansidhar could take you to the thana.'

Sukanta's eyes widened with shock at this unexpectedly direct question. But before he could answer, both men heard a sharp intake of breath from the door, followed by the sound of cups and saucers crashing to the floor.

16

THE INVISIBLE GIRL

The two men started at the loud noise and turned to look at the door. Usha was standing there, looking aghast. Her face had drained of all colour, and her mouth trembled with tension. Sukanta leapt out of his seat when she murmured, 'Dada!' and darted towards her as she teetered on her feet. Pieces of china were scattered on the floor along with the remnants of the tea and muri she had been carrying on a tray. When Sukanta put his arm around her, Usha leaned against her brother for support.

'I told Kamini-di I would get the tray up myself. What was that question about the day of Sarala's murder that Dhananjoy babu was asking you, Dada? You? You had gone out? Where?'

Sukanta turned to the detective with an imploring look in his eyes. 'Dhananjoy babu, may we please get back to your questions in a while? As you can see, my sister needs my help. Forgive me, but I can't leave Usha like this. I beg you. Please.' Sukanta's concern for his sister was apparent in the vehemence of his pleas. Dhananjoy hesitated for only a few moments before agreeing to Sukanta's request.

The girl did appear to have become extremely pale, and even after she was helped to a chair, she seemed to have difficulty breathing. Although Dhananjoy had expressed indifference to Sukanta's account of his past, the truth was that his insides had churned when he heard about Usha's suffering as a child. Recalling his own anger at the world after losing his parents, he could well imagine how the two children might have felt after death had taken one parent and the other seemed to give himself over to uxorious claims.

~

Dhananjoy left the room and walked down the stairs leading away from the sadar khana with several thoughts hurtling in his head. And as he walked, he could feel a pair of eyes watching him leave. It was just a feeling, a stirring of the hair at the back of one's neck. Dhananjoy knew he wouldn't be able to see anyone if he turned his head, so he kept going towards the gate downstairs. While crossing the kitchen, he asked Kamini to send Bama upstairs to help clean the broken pieces of china. When she looked perplexed, he told her Usha debi had slipped and dropped the tray. Once Bama left, Dhananjoy turned to Kamini again and asked her if he could talk to Puti.

It had occurred to him while he walked down the stairs that talking to Puti might produce some more leads. Bansi and he had seen her now and then but never actually sat her down and asked her anything. Given what Bama had told them, she sounded like someone who kept her ear to the ground.

Puti heard his request, and her hands stopped midway through slicing a large piece of pumpkin on the boti. When she looked up at Kamini with the eyes of a skittish fawn, the latter said without any rancour, 'Jaa re, Puti. Go and answer

Babu's questions. And don't worry, you can trust him. He really just wants to find out the truth, not twist our words and turn us into culprits simply because we are poor. Jaa re, go with him. Answer his questions truthfully.'

But the conversation with Puti had to wait since Bama came and informed Dhananjoy that Sushila didi wanted to speak with him. Aah, thought Dhananjoy, so the inquisitive eyes that he had felt following him as he walked away from the sadar khana must have been those of Sushila. He went back inside the house to find out what she had to say.

The two of them were seated just like that first day when Sushila had talked to the police officers from behind a screen. She began speaking without bothering with preambles, and there was no hemming and hawing like the last time.

'Dhananjoy babu, the reason I asked for the interview is this. I wanted to know why you have released Kamini after all that I told you and Daroga babu that day. Shouldn't she have been rotting in prison by now? I saw Daroga babu interrogating her the other day. So, what happened? Why do I still see her cavorting about in the Rajbari?'

'Hmm... you are absolutely right, Sushila debi. What you gave to us was indeed extremely valuable information. But you see, Bansi and I are trying to make a watertight case against the killer so that when it goes before the district magistrate, the culprit won't be able to wriggle out of the punishment they deserve. For instance, we're now trying to find out why Sarala Dasi had dhatura leaves in her stomach on the day she died. Was it Kamini who administered them? We don't know. But we need to find out.'

A loud gasp could be heard from the other side. 'Dha... dhatura leaves, did you say? Is that important?'

'Oh, yes, Sushila debi,' Dhananjoy said promptly and emphatically. 'We feel that it is very important, and we have no intention of ignoring it. Why do you think Ramhari has been taken to the thana? The killer thought they were being very clever, but we'll get to them. Rest assured, Sushila debi, every stone shall be turned. Or in this case, every leaf. We want to be completely thorough. The murderer shall be caught, and we will make sure that nothing short of the noose will await them. I hope I've put your mind at rest now, Sushila debi?' Dhananjoy finished with a smile, knowing exactly the kind of effect his words would have had on Sushila.

There was complete silence from the other side of the screen. The voice that then emerged from there shook a little. 'Yes, yes, of course. And I must go now. You will have to excuse me, Dhananjoy babu. I have not been feeling too well since the morning. I think I need to rest.'

'Yes, of course, Sushila debi. Please rest. You have nothing to worry about. I'll find my way out.'

~

Puti walked a few steps behind Dhananjoy as they went in search of a secluded spot in the garden. After he had settled down on the same bench where he had sat to question Kamini, he turned his attention to Puti. With her round face, bulging eyes and quavering chin, she looked like a child about to receive a stern telling-off. Her toes were curled up, and she was holding her elbows tightly and rocking gently. As though she was putting all her effort into controlling her impulse to flee.

Making his voice as gentle and coaxing as possible, Dhananjoy said to her, 'Puti, there is absolutely no need to be afraid of me. I know you could not have killed Sarala. She was like a sister to you, was she not?'

Puti nodded her head vigorously at this and then added in a whisper, 'She was my only friend in this big house. The only person I could talk to. I know I talk too much, but she never asked me to stop talking or called me an idiot. Bama didi is nice, but she's new. I miss Sarala didi every day.'

The girl's voice was choking with tears, and Dhananjoy remembered Annada daktar's statement that there was no one to mourn Sarala's demise. Here was someone who seemed to be genuinely grieving for her.

He said, 'Well, Puti, since you loved her so much, wouldn't you want her killer to be caught? Surely you agree that your Sarala didi didn't deserve to die in that way?'

When she nodded mutely, Dhananjoy pressed on, making his voice as soothing as possible. 'That's the reason why I called you here. Out of all the people in this house, you were probably the closest to her. More than anyone else, you would be interested in having her killer caught. That is why I need your help. Tell me anything and everything that you feel is important. Anything connected to Sarala.'

Puti blinked several times, and her eyes darted this way and that as she racked her brains for an answer. 'Babu, I can't recall anything right now. All I can remember is that when we talked for the last time that day, Sarala didi had looked extremely happy. There was a radiant smile on her face.'

Dhananjoy remained silent and hoped that the girl might have something more to add. She was scraping the ground with her toenails as she spoke. After a while, he heard her speak in a small voice.

'Babu, can I tell you about something that I heard a few days ago? I don't know if it's important.'

'Yes, of course. Anything. You strike me as being a clever and observant girl. You don't miss much that goes on, do you? I can tell. That's the reason I decided to turn to you for help.'

Puti's face broke into a tiny smile, and she visibly preened at the compliment. After sneaking a glance at him, she continued.

'You know, Babu, you are the first person after my father to call me clever. Everyone else thinks I am a dimwit. I'm invisible to most people. Not worth paying any attention to.' The girl's voice sounded sad rather than embittered as she went on. 'When I was little, my baba loved me the most in this whole world. But then he died of a snakebite one day while working in the fields, and after that my mother couldn't wait to get me married off. And you can see how my life turned out. But I don't really mind the daily toil here. More than anything else, I'm just glad I have enough to eat. Have you ever known real hunger, Babu?'

Dhananjoy shook his head slowly. 'No, can't say I have.'

Puti's eyes had a faraway look. 'No one can describe it to you. My mother and I had to experience it after my father died. It's as if there's something clawing your insides and it won't give up till you feed it. Finally, my poor mother had to go through the humiliation of begging for food from our neighbours. That's why I don't really blame her for marrying me off to a man who was ready to help her with some money. We would have both died if she hadn't.'

Puti had clearly forgotten her fears and was talking quite freely and in a voice that was no longer a mumble that Dhananjoy had to strain his ears to understand. When Dhananjoy saw she was ready to speak without reservations, he gently brought her back to what she had seen after Durga Puja that she thought might be important. Nodding, Puti began to cast her mind back.

It was on the day before Lakshmi Puja. Puti had been asked to clean the corridors and pay special attention to the brass curios. She climbed the stairs reluctantly with a mop and bucket and started cleaning listlessly. She hated cleaning and dusting and wished Kamini-di had asked someone else to do it. But of course, with Sarala didi gone, there wasn't anyone else to help with the cleaning. The new girl who came to help in the kitchen couldn't be trusted to wander around inside the household. With a sigh, Puti wiped one of the large portraits of some ancestor of Ballabh Ray, and that's when she heard the quiet sobbing. Her spine prickled with interest. Finally, something that would make all this dusting and cleaning worthwhile. Who could it be? She inched towards the area from where those sounds seemed to emerge, and after a while, she heard snatches of a conversation. Puti took her mop and began cleaning the spot in front of the room with great vigour. Her ears were on high alert, trying to catch every sound they could. It was Sushila didi who was crying while Rakhal-da was trying to comfort her. Puti couldn't catch whole sentences, but she didn't give up.

'Why are you crying so much, Sushi?... in pain?... ask someone to fetch Annada?'

'Na, go, na, go, I don't have any pain. I...'

'What is it? Have you done something? Tell me...'

'Promise me you... Sarala... I told Ramhari-da. Believe me, I...'

There was complete silence for a few seconds after which Rakhal-da could be heard saying in an astounded voice, 'What?! What did you say?... leaves? But why?'

Between sobs, Sushila said, 'Because I saw that wretched widow licking a bit of a broken clay pot, and I knew... I knew... I have the same cravings. She must have been with child. And I was terrified it might be... I have seen you.'

'Oh god! Oh, Sushila! What have you done!'

Unfortunately, at that point, Puti had spotted Usha walking towards that corridor and had to drop her pretence of being a zealous scrubber of floors and move away. It would have been difficult to fool Usha didi.

Dhananjoy made a few notes in his diary, and when he looked up, he saw Puti was no longer looking as anxious as she had when he had begun asking her questions. In fact, she seemed quite pleased with herself as she tore bits of grass and flung them about, waiting for his next question.

'Puti, that was a lot of help. But I want you to do something more for me. Can you do that?'

And when she nodded quite eagerly, he continued, 'After today's work is over, can you sit alone for a while and cast your mind back to that day when you last saw Sarala? Think carefully about everything that happened. Right from that morning. If there is anything at all that strikes you as odd, I would like to hear it. Even the smallest of things that occur to you. Anything that doesn't add up. Or feels strange when you recall it now. Will you keep this in mind? Who knows, it might be something that will help us crack the case. Bring the killer to justice. Imagine how proud your baba would have felt. Bansi and I will meet you in the evening tomorrow near the pukur here. We would like to hear everything that you can remember. No need to fret now. Later, when all your day's work is done and you have some time to yourself, think about that day. Close your eyes and cast your mind back.'

Puti looked somewhat sceptical as she scratched her cheek. What was it exactly that the babu expected her to remember? But he had praised her, and that sure felt good. People rarely praised her for anything. She wished she could tell her baba that his Puti had helped a police officer from Calcutta. He would have thrown his head back and laughed uproariously. Not to mock her, but because he would have felt ever so happy that the world had finally recognized what he had always known about his daughter. And the other day, Bama didi had told her that she'd even heard about girl detectives! Imagine that! Maybe she could become one of those some day. If all it took was listening in on people's secret conversations, Puti would surely have no problem. And then, her days of being lambasted for every small thing in the smoke-filled kitchen would be over.

'Puti? Dhananjoy babu?'

It was Sukanta's voice that interrupted Puti's happy reverie. Both Dhananjoy and Puti turned to see a dishevelled and grim-looking Sukanta walking towards them.

'Dhananjoy babu, is it all right if you and I continue our conversation that got interrupted earlier? I would like to get it over with.'

'Is Usha debi feeling better now, Sukanta babu?'

'Yes, yes, she is, thank you. She's sleeping. Puti, can you go and be with her for a while?'

Puti sprang up to do as she was told. When Dhananjoy looked at her, she nodded imperceptibly to indicate she would meet him near the pukur later.

After both men had lit cigarettes, Sukanta scowled at his hands for a while and then emitted a noise that sounded like a strangled groan. 'Oh god!' he said after inhaling the smoke of his cigarette. 'The one thing that is guaranteed to give you solace in this wretched world. A cigarette.'

Dhananjoy had felt something akin to hatred for the brazen youth he had met an hour ago. Who tried so hard to impress with his careless charm and rhetorical skills. But the man sitting next to him and breathing heavily seemed like a very different person. His shoulders were drooping, and he seemed to have trouble formulating what he wanted to say. Finally, after another loud groan that sounded like the muffled scream of an animal, he began.

'I have been a complete fool, Dhananjoy babu. A complete and utter fool. I've made so many bad decisions. I told you that soon after I started college, I met my friends who were all interested in philosophy and political thought. That's only part of the truth. What I didn't tell you, what I couldn't tell you is that some of them had a few other interests. Vices actually.'

'Go on, I am listening. As I have said before, I'm not here to judge you for anything. I am only interested in solving a murder. You can trust my discretion. Even if you confess to something that you feel ashamed of, your secret will be safe with me.'

After swallowing a few times and making some visible effort, Sukanta went on. 'This is hard for me to say out loud. Well, along with some of my friends, I began visiting a courtesan called Golaap, and in no time I became besotted with her. I will cut a long story short here. Golaap was fond of expensive gifts. Paying her a visit seemed to require more and more money, and I didn't really have much. I began to borrow, and since I am Ballabh Ray's nephew, people lent me money. But then, loans have to be returned, don't they? I became desperate, and that's when I sank even lower. Into a hole I just could not climb out of. I started going to a gambling den in Calcutta's Black Town.

'Believe me, Dhananjoy babu, I turned to Swadeshi with the conviction that I had found the antidote to all my sins. That it would keep me on the straight and narrow. But in time, even though I managed to forget Golaap, the addiction to gambling refused to loosen its grip. Once I had dipped my toes into that murky cesspool, it just kept pulling me in. I have lost so much money and sunk into terrible debts and yet I am unable to stop. I loathe myself, loathe the fact that people see me as the upholder of a noble cause – Swadeshi – whereas I struggle with such a horrible weakness, but nothing has helped. I would even tell myself that I was gambling to get money for the great cause. But I was only being delusional. I gamble because I'm addicted to it. There, I have said it.'

'I'm a little confused, Sukanta babu. Where does Sarala come into all this?'

Sukanta scratched his birthmark, stood for a bit and sat again. A group of monkeys sitting on a mango tree nearby watched the two stern-faced humans for a while before going back to raiding the bounteous fruit trees for food.

'Oh god! I really wish I didn't have to talk about all this. It's so painful to hear the details of one's ignominy being uttered aloud. How could I have plummeted to such depths? What must you think of me? My only excuse would be that I owe a lot of money to a Kabuliwala, and he has been threatening to break my bones if I don't pay up. May even kill me. Sometimes, though, I feel death might just be preferable to all this. I know I deserve to die.'

17

CONFESSIONS AND CONTRITION

Dhananjoy was beginning to feel a little exasperated by the amount of time the young man was taking to get to the point. He really didn't care for all the pathetic moaning and wallowing in self-pity that was going on. Tears and snot were flowing down Sukanta's face. Perhaps he needed to be a bit more compassionate, Dhananjoy chided himself. But all he could muster was some contempt-mingled pity for the man who was almost doubled over with pain, his arms wrapped around his middle. It looked as if Sukanta was afraid it would come spilling out of him and create a mess on the ground if he did not hold it in. Finally, in a desolate voice, he said, 'Sarala was a witness to one of the darkest, most despicable moments of my life.'

That day, Sukanta had been feeling particularly desperate. Two days ago, when he had stepped out of a friend's house in Calcutta, a shadow had separated itself from the trees behind one of the lamp posts and then moved swiftly to stand right in front of him. It was his bête noire, the Kabuliwala, barring his progress, arms folded. Sukanta's heart did a somersault, and for a minute, he thought of making a run for it. Just then, the collar of his kurta was seized and pulled so that Sukanta found himself staring straight into the ferocious eyes of his tormentor. Sputtering with fear, Sukanta begged the broad-shouldered Kabuliwala to give him a bit more time. The Kabuliwala looked at him coldly and then raised two fingers to indicate that he wanted his money back in two days. After he left, Sukanta had collapsed near the lamp post, weeping, with his cheek pressed against the cold metal, till hysterical giggles rose within him at the thought of how his young followers would react if they could see him there.

And so, he told himself, he had no choice. He would have to steal from within the Rajbari. Feeling like an utter cad, the very next day, he crept into Ballabh Ray's room and stole one of his gold rings kept inside a drawer. Mama had been sleeping, unaware of what his dear nephew was up to. Till he picked the ring up from the table, Sukanta's heart had raced wildly, and he had felt bile rising to his throat. But once the deed was done and he had pocketed the loot, a curious sense of calm descended on him. Mama would hardly miss one of the many ornaments that he possessed. What use did he have for them anyway? He'd always had a great fondness for Sukanta and would forgive his nephew even if he did find out about his breach of trust. Mama would in fact have approved of all his shenanigans as part of a young man's rite of passage. These were some of the things he told himself to ease his conscience.

But just when he thought he had escaped the consequences of his act, reprisal stared him in the face in the form of Sarala. True to form, after returning to his own room that day, he had simply flung the ring on one of the shelves. Relieved at having been able to steal it successfully, he thought he could afford not to worry about hiding it immediately. Who knew that Sarala would come to clean his room that very day and find it lying there. He had just come back after taking a bath, combing his hair and whistling, when he stopped at the entrance of his room. Sarala was holding up the ring and staring enquiringly at him. She knew whose ring that was and had connected the dots. The flash of alarm in his eyes only confirmed her suspicions. It was too late to make excuses. He thought of being brazen about it, his mind racing like a rat caught in a maze, but her steady gaze made him falter. All he could do was beg her to be silent.

'So, what was the price of her silence? I'm guessing there was a price?'

'Yes, money, of course,' said Sukanta with a bitter smile. 'She wanted money.'

'When I told her I had no money, which was why I had stolen the ring, she came up with a solution. She wanted a share of the money I would get after pawning or selling the ring. She even knew someone in the village who could do it. She gave me his details and told me to go to him with my face partly covered with a piece of cloth. She said people who wanted to keep their identity concealed went to him in that manner. He never asked questions.' Drawing a deep breath, Sukanta concluded, 'That's where I had gone on the afternoon that she was attacked. And now, you know everything.'

'Would I be right in presuming that you were not having an affair with Sarala?'

'What! What did you say? Of course not! Whatever gave you that idea?' Sukanta looked at him with incredulous eyes and then laughed mirthlessly. 'Is that what you have been thinking, Dhananjoy babu? Oh, no, no. I used to talk to her now and then, like I talk to everyone. But that was all. Nothing of what you're suggesting happened.'

'Sukanta babu, what you have just told me actually gives you a very strong motive for killing Sarala. She was blackmailing you. So, when you set off that afternoon, you must have known that was the day she usually went back home. Who's to say you didn't lurk in the foliage to finish her off? From where I'm standing, it definitely looks like you had motive and opportunity. I—'

The rest of Dhananjoy's sentence was lost as a loud shout – 'Dadababu, Sukanta dadababu' – could be heard, and Puti came running towards them. 'Dadababu, Usha didi is awake, and she says if you don't go to her immediately, she'll come down here.'

After appealing to Dhananjoy to be excused, Sukanta rushed off with Puti towards the inner quarters of the Rajbari.

Later in the afternoon, Bansidhar looked a little vexed when Dhananjoy asked him about Sijad.

'I had underestimated that boy, Joy. He is badly injured, but he refuses to give up the names of his attackers. He looked at me with those soulful eyes of his and insisted that they were childhood friends and had simply been involved in some horseplay. His getting hurt, he claimed, was just an accident. There were no malicious intentions on anyone's part. So, nothing to report. Both Daktar babu and I sat next to him and spent an hour trying to convince him to tell us their names, but the boy turned his face to the wall and remained adamant. Said there wasn't anything to tell. It was all just a bit of rough and tumble that got out of hand.

'Finally, Hakim chacha told us to leave him alone since our efforts were clearly going to be in vain. Poor Chacha! The man had become nearly mute with shock. Kept stroking the boy's head and thanking god that he was alive. The good news is that except for a fractured arm, Sijad only has surface wounds. No other bones broken. Annada babu said he should be fit and fine in a few weeks. When we were coming away, Sijad held Daktar babu's hand, and I could see tears in his eyes. All he said was, "Daktar babu, I'll come back to trouble you as usual once I'm feeling better. Don't think you can be rid of me so easily."'

'What did Daktar babu say?'

'He said, "If you are not back in my dispensary to assist me after a fortnight, I'll break your other arm as well. And you know me. I'll come and make good that threat. So, make sure I see improvement every day when I come to see you, do you understand, young man?" Later, as we were walking back, Annada babu said only one thing, "Sukanta has a lot to answer for. I'm not going to spare him. That bloody fool doesn't know that he's stirring up a hornet's nest with all his rabble-rousing."'

A sigh escaped Dhananjoy before he could hold it back. He said heavily after a moment, 'I'll go and see the brave fellow tomorrow morning. You know, Bansi, that first morning at Daktar babu's place, when I saw Sijad squirming upon hearing our questions about the corpse, I had judged him as being too squeamish to become a doctor. But he has proved me wrong.'

'Yes, Joy, I think so too. And he'll be very pleased to see you tomorrow. But tell me what you found out. Anything I should know before tomorrow's interrogation of Ramhari?'

He could scarcely believe his ears when Dhananjoy told him all that had happened at the Rajbari that day.

'What! Sukanta has a gambling habit? And was being blackmailed by Sarala? So, he has been leading a double life, is it? Goes around pretending to be a Swadeshi activist and keeps his other self hidden from all his followers and devotees. What a two-faced charlatan! And what about Sushila? Surely, what Puti overheard was her confessing to her husband. Telling him that she had instructed Ramhari to kill poor Sarala! Isn't it? So, Ramhari drugged the girl and then struck her with a brick. Is that what this means?'

Dhananjoy didn't look entirely convinced. 'I don't know, Bansi. I'm not sure. I'm not discounting it and yet... Let's wait and see what Ramhari has to say. But something tells me that the lathiyal would not have gone so far as to kill a helpless woman by striking her from behind. Besides, he is past his prime and an opium addict. Kamini had said he is half-asleep most of the time after sunset. Would he have been able to commit a murder that required precision and planning?'

~

The next day, once Ramhari was arrested, he broke down after a few hours of being questioned in the thana and admitted to giving the dhatura leaves to Sarala. After some more thrashing by the jamadars, he further admitted that he had sent one of the younger lathiyals to follow the two police officers. One of the zealous youngsters had thrown the stone at Dhananjoy to scare him off and scuttle the investigation. But Ramhari refused to own up to the blow that had killed Sarala. Finally, when both his eyes were swollen and there were bleeding gashes all over his body, he beseeched Bansidhar to ask his men to stop the beating.

'Babu, listen to me. Ask your men to stop. I really can't own up to something I didn't do. I'll tell you the truth, but you have to promise me that you won't ask me why.'

Bansi told his jamadars to step back and then turned to Ramhari again. When the lathiyal had been brought in, he had sat in front of the daroga, exuding a great deal of bravado. His bulky arms had been crossed over his broad chest, and his eyes had been full of fire. From time to time, his stubby fingers would stroke a scar that ran across his substantial biceps. All that had now changed. The man was on the ground, moaning in pain and clutching his arm in a way that suggested a few broken bones. It unsettled Bansi to see the giant of a man reduced to a gibbering wreck. Had his men overdone the beating? Bansi sat next to the lathiyal and said, 'I'm not making any promises, Ramhari. Just tell me what you know. Was it you who killed Sarala? You were the last to see her alive, weren't you? As she walked out of the estate? Maybe you followed her and then bashed her head in. Who knows how to do such things better than you?'

'Daroga babu, I'll tell you everything, but please don't accuse me of smashing a woman's head. I can never do something like that. I might have committed many sins in this lifetime but never killed a defenceless woman by hitting her from behind! No, Ramhari Das could never do that. Besides, my weapon of choice is a lathi. I would never use a brick. Daroga babu, it is true I had given those dhatura leaves to Sarala. I had found out she was with child, and I knew the kind of scandal that could cause. If word got around, that bastard dewanji would have used the information to make life hell for our Radha didi. Insinuate all kinds of things about the people of the Rajbari. And that's why I thought I would give Sarala those leaves and kill the child inside her. Believe me, I didn't have anything to do with that blow to her head. One of the younger lathiyals lobbed that stone at Dhananjoy babu after seeing the two of you at the haat and then following you. It's true, I had asked him to follow the two of you. I had panicked when I heard about your friend, a detective inspector from Calcutta. I thought the man has walked in from the big city to make trouble for all of us. I regret all of it. But, Daroga babu, I didn't kill that girl. Believe me, I didn't.'

'Why would she even take those leaves from you?'

'I... I told her that her paramour had asked me to give those leaves to her. That he had said they were good for her... and she trusted me. She looked a little puzzled at first, but then she had never had anything to fear from me, you see. She called me Ramhari-da and believed that I was like an elder brother to her. And so, she just took them from me without any further questions.'

He had seen her walking towards the gate and realized she was on her way home. To Ramhari's surprise, Sarala seemed to be brimming with carefree joy rather than any kind of anxiety. Why was the girl not worried about the consequences of everyone finding out that she was with child? Sushila didi was convinced, for some reason, that the child was Rakhal babu's. Ramhari had tried arguing with her, but he knew the stubborn set of that jaw since she was a child. No amount of reasoning was going to make any difference. She said she wanted to die every time she thought of the child growing in that other woman's womb. Ramhari had finally relented when she talked of how the scandal of Sarala's pregnancy would sully the reputation of the Rajbari and leave Thakurani utterly shattered. He would have to do this to protect Radharani. She deserved some peace of mind after all that she had gone through in life. And so, he had taken those leaves from Sushila and given them to Sarala.

'What are these leaves, Ramhari-da?'

'Not sure, Sarala. But someone from within the Rajbari asked me to give them to you secretly. He said you'll know what they are meant for. They're good for you, he told me. You must start chewing them as soon as possible. I really can't say more than this.'

Sarala's perplexed face gradually became suffused with joy after hearing this. She put a couple of the dhatura leaves in her mouth. Then she began walking down the path where death lay in wait for her.

After his confession, Ramhari sat in a corner with his arms wrapped around his knees, which were drawn close to his chest. To all further questions, his answers remained the same, and he refused to say anything that changed this account. Bansidhar realized the futility of asking him anything more.

At least the mystery of the dhatura leaves and the question of who had hurled the stone at Joy had been solved. But it was clear that however much they might press him, Ramhari was not going to spill the truth about Sushila's role in the entire thing.

~

In the afternoon, when Bansidhar related all that had happened in the thana to Dhananjoy, he listened to him with his eyes focused on something far away. Then he said, 'Bansi, I'm really glad I went to meet Sijad today.'

Baffled by this non sequitur, Bansidhar nodded bemusedly and then asked him what they should do next. Dhananjoy, who had had an abstracted air till then, dug the heels of his hands into his eyes for a while and then sprang to his feet with a loud exclamation. 'Bansi! Something's just struck me when you related the stone-throwing incident. I had forgotten how fear and panic can make people behave in dangerous ways. What a fool I've been. Get up, get up now. We have to go.'

'What? Where? Where do we have to go, Joy? What are you talking about?'

Dhananjoy gripped Bansi's arm and said, 'There's not a moment to lose, Bansi. We have to set off for the Rajbari right now. I thought I was being very clever when I asked Puti to mull over everything that she could recall from that day and think of anything that strikes her as being odd.'

'What day? The day of the murder? But so what?' Bansi, feeling quite dazed by his friend's mercurial behaviour, was putting his arms again inside the shirt that he had just discarded after returning home.

'Don't you see? If Puti does actually recall something and then unwittingly mentions it to the killer... no, no. I have a terrible foreboding about how this could end. If something were to happen to that girl, I'll never forgive myself. Never.'

~

Kamini had stepped out of the kitchen to search for Puti. A hand placed on her forehead screened her eyes from the sun blazing down from the clear skies. Where had the silly girl gone? She had had a distracted air all day and had even received a bit of a dressing-down from Kamini. Must have gone off somewhere to sulk. With a sigh, Kamini turned to Bama.

'Hain re, Bama, have you seen Puti? I had told her to remember to take the tea to Usha didi's room, but she seems to have disappeared. She knows Usha didi likes her tea exactly as the clock chimes four. Where is the wretched girl? Tonight, Thakurani will be returning, and I had thought of making something special. She'll be extremely upset when she hears about Ramhari-da's arrest. It's almost as if someone's cast an evil eye on this household. Everything seems to be going to pieces. I knew that wretched girl, Sarala, was bad news. Just knew it. I started getting bad dreams soon after she arrived. Full of terrible omens. More than anything else, I can't bear to think of Thakurani's suffering. After all the work she did to get everything together...' Kamini was clawing her hands fretfully by the end of her speech.

Bama let her run out of steam before saying, 'I'll carry Usha didi's tea, Kamini-di. Give it to me.'

'Yes, yes, you take it. Just when you think this girl Puti is becoming more responsible, she disappears. I—' Kamini stopped speaking suddenly when she saw the two detectives rushing towards the kitchen. What now? Why was the tall detective running as though chased by a mad dog, with his portly friend trailing in his wake, huffing and puffing?

Dhananjoy's hair looked even more wild and dishevelled than usual. His agitation became apparent when he looked at the two women and shouted, 'Where is Puti? Is she still here, Kamini-di? Or did she leave for the pukur?' There was a vein throbbing on his forehead, and he breathed noisily as he waited for the two women to respond.

Both Kamini and Bama stared at them with their mouths open and then looked at each other. What was going on? As soon as Kamini said, 'Na, she's not in the kitchen,' Dhananjoy shot off in the direction of the pukur, with Bansidhar trying to keep up with him. The two women gaped at the receding figures before turning to look at each other and then deciding to follow the men. This was way too intriguing to miss. What did the two police officers want with Puti that was making them run in that frenzied manner?

18

MEETING AT THE PUKUR

Sprinting through the Rajbari garden, Bansidhar could feel branches and twigs whipping against his body and scratching his cheek. He was sure his face would be covered with cuts and grazes. And the uniform was going to have quite a few holes. His breath was raging through his chest, but there was no time to stop. With Dhananjoy running like a hare in front of him, not stopping even when he stumbled on protruding tree roots, how could he give up? Daroga Bansidhar's heart was going *thump*, *thump*, and he sincerely hoped that he wouldn't collapse midway with the exertion and let his friend down. Not to mention, become the laughing stock of the village. He regretted every extra spoon of ghee and sugar that he had ever reached for. Saroja was right. He needed to rethink his eating habits and become lighter and faster.

And just when he thought he would faint if he took one more step, he heard Dhananjoy shouting, 'There, there, I can see her. Puti... O Puti! Why? Is that Nityanand I see with her?'

Dhananjoy had been right in fearing the worst. Someone had been rattled by the thought of what Puti might recall.

Rattled enough to attack her. For the young cook was lying near the pukur with blood seeping from a wound in the back of her head. The gaunt yogi was kneeling next to her with a face blanched of all colour.

'What are you doing here, Maharaj? How did you know Puti would be here?' Dhananjoy's voice was sharp as he turned to look at Nityanand.

'I... What do you mean, Dhananjoy babu? I was simply taking a walk, and as I reached the pukur, I saw the poor girl. Lying in a pool of blood. I froze. And then, within a few minutes of my reaching here, Bansidhar babu and you came running. Believe me, I have no idea how this might have happened!'

Dhananjoy's eyes were narrowed to slits as he asked, 'How could you have reached a few minutes back? We didn't see you in front of us.'

'That's because I took the other path from behind the Rajbari. I have always used that route to get here. It's the closest to Zamindar babu's room, and I like walking through those wooded grounds.'

All of them turned their attention to the wounded girl and called her name, and after a while, Puti emitted a low, piteous moan and her eyelids fluttered a little.

Kamini and Bama had also reached the spot where the young girl lay. Catching sight of the growing pool of blood under Puti's head, Kamini clutched her mouth in horror. She sank to the ground and began stroking the young girl's hand. Bama had rushed to the pukur and scooped up some water, which she carried back in the corner of her sari. She clearly knew how to be calm in a crisis and do what was required.

When the water was splashed on her face, Puti opened her eyes again, but she was unable to focus. Bama looked at Dhananjoy and said, 'Dhananjoy babu, I saw Daktar babu walk into the estate an hour ago. Perhaps to check on Sushila-di. Shouldn't we fetch him?'

Dhananjoy turned to Bansidhar and shouted, 'Go, Bansi, go ask someone to get Annada babu immediately. Puti needs medical attention. Go! Now!' Seeing Bansidhar looking red-faced and panting, fit to burst, Bama offered to go in his stead and ran swiftly in the direction of the house. Puti looked at them with bleary eyes, and then, clutching Dhananjoy's sleeve, she muttered in a barely audible voice, 'Babu, Usha didi, tea... tea... the clock... at the stroke of four...' And then she lost consciousness.

Dhananjoy went very still, although his flaring nostrils and accelerated breathing betrayed the tension inside him. After clearing his throat several times, he said, 'Kamini-di, do as I say. Keep Puti's head elevated. We need to staunch the blood.' Nityanand had been carrying a piece of cloth on his shoulder, which was quickly placed on the wound. Puti's head was on Kamini's lap, and she was asked to keep applying pressure on the cloth. Looking at the helpless, wounded girl, Kamini started weeping in earnest.

'Babu, I had been berating this girl for being forgetful of her duties, and here she is worrying about Usha didi's tea. Even in this condition. I misjudged her. I've been completely wrong. Oh, Puti, open your eyes. I'll never scold you again, I promise. Just don't be like this.'

Bansidhar drew a noisy breath through his teeth. 'Kamini-di, calm down,' he said. 'Don't cry so much. Puti will recover. Bama will make sure that Annada babu comes soon. Joy, say something.'

Dhananjoy's voice was racked with pain when he answered, 'This is all my fault, Bansi. I should have asked her to be careful. I was so hung up about catching the killer that I didn't stop to think that I could be endangering the life of this poor, innocent girl. It's all because of my puerile idea that she came here alone. And now she lies bleeding. What have I done, Bansi?'

The girl's breathing was becoming shallow and the pallor of her face was turning waxen. If the doctor didn't arrive soon, Puti's chances of waking up would become slimmer by the minute. They sat waiting for what seemed like hours before they heard voices and then saw two young lathiyals of the estate come running towards them. Bama and Annada babu were behind them. They all helped carry Puti inside and laid her on a mattress in one of the rooms near the kitchen.

Both Dhananjoy and Bansi went in along with Daktar babu, and he asked the others to stay outside. Kamini seemed to be in a state of shock. Dhananjoy asked Bama to make some sugary tea for her. Nityanand looked like he was in a trance. Hearing all the commotion, Rakhal babu had stepped out and now stood blinking as though unable to wrap his head around what was going on. Usha had also come out of her room. Her eyes widened, and her hand flew to cover her mouth when she saw the bloodstains on the clothes of the detectives.

~

When Annada babu finally came out of the room where Puti had been placed, wiping his hands on a piece of cloth, his face looked grim. Dhananjoy and Bansidhar were right behind him, and all of them had lines of exhaustion etched on their faces. The daroga was rolling his shoulders and massaging the back of his neck.

In a low voice, the doctor said to those who had gathered to find out how Puti was doing, 'I have examined Puti's wound. It is a severe injury, and Puti is still unconscious. Someone had hit her from behind when she least expected it. But thankfully, the blow wasn't as strong as it was in Sarala's case. Puti will survive. But she needs time to rest. I don't see her coming out of her unconscious state before tomorrow. Or maybe even later. Those of you who believe in god, pray for the poor girl. Her life hangs by a thread. And even after she does recover, who knows whether she'll be in any state to talk or move her limbs. I hope that the monster who did this to her rots in hell.' Bansidhar thought that in the stillness that surrounded them, he heard someone let out their breath loudly after Annada babu finished speaking.

~

'Don't beat yourself up over this, Joy.' Bansidhar placed his hand on his friend's shoulder, which had sunk extremely low as they sat in the Rajbari baithak khana. Dhananjoy had his fingers steepled over his mouth as he stared with fierce concentration at the floor. Annada babu had gone up to meet Thakurani, who had returned home in the evening. After a while, they heard Kamini addressing them in a gentle voice.

'O Babu, the two of you need to eat. It has been so long, and we don't know if Puti will wake up tonight. Didn't you hear what Daktar babu had to say? One of the lathiyals will be right outside her room all night. I can't bear to see the two of you like this. It must be hours since you have eaten anything.'

When Dhananjoy raised his eyes to look at her, Kamini almost took a step back upon seeing how distraught he looked.

'Kamini-di, do you really think I can bring myself to eat, knowing that Puti is in that condition because of me?'

Kamini was silent for a little while, and then she spoke in a voice that trembled a little.

'Babu, I know you are blaming yourself, but you're not responsible for the terrible things people do. There was no way you could have known what would happen to Puti. Why don't you look at it this way? If you hadn't reached the pukur to save her, she wouldn't have been lying downstairs recovering from her injuries. You have always addressed me as didi. As your didi, I now order you to have some food. I will bring it myself. Nothing elaborate. Bit of rice and vegetables. But I insist that you eat.'

Kamini's face broke into a smile when she saw Dhananjoy nodding in response to what she said. He called her back as she was about to leave and said in a stern voice, 'Kamini-di, we have a request. Please tell Thakurani that I want to see her. Things are getting out of hand, and I would like to talk to her. In fact, I would like to address everyone who is here at the moment. Can you please arrange that? I'm sure if you talk to Thakurani, she can make it happen.'

~

After a while, when the two detectives entered the sadar khana where they had first sat with Thakurani, they could see that Kamini had managed to get everyone in that room. Both Thakurani and Sushila were sitting behind a screen while all the others – Rakhal, Sukanta, Usha, Nityanand, Annada – were sitting in various chairs and sofas. Daktar babu had just finished smoking and was crushing the stub on a plate, rubbing it back and forth with unnecessary vigour. His left eyelid was twitching slightly. All the faces were sombre, and yet, Dhananjoy knew that one of them had killed Sarala in cold blood and had attempted to silence young Puti as well.

He took a long breath, squared his shoulders and drew himself up to his full height before addressing the faces that were turned towards him.

'Thakurani, with your permission, may I speak?'

Thakurani's gravelly voice responded from behind the screen. 'Of course, Dhananjoy babu, please tell us what you want to say. We are all deeply disturbed by everything that has happened.'

'Yes, Thakurani, one murder and another attempted murder are indeed enough to shock anyone. Both victims are women, young widows trying to earn a livelihood to survive with dignity in a world that shows little compassion towards them. Sorry, I don't mean to give a speech. That's more Sukanta babu's forte, is it not?'

Sukanta smiled thinly at this comment and scratched his temple. Dhananjoy continued to speak.

'When I came to this village, to spend time with my old friend and stay away from the kinds of crimes I have witnessed in the city, I had naïvely assumed that evil couldn't possibly touch this quiet village. But this case, which I got involved in only to help my friend Bansi, has taught me never to make that mistake again. How can human nature be any different here? And so, I have come to realize that the desperate desires and dark impulses that drive people in the city to commit crimes are the same everywhere.'

When the sound of someone clearing their throat was heard, the detective stopped and then said, 'I shall make it short. I know now that one of you has committed both these evil acts. What I also know is that many of you have not been completely honest with us when we asked you questions. Harbouring those secrets was way more important for you than justice for a dead girl. And that is partly the reason why another young woman is fighting for her life in that room downstairs.'

After a few moments of stunned silence, almost everyone began to talk at the same time. Most of them were protesting their innocence in outraged tones and challenging Dhananjoy's claims about their nursing guilty secrets. Sushila's voice was the loudest. 'Didi, are you going to sit here and let this arrogant man bully and threaten us in this manner? I don't want to be here for another minute. We have all been so helpful, and look at the impertinent way he talks to us! How dare he? Who does he think he is, talking to us as though we are like the common crooks that he encounters every day in his work? He seems to have forgotten the difference between those who live in the Rajbari and the bajaria crooks. Didi, say something!'

Rakhal stood, extending his hand in the direction where his wife was sitting, as though he wanted to stem the flow of her angry screeching. But he sat down when Thakurani's severe reprimand could be heard. 'Sushila, stop this kind of talk at once. It was I who had asked Dhananjoy babu to do his duty and conduct his investigation to the best of his abilities. I don't see any impudence in what he is saying. If the murderer is somewhere amidst us, don't we want that person to be caught? He is right when he says that Sarala and Puti both deserve justice. So what if they worked in our kitchen? My father, who raised you as well, taught us that every form of life is precious. And anyone who acts with impunity deserves punishment. None of us is above the law, do you understand, Sushila? No one has the right to kill or injure another human being. He would have been very disappointed by your behaviour today. I request everyone to be seated and to be silent so that Dhananjoy babu can continue with what he is saying.'

There was steel in her voice, and everyone subsided in their seats without another word. Sushila continued to mutter angrily for some time, but after a while she fell silent as well, like all the others. Bansidhar thought that he could finally understand the meaning of that English idiom about pin-drop silence. He was sure he would be able to hear a pin drop in the silence while everyone held their breaths and waited for his friend to continue speaking. Even the cicadas chirping outside seemed to have quietened to let the man's voice be heard without any distracting background noise. There was a glint in Dhananjoy's eye as he looked at all of them and then began speaking.

'As I was saying, there are questions that are still unanswered because many of you have not come clean. Let me begin with you, Nityanand Maharaj. Have you been completely honest with us about your relationship with Sarala? I ask Sukanta babu. Is it possible that something happened on that path to the village? You were on it the day of Sarala's murder, weren't you? Have you told us everything? And what about you, Usha debi? Would you care to explain why you had an altercation with Sarala when she went to your room with a glass of milk one night? Or why you thought fit to place a nail on the stairs so that Sarala would hurt her foot or fall down the steps? You, Sushila debi? Have you and your husband told us the complete truth? Ramhari is in prison, but were his actions driven by his own impulses? Rakhal babu, were you honest with us when you talked to us about your past? About your father? And Daktar babu? Why, may I ask, did you neglect to mention to us your argument with Sarala a week or two before her death? Didn't she threaten you when you said you would tell Thakurani what you had found out about her?'

Sushila could be heard sniffing loudly and weeping at the end of this thunderous fusillade of questions, while the two young men sat with grave faces. A muscle could be seen working along Nityanand's jaw. Rakhal had shot a look of exasperation at his crying wife and clenched and unclenched his fists. Even Annada Charan looked pale and drawn. Usha was staring at her dada, eyes shining with unshed tears. Sukanta sat ramrod straight, looking out of the window as if he could see something extremely compelling in the darkness outside.

After a while, Rakhal babu asked in a distressed voice, 'I really don't understand how my account of my father can have anything to do with this. I—'

Dhananjoy's head snapped towards him as he said, 'Maybe it doesn't, Rakhal babu. But I don't like lies and half-truths when there's a murder inquiry going on. They make me suspicious.' Rakhal fell back in his chair after hearing Dhananjoy's sharp words.

When the silence around him remained unbroken, Dhananjoy turned to Bansi and said, 'Bansidhar, let's go. I don't think they will tell us anything.' Then he turned back to the others and continued, 'But let me tell all of you something. I have gathered quite a bit of information, and I have scarcely any doubts about who the killer is. I'm only waiting for Puti to regain consciousness and tell us if she can recall anything about the person who struck the blow. When we were in her room with Daktar babu, she came to for a few seconds. And when I asked her if she knew who had struck her, she nodded before fainting again. So, the killer just has a few hours more before Puti opens her eyes. If they confess, Bansidhar and I might be able to talk to the magistrate and ask for some relief for them. Else...'

In the silence that followed, Daktar babu rose from his seat, his body rigid with suppressed fury. It was quite clear that he had taken umbrage at the way in which Dhananjoy had included him in the circle of suspects. Back stiff and bristling with indignation, the doctor glared at the two police officers before pirouetting on his heels and marching out of the room. Bansidhar couldn't help feeling more than a little upset and wondered if his friend had crossed the line of decency when he had chastised Daktar babu, but he kept his counsel. Joy only wanted to find the truth, and that sometimes did involve crossing the line of decency and decorum. It came with the territory, Bansidhar told himself with a sigh.

The tension in the room was something that Bansidhar felt like a physical thing. Nobody spoke, but it was obvious that they were all mulling over the detective's words as they gazed at the floor despairingly. When the two policemen rose from their chairs to take their leave of Thakurani and began the long walk down the corridor, it was Nityanand who addressed them in a choked voice.

'Dhananjoy babu, Daroga babu, stop! Arrest me, Daroga babu. It was me. I am guilty of Sarala's murder.'

Several pairs of stupefied eyes swivelled towards the young yogi. A loud gasp could be heard from behind the screen where Thakurani and Sushila sat. The shock couldn't have been greater if someone had suddenly hurled a stone into their midst. Nityanand's face was deathly pale, and his breathing was laboured. He stood, clasping the back of a chair, and looked like he was under enormous strain and might collapse any minute.

19

THE KILLER STRIKES AGAIN

Dhananjoy's voice was even as he gazed at the man who had confessed to the murder. 'Is that so? Are you sure you mean that? Do you mean to say that you were the one who crept up behind Sarala Dasi on that fateful evening and hit her on the head? Hit her so hard that the poor woman's skull nearly caved in? In that case, can you tell us, what you hit her with?'

Nityanand winced at the detective's words but then pressed on. 'Why, I... I... used a... a heavy branch that I had found on the ground... I think I...' The yogi's voice trailed off.

'No, Maharaj, Sarala wasn't hit with a branch. And you did not kill her.'

Nityanand's face crumpled. His forehead was dripping with sweat even though it wasn't that hot inside the room. 'What does it matter, Daroga babu, what was used? I'm confessing to the murder. It was my cowardice, my deception that killed the poor girl. Whatever you might say, Dhananjoy babu, I killed her.' The calm yogi's voice verged on hysteria. It rose with every word he uttered.

In a slow, thoughtful manner, Dhananjoy said, 'Come, wipe your tears, why don't you? Let's go and sit in the baithak khana downstairs. You can tell us properly what you mean. Get that weight of guilt and sorrow off your chest, which has been driving you mad.'

~

Once they sat in a room downstairs, they could see that Nityanand's eyes were still glistening. Both detectives waited for him to collect his thoughts. Sitting close to him, Bansi saw that the young mendicant had become painfully thin. A dark stubble was apparent on his emaciated cheeks. After a few minutes of sitting with his head hanging down, his shoulders hunched, the yogi straightened his spine, looked directly at the two men in front of him and began to speak.

'Dhananjoy babu, I am a sinner. I deserve to be punished. I committed the sin of falling in love. So did Sarala. We both committed that sin. She was a widow; I am a mendicant who is supposed to have transcended desires of the flesh, and yet...'

After that first time when Sarala had heard Nityanand sing, she knew she would not be able to stay away for long from that magnetic voice and, more importantly, the owner of that voice. The next time she saw him, he had been walking near the pukur and singing to himself. His eyes were half-closed, and he sang with full-throated ease, unaware of the secret listener. She watched him for a while and then stepped out from behind the tree where she had been hiding. He was completely taken aback at first, but when she said she just wanted to hear him sing, that it made her forget her aches and pains, he invited her to sit. By the time he had finished singing, he could see tears coursing down her cheeks. And so he decided to keep sitting there rather than rush back to the house. They were both outsiders in that mansion, lonely despite being surrounded by people. Neither of them was used to talking too much in the Rajbari. They were there to stand and serve. To speak when spoken to. And so, to begin with, their conversation was full of hesitation and silences.

But in due course, that changed. They soon found out they had certain things in common. And the greatest discovery, of course, was the fact that they could talk without reservations and fear of judgement to another human being in that mansion. Having spent most of their lives clamping down on their feelings, it seemed like they could finally exhale in each other's company. Their meetings were few and far between, but when they did meet – and the pukur became their chosen place – they found they could not stop baring their hearts to each other. They had no name for their relationship, and yet, it became such an important one in their lives.

'I know you will find it very hard to believe when I say that, to begin with, we only sought each other out for some companionship in this large estate. We have our work cut out here, and yet, I suppose, once we met each other, we realized that we wanted something more. Wanted someone who would not just see us as the kitchen hand or the yogi whose sole purpose in life is to help Ballabh Ray get better. We had both been trapped in violent relationships in the past. Perhaps that made us recognize a kindred spirit. We formed a powerful bond that neither of us could deny.'

Bansidhar said nothing, but inwardly, he scoffed at the very idea of friendship between a man and a woman. Of course, there could be no such thing. Was the yogi that naïve? It was like claiming that ghee and fire could be friends. He kept a straight face and stopped himself from snorting loudly. Dhananjoy, meanwhile, was nodding, and Nityanand looked grateful when he saw the glimmer of compassion and understanding in the tall detective's eyes. By now, tears fell openly from his eyes as he continued in a bleak voice. 'Believe me, Daroga babu, neither of us thought or expected it to go any further than that. And yet, and yet... it did. We were both mortified, but we couldn't resist the power of what we both felt. Why does God test us so? Why?' The yogi's chin was trembling. His fine, sculpted features were contorted in grief that he was finally able to express. When Bansidhar asked, 'So, Maharaj, was the child yours?', he nodded mutely in assent.

'We need you to tell us about that. When did you get to know?'

'About two or maybe three weeks ago. Not more than that. Sarala had told me and then looked at my face expectantly. She said she had already visited Daktar babu to confirm what she was sure she could feel. When I looked dumbfounded, she said she had made sure the doctor would never talk about it to anyone in the Rajbari. Especially to Thakurani. So, she could keep her job till we decided what to do. I really didn't know what to say, Daroga babu. I was numb with shock, while she went on and on about how she had heard Sukanta talk about Vidyasagar and the widow remarriage law and that there was nothing to stop us from running away to the city and getting married. Apparently Sukanta had also told her about something called *Teen Ain,* or the Act III of 1872, which she was convinced would facilitate our marriage. I could see the euphoric expression on her face. That disarmingly open face with which she looked up at me, expecting me to echo her innocent joy! I didn't want to disappoint her. But she must have seen that I had baulked when she started talking of the child and her dream about our life in the city. I told her I would need some time to think about it. Her face fell, and she walked away silently. After that, whenever we met, she would ask me how much more time I needed to make up my mind. I'm fairly certain someone overheard us once, during one such meeting in the night. Finally, I told her I was ready to take the leap. You should have seen her excitement. She was like a child herself. I can never forget that incandescent smile on her face!'

'But did you really want to go along with what she was suggesting, Maharaj?'

Sarala Dasi's lover wiped his eyes and said disconsolately, 'No, you are right. I couldn't think of my future the way she was planning it for us. Run away to the city, get married, get a job, raise a child together... all of those things filled me with the deepest dread. But I never ever thought of doing her any harm.' The last bit came out like a cry of pain.

'Maharaj, I have to ask these questions. In our line of work, we cannot trust anyone. It is nothing personal. Look at it from my point of view. The victim was a pregnant widow. You know only too well the kind of repercussions that follow when news of this kind travels. Mostly, the poor women try to abort their foetuses. And can you blame them? As always, it is they who have to carry the burden of shame and public disgrace. And the sarkar, with its anti-abortion law, has only made things worse for them. Listening to you, I can't help but admire Sarala Dasi for having thought of a future for herself and her child.'

Nityanand's head hung low again. He said in a toneless voice, 'Yes, I was the coward. She, at least, had dared to dream of something different. You should have seen her. Her resolve to have a new life was unclouded with doubts or confusion. And I was about to let her down. I was weak. The enormity of the responsibility frightened me out of my wits.' The contrition on his face was moving, and yet, Bansidhar couldn't really feel sorry for a man who wanted to turn his back on his unborn child. That, to him, seemed like an unforgivable sin, far greater than the illicit affair.

Dhananjoy said after a few moments. 'So let me ask you again, since, as you have just told us, the news of the pregnancy had rattled you completely and you had no desire to marry her and raise the child, what *was* it that you were planning to do?'

Nityanand was walking back from what was going to be his last meeting with Sarala. He had met her at their usual meeting place – near the pukur – and listened to her talk about how they should begin planning their departure soon. The poor girl really believed they had a future together. She had even organized some money, she said, which would take care of their needs in the initial days in the city. They would get swallowed by the city's multitudinous crowds and begin their lives afresh. How could he tell her that she was living in a fool's paradise? He could never be a husband or a father. Why had he gotten entangled in all this? he thought. He still had feelings for her; there was no denying that. Even now, as he saw her face brimming with hope and joy, he wanted to fold her in his arms. No, he could not bring himself to tell her that if she went to Calcutta, she would have to make the journey alone. Let her have her few moments of joy before he made his escape.

'I was planning to run away, Dhananjoy babu. I was going to escape from the Rajbari and never return. I am a cowardly escapist. She was offering me the one chance of becoming a responsible adult, and what did I do? I deceived her. And then someone killed her, and despite my shock and grief, I just decided to keep quiet about everything that had happened between us. The woman I loved had died, and all I could think of was saving my reputation!'

Clutching a fistful of hair, he continued in a hoarse whisper, 'I even felt a little relieved that the problem had gone away of its own accord. That I didn't need to do anything. What sort of a man am I, Dhananjoy babu? Don't you think I deserve to be in prison? Not a single day goes by when I don't feel disappointed in myself. That wisp of a girl was so courageous, so full of hope. And I was so weak. I lied to her, lied to you when you asked me questions. Sleep eludes me every night. I simply walk up and down the corridor in the hope that I'll feel exhausted and fall asleep. And yet, on most nights, I don't sleep a wink. I think I have heard Sushila debi complain to Rakhal babu about the incessant sound of footsteps she can hear every night.' Here the yogi stopped to draw a long, shuddering breath. 'In a way, I'm also responsible for Puti's injuries, am I not? That poor girl would not have been in this situation had I told you everything truthfully. I can't even begin to describe what I felt when I saw the girl bleeding near there. I had stopped going to the pukur since Sarala's death. That used to be her favourite place. In fact, I went back there for the first time after her death and that shocking sight was waiting for me. For a moment, I thought my guilty mind had conjured the image of Sarala's broken body in that very place where we had loved each other.'

Nityanand finally ran out of steam and slumped back, striking his mouth repeatedly with his fist. Dhananjoy sat with his arms folded and reflected on what the yogi had just told them. Looking at him, it was evident that guilt was eating him up from within and turning him into a husk of the self-composed, serene man they had met earlier. His tears had dried and left tracks on his cheeks. All that Dhananjoy could feel was a diffused fury on behalf of Sarala, who had loved and then been so tragically betrayed.

'One last question, Maharaj. You would have had the strongest motive to kill her. If I were to believe what you just said, who else do you think would want her dead? And why? Even if you didn't know it then, have you thought of something now?'

The yogi batted his inky black eyelashes in what seemed like confusion. 'No, nothing, Dhananjoy babu. Believe me, I have thought a lot about this. Who would have wanted her dead? What reasons could they have? If Sarala were to be believed, she had not told anyone about our love or her pregnancy. Except, of course, Daktar babu. But what reason could the doctor have for snuffing out her life? Then who? And why? I keep going round in circles and yet have no answers.'

'All right. So, what will you do now, Maharaj? Do you still want to continue being in the Rajbari for some more time? I will, of course, have to ask you to wait till the culprit is found.'

Nityanand sniffed loudly and then shook his head. 'I doubt I can be here for very long. I'll wait for the investigation to be over, after which I shall leave. As to where I'll go, I will write to Gurudeb and implore him to call me back. Once I'm there, I'll tell him everything and beg for forgiveness. If he allows me to meet him or to stay in the ashram, I'll spend my life serving the ashram. Else, I'll begin my journey to the Himalayas. Maybe I'll find some peace and forgiveness amidst those tall, majestic peaks.'

~

After the ashen-faced yogi had left them with painfully slow steps, Bansidhar turned to Dhananjoy and said, 'So the mystery of who the child's father was has been solved. But I don't think he killed her. I believe Nityanand's account of what happened. What do you think?'

Dhananjoy made a noise at the back of his throat, took off his spectacles and nodded slowly. 'Yes, even though till the murderer is found, everyone's a suspect. Like you, I am fairly certain that Nityanand didn't kill her. Running away from the Rajbari would have been an easier solution for him. Leaving her holding the baby, quite literally. A real coward. Terrified of committing to a relationship.'

'Another trail run cold as far as we are concerned,' said Bansidhar with an air of defeat. Then, after a few minutes of silence, he turned to his friend with a question. 'Achha, Joy, have you considered the fact that even Thakurani would have had a massive stake in Sarala's death? After all, the scandal surrounding the cook's pregnancy would surely also have besmirched the Rajbari's reputation? After Ballabh Ray's accident, she has been trying so hard to restore its stature. She wants people to respect the Rajbari and not just fear it. Or gossip about it.'

'You are absolutely right, Bansi. I thought of this a couple of days ago. If Sushila could get Ramhari to give those dhatura leaves to Sarala, surely Thakurani could have sent someone that evening to attack her. She is, after all, the most powerful person in this household. She had seen how self-assured Sarala had become and might have wondered if it was Sukanta who was the cause of the young cook's nonchalance. If the news of the pregnancy had somehow reached her ears, she might have decided that the best way to silence the possibility of a scandal would be to kill the pregnant widow. You are right about that.'

'So why do I get the feeling that there is a "but" somewhere in your sentence?'

'Just this. If she had wanted to bury the scandal, she would not have asked whoever she sent on the mission to leave the body on the road. She would have given him explicit instructions to bury the body and remove all traces of the murder.'

Bansidhar could not disagree with what his friend was saying.

'Sarala's disappearance would not have caused so many problems. It would have been easy to claim that once the young widow found out about her pregnancy, she wanted to go off somewhere to hide her shame. The body on that path only complicated matters for the people of the Rajbari. Now there are police officials here, looking askance at the members of the household, questioning suspects. It is the opposite of what the Thakurani would have wanted had she planned to protect her family's reputation. She is an extremely intelligent person who makes her decisions after a great deal of reflection. She would not have panicked or done something like this in a fit of rage that leaves the people of the Rajbari and its reputation sinking in an ever-deepening morass.'

Bansi scratched his head and said, 'You're right. She is definitely not the kind to make impetuous decisions. It has to be someone else.'

Both men were beginning to feel the effects of the long day that had taxed them physically and emotionally. But Bansidhar had one more question for his friend before retiring for the night. As they got up to leave the room, he reached out and held Dhananjoy's wrist.

'What now?' Dhananjoy turned towards him with surprise.

'When you were addressing that assembly inside, you seemed to suggest that you know who the killer is. Is that true? Have you worked it out already?'

With an impish smile, Dhananjoy said, 'I won't say I am completely sure I have figured it out, but I have my views on the matter.' Then he added somewhat ruefully, 'You are right, though. I was bluffing a bit in there. I wanted to shake them up. That's why I said that once Puti was awake, they didn't have much of a chance. I have set the cat among the pigeons. Let's see what turns up now.'

~

After everyone had left for their rooms, Dhananjoy sent a message to Thakurani requesting her to let Bansi and him spend the remainder of the night in one of the rooms downstairs. Thakurani agreed with alacrity and asked Bama to prepare a room close to the one where Puti had been brought in. Daktar babu was also going to sleep in the Rajbari but he refused to talk to the police officers. The two of them looked in on Puti one last time and then walked to the room where they were going to spend the night. Bansidhar was yawning quite loudly by the time they were ready to call it a day.

Even though both men were dreadfully exhausted, sleep evaded them for a while. After tossing and turning for some time, Bansidhar sat up.

'Joy, you never got the time to tell me whether you found the answer to the question that you said had been bothering you.'

Dhananjoy also sat up, and after blinking for a few seconds he raked his hands through his hair, making it untidier. And when he spoke, it felt as though he was speaking more to himself than addressing his friend. 'I did find out something. Perhaps not important at all. A lie that someone told us. Unrelated to the murder you'd say, but lies always bother me.'

Bansidhar lay back on the bed and said glumly, 'I'm way too tired to make sense of what you said just now. Maybe tomorrow, if you explain it to me after I've had some food, I'll understand better.'

Assured that the explanation would make far better sense the next day, the daroga closed his eyes. After a while, Dhananjoy could hear his friend's snores. Staring at the tall palm trees swaying outside the window next to his bed, he felt certain the truth lay within his grasp. Not much longer now... not long. The bed and the pillow were invitingly soft, and gradually his eyes began to close.

And then they flew open. Their room being close to the one where Puti had been brought in earlier, Dhananjoy felt certain he had heard footsteps. Or was it a noise made by a door being opened surreptitiously? It was definitely some sound that put all his senses on high alert. He stepped out of the mosquito net that was hanging on his bed and then gently shook his friend's shoulder. Bansidhar was not a light sleeper like him, and the gentle shakes had to turn into rough jerks before he opened his eyes reluctantly. But once he saw Dhananjoy's face and the finger placed on his lip, he knew something was up and prepared himself for whatever awaited them.

Bama had given them a room where the door moved noiselessly, and the two men were able to step out without making any sound. The first thing they noticed as they moved with careful steps towards Puti's room was that the lathiyal posted outside was sound asleep. Even though his hand still grasped the lathi, his head hung low and his eyes were shut. Could he have been drugged? But there was no time to dwell on such questions for both men could see that the door to Puti's room was slightly ajar and someone was inside.

20

A LIFE LOST

There was not a moment to lose. The person inside had to be the killer. Attempting to finish what he couldn't achieve near the pukur earlier in the evening – silence Puti forever. The detectives exchanged glances as they stood on either side of the door. And then, as Dhananjoy raised his hand as a signal, both rushed into the room. The face of the figure was covered with a thick cloth, but the dhoti indicated that it was a man. Who was he? That was still not very clear. In the moonlight flooding the inside of the room, they could see that the intruder had plunged a knife into the chadar-covered shape on the bed. Since no blood had spurted out, it didn't take the killer long to realize that the two policemen had foreseen something like this might happen. Puti was not lying on that bed. A few pillows had been arranged artfully where she had lain earlier. She had been moved to a different room. It was all a trap set to catch him.

A pair of eyes, engorged with shock, looked up at the two detectives who had entered to grab him. He knew his game was up. And then, just as Dhananjoy and Bansidhar began advancing towards him, the man who had been planning to kill Puti leapt across the narrow bed, pushed Bansi out of his way and shot off in the direction of the door. Bansi was left clutching the cloth that had covered the man's face. Before the two detectives could gather their wits, the assailant was out of the room.

As he ran out, he stumbled on the sleeping figure of the lathiyal stationed outside, who woke up immediately, rubbed his eyes and stared open-mouthed at what was going on. The killer quickly gathered himself after losing his balance and sprinted away.

Dhananjoy shouted, 'Stop, stop, Rakhal babu. You can't go anywhere. There are lathiyals posted at every gate.'

Upon hearing this, the figure running in front of them rushed off towards the staircase. By now, the noise had woken up many others, and figures emerged from various rooms to see what was going on. All that people could see in the dark were shadows rushing. Only Sushila could be heard shrieking, 'What's happening! Are there intruders in the house? Are we being robbed by dacoits? Where are those two useless policemen now? My husband! I can't find my husband. Oh, lord, have the dacoits done something to him? Has he been abducted? Oh, Didi, what's going on?'

It was apparent to the two detectives that the man in front of them was not going to turn himself in easily. He kept running up the stairs amidst all the shouts and screams that emanated from different parts of the household. They heard him stumbling and cursing, but he didn't stop.

Bansidhar shouted to Dhananjoy, 'Where's he going, Joy? There's nowhere for him to escape. What the hell is he doing?'

'I think he's headed for the terrace, Bansi.'

'What? The roof?' And then as realization dawned, he shouted, 'Oh god! No!'

Dhananjoy was right. When they burst through the door leading to the terrace, they could see Rakhal standing near the edge of one of the low walls. As soon as he saw them, he climbed up and stood on the wall, poised to plunge to certain death below. He held on to a protruding part of the wall for support. Bansidhar had bent double to catch his breath after they stopped running. When he looked up, he gasped. In the moonlight, Rakhal babu's face was clearly visible. His eyes looked even more bulbous than usual, and his mouth was drawn back in what seemed like a terrifying, rictus-like grin. The gentle face was completely transmogrified into something unrecognizably hideous.

Behind Dhananjoy and Bansi, most of the other inhabitants of the Rajbari had gathered, and there were audible sounds of surprise from many of them. Only the loquacious Sushila was completely silent. Her hand was clapped to her mouth as she tried to take in what she could see in front of her. And then, all that she could utter was a prolonged whimper, 'Oh no! Oh no, no, no, no!'

Dhananjoy raised his hand to ask the people gathered behind him to be quiet. Soon, there was deathly silence, and other than the sudden screeching of a flying owl, nothing else disturbed the tableau of still figures.

Dhananjoy looked at Rakhal and said, 'Rakhal babu, we beg you not to take that step. If nothing else, please think of the child that awaits its father. Don't you want to cradle that little innocent baby in your arms? Watch it grow up? I remember how your eyes had filled with tears when you recalled your closeness to your father. Do you want to deprive your child of that important presence in his life? We know you'll be a marvellous father. Once you have served your sentence, we—'

'Stop! Stop talking, Dhananjoy babu!' Rakhal's scream was heart-wrenching, as much a cry of pain as it was a furious injunction. Were those tears glittering on his cheeks? Bansi wasn't sure. Transfixed, he watched the figure standing on the wall, swaying ever so slightly and glaring with bloodshot eyes at all of them.

'I want you to stop talking. Just don't speak. I really have had enough of people telling me what to do and what's good for me. Treating me like a project they need to work on. To improve. Wear this, do that, go there. Enough, I say! I don't need your words of wisdom, Dhananjoy babu. Who do you think you are, coming here and telling me what to do? Pontificating about fatherhood! Yes, I loved my father. Worshipped the ground he walked on. And do you know what he did?'

After a few seconds of utter silence, he shrieked again, 'What, I ask you, did he do, Mr Detective?'

In a soft voice, Dhananjoy answered, 'He killed himself!'

'Louder please, Mr Detective! So everyone can hear you. Weren't you shouting at me earlier in the sadar khana for lying to you? Well, let everyone hear the truth. Spit it out!'

'He killed himself.'

'Bravo! Well done! Right answer, Pandit moshai's son. Absolutely correct answer. Your father would have been proud of you. Garlanded you, applauded you if he had been around.' Rakhal burst into gales of wild laughter after this. Once that stopped, he roared, 'At least yours died of an illness. Not like mine, who simply abandoned me. Who went and killed himself. Yes, yes, I know I had told you that he had died in an accident. I lied. Yes, I lied. As you have found out, Dhananjoy babu. How could I admit to anyone that my father didn't think his son was worth living for? Do you know what it is like for a child to live with that knowledge? To open one's eyes every morning and remember that even though he doted on me, I was not enough for him? That ultimately, he cared so little that he hanged himself and left his lifeless body for his only child to discover? A son who had no one else in this big, wide world but him? Who does that, Dhananjoy babu, tell me. I was just sixteen when I had to cut my father's body down from the branch of a neem tree in our courtyard. He hanged himself in the night while I was sleeping. How very considerate, don't you think? To imagine that it would be perfectly fine for his son to discover him like that early the next morning. I have never been able to pass a neem tree without feeling sick. Who does that to their child?'

Her back pressed tightly against a wall, Sushila was sobbing quietly. This could not be happening, she thought. She had never seen her husband look like this. Never heard that voice. It was the first time, she realized, that she had heard him sound so pugnacious. And yet so miserable. There was so much she didn't know about him. She had never really tried to find out. Sometimes, when the long silences between them made her nervous, she tried to fill them with her own endless prattling. Why had she never asked him what was going on in his head? She blindly assumed everything would be all right once the child was born. What was the point of lamenting now? He wasn't even looking at her. She wanted to fall at his feet and howl for forgiveness.

Thakurani's voice could be heard now, addressing her brother-in-law. 'Rakhal, please don't do this. We all love you. Every one of us. Think of Sushila, I beg you.'

Rakhal babu shook his head. 'Sushila will be fine, Didi. You know that. She'll have this life full of creature comforts, she'll have all of you, she'll have her child. Sushila was never really interested in me. She wanted a husband, that's all. And truth be told, I have never been able to love her either. I have tried. I really have. But she never really tried to understand me. I have tried to love her, but I couldn't. And then, I gave up, and I thought I would never know what it was to love. Told myself that it didn't matter. And just when I had convinced myself I would never find out what true love is, I did. I did. Dhananjoy babu, I did. It was a wonderful, glorious thing! All I wanted all day was to catch a glimpse of that face. But of course, I could not have that love returned. I was born to remain unloved. That's the truth, Dhananjoy babu. My sincere love has never been seen as worth returning. Poor Rakhal-da, poor Rakhal babu... stammering and twitching... poor thing, let's pat him on the head like a dog and then forget all about him. That's how I am regarded. And that's what's turned me into this... this thing that you see in front of you. How can someone who feels as though his insides are completely charred, love a child? And then, what if one day I find even that child looks at me with a distracted kind of affection? Oh, no, no, Dhananjoy babu. I can't go through that again. Don't ask me to. Yes, I killed Sarala, and today I was out to kill poor Puti. I hate myself. I can still remember the perplexed look on Sarala's face right before the light went out in her eyes. Just for a split second, and yet, it is etched in my mind. Not horror, not fear. No, it was pure incomprehension. That look haunts me, Dhananjoy babu. Why does the memory of that expression not fade? I just can't go on like this. It's... it's just...'

The sentence remained incomplete as Rakhal clawed his cheek with one hand and stared with an air of despair around him.

'Dhananjoy babu, I carried a letter today in my pocket, which is meant for your eyes alone. Please don't let anyone else read it. And destroy it after you are done with it. When I set out today to finish what I couldn't complete near the pukur, I carried the letter with me. Perhaps some part of me knew you would stop me. You were drawing closer to the truth. I could feel it. You were not going to give up till you had dug up everything. And in a strange sort of way, a part of me is glad that you did. That you have... have uncovered the truth. Unmasked the devil!'

The voice died down for a few minutes but could be heard again after a while. Never had Bansi heard anything like it. It was like listening to misery in its purest form. Misery that rose from the turbid depths of the murderer's consciousness.

'I'm exhausted, Dhananjoy babu. I can't tell you how exhausting it is to lie to everyone all the time. This wretched life of pretence. Of knowing that I'll never be anyone's best-loved person and pretending that I'm all right with that. I'm glad it's going to be over. I had resented your coming and investigating the case, Dhananjoy babu. But now I feel you have done me a favour. You have set me free! I feel I can fly now. I'll finally have some peace. All I want is for you to read the letter in my pocket.'

Then, just as Sukanta stepped forward with a cry, 'Rakhal-da, don't do this...' Rakhal looked at him with an anguished expression, shuddered as if a spasm of pain had shot through his body and stepped back to his death. Dhananjoy heard screams from around him and then the sound of Sushila dropping to the floor in a faint.

~

A day had elapsed since the horrific tragedy. The people of the Rajbari were still reeling with shock and grief. Bansi and Dhananjoy were sitting in one of its rooms, waiting to take statements and trying to make sense of all that had happened in the night. Annada Charan had also arrived and was checking up on Puti.

Young Puti was recovering at a good pace. Her breathing had become quite stable, and it seemed that she might open her eyes soon. Sushila and her unborn child were also fine. But after being brought down from the terrace, she had withdrawn completely into an impenetrable silence. The fidgety, garrulous woman who could barely sit still had turned into a figure of stone. Her long hair, which she loved tying up in intricate plaits, lay in a wild, tangled mess about her shoulders as she sat, gazing wordlessly out of the window. Thakurani was with her, and it was she who talked while stroking her sister's back. Annada Charan had prescribed some medicines. But even the doctor knew that they were powerless to heal the real damage – the one that lay within. He could only hope that the child in her womb would ultimately help her return to normalcy.

When Bansi saw Daktar babu walking down the staircase, he rushed out, grabbed his hand and requested him to join them in the baithak khana. Annada babu thought about making a curt gesture and walking away. But he was quite curious about how the Calcutta detective had worked out the answers to some of the questions related to the case. So, he allowed himself to be persuaded by Bansidhar. Besides, even though he had reacted in an ill-tempered manner that evening to Dhananjoy's angry queries, he knew that the detective had only been doing his job. And that he had been right in accusing the doctor of not being entirely honest in his answers about his dealings with Sarala.

Bansidhar's head was also bursting with questions. For once, he was willing to ignore the sounds of hunger that his stomach was making. He needed hot food to help cope with the disturbing memories of Rakhal's broken body sprawled in an expanding pool of crimson. But more than that, he wanted Dhananjoy to tell them how he had pieced the puzzle together. And yet, when Kamini entered the room with plates full of food, Bansi couldn't stop himself from smiling. It was like watching the Goddess Annapoorna herself stepping into the room to feed hungry humans. Usha had also walked into the room behind her and helped serve the food.

Even after their meal was over, Usha hung back. Her face was flushed, and the puffed and red-rimmed eyes suggested fitful sleep and bouts of weeping.

'Daroga babu, Dhananjoy babu, I request you to let me sit here for a while. I know you are discussing the case. I would like to know what drove Rakhal-da to do what he did. My head has been spinning since the incident on the roof. We all liked him so much. Despite what he said, we did love him. I find it so hard to believe I'll never see him again. All this just doesn't make sense.'

'Yes, Usha is right, Dhananjoy babu.' Sukanta had also walked in as his sister was talking. Nityanand stood behind him, near the door, like a ghostly shadow.

'We want to hear your explanation about what happened. Rakhal-da wouldn't have harmed a fly. So, what prompted him to...?'

Just then, Kamini and Bama came to the door to ask if they needed anything more. Dhananjoy got up from his chair and went up to Kamini. 'Kamini-di, why don't you come and sit with us? The past few days have been rough for all of us. We were just going to discuss the case. You are welcome to join us. Bama, you, too. In fact, I would like everyone to know about your invaluable help.'

Kamini looked curiously at Bama but then shook her head. 'Na, na, Babu. I need to be with Thakurani. She's putting up a brave front while looking after her sister, but I know her heart is bleeding. Everyone will point fingers at the Rajbari, say that it is cursed. She needs someone beside her, doesn't she? Let me go to her. Bama, you stay here.'

Bansidhar then said, 'We can begin now. Dhananjoy, we are all agog to hear what you have to say.'

Annada Charan raised his hand and interrupted them. 'First things first. Dhananjoy babu, did you know that it was Rakhal who had killed Sarala? Before Rakhal's confession?'

Dhananjoy looked at all of them and nodded. 'Yes, the time has come to answer all questions. Why don't you all sit down? I'll give my explanations. I'm not sure how convincing all of them will be. But let's begin.' Once everyone had settled down and Dhananjoy saw the expectant faces turned towards him, he began.

'First, Daktar babu's question. Whether I knew it was Rakhal babu? Yes, I had started to suspect him. Everyone had lied to us, but his lies seemed the most carefully crafted and elaborate. They smacked of planning and premeditation. Especially the one about going off to Calcutta and not being here during the murder.'

'But his alibi was watertight, Joy. Puti had seen him leave at four from the uttor dorja and bid him farewell. Then Sijad and Chacha saw him on his way to the station. Ahir, our station master, had also confirmed that he waved him goodbye. They had exchanged pleasantries, he said. Sarala left the Rajbari using the dokhin dorja nearly half an hour later and took the path going to the village. Which would be four-thirty or thereabouts, right? It had just started getting dark. So how?'

Bansi's bafflement was reflected on all the other faces in front of Dhananjoy.

'Yes, yes. And truth be told, I had thought of leaving him out of the list of suspects initially. But when I stared at my notes, I felt something was not adding up. I looked and looked at my notes till they became a blur, and yet nothing jumped out. But that feeling kept bothering me. I could not put my finger on it for the longest time. And then, it suddenly stared me in the face.'

'What, what was it, Dhananjoy babu?' This time it was Annada Charan, unable to contain his curiosity. Dhananjoy remembered the way Daktar babu had prolonged the suspense in his dispensary with his tea-making and toyed with the idea of serving revenge as a cold dish. But then he changed his mind and smiled.

'Be patient, Moshai. I'll tell you. It was a stray remark by Hakim chacha. Yes, I'm grateful to the voluble Hakim chacha for helping me solve this mystery. When I recalled his remark, I knew what the bee buzzing in my head had been trying to tell me. Hakim chacha had said to me that he had been teaching a reluctant Sijad how to catch fish in the dighi that afternoon. And then Chacha said he had felt a hand on his shoulder late in the afternoon. It was Rakhal babu walking to the station who had startled them from behind. And then they chatted for a bit before he walked on.'

'Yes. So?'

'Think, Bansi. Puti had confirmed that she had seen Rakhal babu walk out of the uttor dorja, which is the one that the Rajbari inhabitants normally use. He said to Puti that it was four and he needed to be at the station to catch the five-thirty train. If you were walking from the uttor dorja to the station, on what side would the dighi be as you walked? Think!'

Usha exclaimed in an excited voice, 'Oh, yes, yes, I see what Dhananjoy babu means. He would not have been behind Chacha as he caught fish. That route from the uttor dorja would have been on the other side of where Chacha would have been sitting. And that road is also slightly curved. If Rakhal-da had taken it, he wouldn't have been behind Chacha and Sijad as he walked to the station. He would have been in front of them.'

'Exactly! Sijad, especially, would not have missed him. He wasn't as focused on his fishing as Chacha would have liked him to be. He would surely have looked up and seen Rakhal-da on the other side, and felt glad about the distraction. In fact, when I went to visit Sijad the other day, I asked him again about their encounter with Rakhal that evening. And he confirmed that both he and his dadu had been startled by Rakhal's hand on their shoulders. But there's more. And that's where Puti comes in.'

21

THE TYING OF LOOSE ENDS

This time it was Sukanta who leaned forward in his chair and said, 'Yes, I have been wondering about that. Why Puti? What could poor Puti have known?'

'I'll explain that in a minute. But before I do, I wanted to find out from Usha debi why she had shouted at Sarala. Why did you throw away the glass of milk she had taken up for you. Why did you do that? And what about the nail that caused Sarala's foot to bleed?'

The young woman who had been watching the detective with avid eyes as he explained things now lowered her gaze. After a few minutes of staring at her fingers, she looked up and said, 'I need to come clean, don't I? You're right. I did not tell you everything that day. Well, the thing is, I thought Sarala was trying to make Dada fall in love with her and that Dada was becoming smitten with her. I had seen them chatting and laughing now and then, and I assumed...'

Sukanta's jaw had loosened a little as he turned to his sister. Usha didn't look at him but reached out and held Sukanta's hand. 'I'm truly sorry, Dada. I don't know what I was thinking. It's just that...'

'Yes, go on. What were you thinking?' Sukanta urged his sister. The look he gave her was full of reproach.

Usha's voice was faint, tear-choked. 'I had once overheard Sarala asking you about Vidyasagar babu's attempts to get widows married. And when she asked you in an earnest voice whether you supported his ideas, I began imagining all kinds of things. I was sure she wanted to ensnare you.'

'Ensnare me? What!' But after the outraged exclamation, Sukanta sighed in a defeated manner and leaned back in his chair. 'Well, who am I to shout at you? We have all made mistakes. Bad decisions. Some more terrible than others.'

Dhananjoy shot a searching glance at Usha. 'So, Usha debi, you were so angry you planted a couple of nails near the stairs just before Sarala came out of Sushila's room, right? She had already cleaned the stairs under Sushila's hawk-eyed inspection, and so she didn't pay any attention to the nails and stepped on one. You got that idea from one of the novels you had been reading, isn't it?'

Usha's voice was so low they all had to strain their ears to hear her. Her chin was practically tucked into her chest. 'That day, when you asked me about that book, I knew you had figured it out. I really wasn't thinking straight that day, so consumed was I with my need to protect Dada.'

'Those stairs aren't too many, so she wouldn't have died even if she fell down those steps. But even so...'

Usha's knuckles had turned white. 'I know, I did an unforgivable thing. I would never hurt anyone. But something was driving me to behave in that despicable manner. It was like a red mist had descended over my eyes. Oh god! What was I thinking! And the girl hurt her foot quite badly. I got quite scared by how deep the cut was and asked her to go to Daktar babu.'

'And more recently? When she went to your room to give you milk? You gave Sarala quite a dressing-down that night, am I right?'

With a sigh that seemed to have been wrung out of the very depths of her being, Usha turned her doe-like eyes to the detective, who was implacable in his pursuit of the truth. Like the mythical Sita, she wanted nothing more in that moment but for the earth to part and swallow her. 'I'm mortified when I think of all those things, Dhananjoy babu. I need to stop being an overprotective sister. I behaved so badly that day. I went berserk and called her all sorts of names. I, who hate the ugly words used by writers to revile women, felt no compunction about hurling those words at Sarala that day. No wonder she rushed out of the room in tears. How could I have done that?' Usha rubbed her face repeatedly. Bansi noticed unshed tears glittering in Nityanand's eyes.

Steering the conversation back to Puti, Bansi urged Dhananjoy to explain why he had feared the young woman's life might be in danger.

'Well, to be honest, when I had told Puti to try and remember whatever she could about that day and tell us if there was anything that bothered her, I wasn't sure what to expect. But by the afternoon, I started feeling anxious for her. Which is why I rushed to the pukur to make sure she was all right. For my fear was that the killer might panic. Might think that some specific question could trigger a memory in Puti. By then, Rakhal babu was probably becoming frantic with worry that I was closing in on the truth. I'm sure he had seen me questioning Puti and felt nervous about what she might recall about that day. You see, a very important part of his alibi hinged on Puti's statement.'

'So what was it that she had recalled?' Even though it was Bansi who asked the question, everyone in the room waited for Dhananjoy's response.

~

Dhananjoy looked at his hands for some time and then addressed his friend.

'Bansi, do you remember Puti talking of Usha debi's tea the day she was struck? Just before losing consciousness?'

The people gathered in the room exchanged baffled looks. What could Usha's tea have anything to do with the murder?

Bansi said after a bit. 'Oh yes, Joy. I think I do. She was incoherent, but she did mumble something about Usha and her tea and the time. But—'

'Wait, hear me out. At the time when Kamini-di said that Puti had remembered it was time to give Usha debi her tea, I didn't have reason to think otherwise. But later, I wondered if Puti was trying to tell me something very different. Something she had recalled from the day of the murder. I had asked her to remember anything that didn't quite add up, and so, when she saw us, she was trying to tell me what she had recalled.'

'Why, what was it?'

'She remembered that when she met Rakhal babu near the uttor dorja, he had looked at his watch and said he needed to hurry since it was exactly four o'clock. But then, when she carried Usha debi's tea upstairs, which would have been at least fifteen minutes or maybe a bit more after meeting Rakhal babu, she had heard the trusty grandfather clock strike four. Usha debi might even have praised her for being right on time. Puti would have been so relieved and happy that everything else slipped from her mind. Besides, that was the time when Durga Puja preparations were going on at a frenetic pace. Kamini-di's instructions about not dawdling anywhere would have been ringing in her ears, so she must have rushed back to the kitchen and then met Sarala afterwards as she walked out of the Rajbari for the last time. Not surprisingly, it was only when I asked Puti to take her time and carefully go over everything that she could remember from that day that this discrepancy of time came back to her. How could Rakhal-da have talked of the time being four when clearly the chiming of the Rajbari clock suggested otherwise?'

'That's brilliant, Joy! I can't believe you thought of all that. Bravo, my friend.'

Annada Charan said, 'So, Rakhal babu had needed Puti to confirm that he had left the Rajbari at four. But he had actually left at least fifteen minutes before four since he had to take a detour and hide himself in the thicket and wait for Sarala to pass that way. Am I right, Dhananjoy babu?'

'Spot on. That's precisely what must have happened. For Rakhal babu needed someone to hear that he was leaving the mansion at four, and he must have thought that meeting Puti near the gate was an immense stroke of luck for him. So, he would have made an elaborate pretence of looking at his watch and announcing that it was four and time for him to leave. When Bansidhar came here to take everyone's *ijahar*s, that's all Puti remembered. Rakhal babu's gamble paid off.'

'Yes,' said Bansidhar, 'I remember that first statement. He told me that he left at four, and then, when he turned towards Puti for confirmation, she simply nodded.'

'So, this is what happened. Rakhal babu set off fifteen or twenty minutes before four despite what he announced to Puti. He probably assumed no one would pay that much attention to the inconsistency, especially since Puti herself would also remember what he would have said to her more than once. Casually inserted it in his chats with her, so that that was what became the truth for her. She forgot all about the grandfather clock. The power of suggestion as it is called.

Anyway, after that, he took the path that cuts through the dense foliage. He then took the other route that leads from the dokhin dorja to the village. And also, the train station.'

He turned to Bansidhar and said, 'Remember, Bansi, I told you about my chat with Haridasi Boishnobi? When I met her by chance that day?'

'Yes, yes, I remember that,' Bansi said, a little bewildered by the leaps made by his friend's excited mind.

'That day when I met her, she had been going to the Rajbari. At the end of our chat, she had moved in a direction that didn't make sense to me. But later, it struck me that she might have been taking a different route to get to the Rajbari. The next day, when Bansi went to help Daroga Shyamacharan, I used my time to explore all the routes between the village, the station and the Rajbari.

'Coming back to Rakhal babu's movements that day. He used that path in the copse to reach the other side. The side that flanked the path from the dokhin dorja to the village. The path that Sarala would take every week to go home. Then he hid and waited for his prey.

'He had probably also asked her earlier that day whether she was going home. And he knew about her fear of ghosts and that she would walk home before dark. So, brick in hand, he waited behind a tree. And then, sure enough, there was Sarala walking down that path, preoccupied with her happy thoughts and probably a little disoriented after chewing on the dhatura leaves. Her reflexes not as sharp as they would have been under usual circumstances. It was not too hard for Rakhal babu to creep up behind her and strike the fatal blow.'

Usha was listening to him with rapt attention and said, 'But, Dhananjoy babu, wouldn't he have got blood on his clothes? How did he take care of that?'

Bansi was a little appalled by the ease with which the girl could ask such questions with no trace of squeamishness. No doubt, she was canny. That he had to admit with grudging admiration. But this unhealthy obsession with crime and gore was simply not appropriate in a young woman. Indeed, her eyes shone as Dhananjoy explained the puzzle bit by bit. These modern, educated women were truly beyond his comprehension.

While Bansidhar sniffed with disapproval, Dhananjoy looked happy to be asked the question. 'Yes, Usha debi, you are right. I did think of that. But then, there wouldn't have been a great deal of blood since he hit her from behind and she fell face forward. Most of the blood would have spilt on the ground where she fell. Once Rakhal babu became a suspect, I sent a letter to the Calcutta guest house where he stayed that night. It was Sijad who carried that letter for me. I had asked him to wait there and bring back the guest house owner's response in writing. In the letter, I had instructed the owner to ask the guest house *dhobi* whether he had received any bloodstained clothing for washing a few days ago from one of the guests. When threatened with the possibility of a police interrogation, it didn't take the dhobi long to remember the slightly bloodstained clothes that a particular babu had given to him for washing. The babu had told him he had a gash on his hand which had bled.

'While walking to the station, Rakhal babu was carrying a small suitcase. The bloodstained kurta went into that, and he wore a fresh one for the journey. On the train, he cut himself with a piece of glass. He must have shown his cut to the dhobi to allay his suspicions. As I said, this was a meticulously planned murder. And Rakhal babu took great pride in his planning and his careful eye for detail.'

'So that's the real reason for Sijad's Calcutta visit that day.'

Annada babu turned to look at Bansi and saw that his brow was creased with worry.

'What is it, Daroga babu? Why the lines of worry on your face after everything has been solved?'

'I was thinking of how close Puti came to losing her life. And what would have happened if we hadn't kept pillows on that bed where she was supposed to be to dupe the murderer. Another young woman would have been killed. And, Joy, what if we had missed Rakhal babu that night?'

Dhananjoy tilted his head back and rubbed his cheeks with his hands, as if to shake off the overpowering sense of exhaustion that had begun to assail every part of his body. His eyes felt gritty, and he could sense the beginning of a headache.

'Yes, Bansi, you are right. For all our research and chasing of leads, more often than not, luck does play an important part in investigations. So much of what we ultimately achieve can be chalked down to blind chance! Being in the right place at the right time!'

Usha, who had been replaying in her mind Rakhal's final words on the roof, said, 'So why did Rakhal-da kill Sarala? He talked of love. Was he in love with her? Did she rebuff him? Is that what he meant?'

Dhananjoy stood and exhaled loudly. 'Yes, we will have to assume that's what he meant. He appeared to be a diffident man, but something must have snapped. Let's just leave it at that. What would be the point of speculating? The mysteries of the human mind... those are the hardest to plumb.'

Annada Charan said, 'You will get some of the answers in that letter that Rakhal has left for you. But you seemed to know that his father had killed himself. How did you know about that? That would have been one of his most painfully guarded secrets.'

'Yes, well, I can't quite say why I felt he was being a little economical with the truth when he talked about his father that first day when we met. Maybe there was something about the way he blinked repeatedly or the way he kept glancing to his left. I felt there was something he was trying to hide. Something about his father. On one of those days when Bansi had work at the thana, I went to Badalgram. Where Rakhal babu lived before coming to Rajapur. I talked to an old neighbour of his, and he told me about his father's suicide. The old gentleman I met had helped the young Rakhal cut the rope and bring down his father's body. He said that Rakhal was not quite the same after that incident. He became withdrawn, anxious, difficult to talk to.'

The room sank into silence as all the people gathered there absorbed everything they had just heard. Usha drew in a breath and cried out suddenly, 'I am so confused. I can't help thinking that I'll miss Rakhal-da. I keep remembering his gentle, endearing smile, his eagerness to help if he saw me struggling with a problem. He was such a decent person. Do I now have to believe that all that was false? Remember him only as a murderer? But even when I remember him on that roof, I feel more sorry for him than anything else. And yet, he...'

Sukanta held his sister's hand, but even he had no answers to what she said. Dhananjoy said in a mild voice, 'Usha debi, it's only in detective fiction that crimes are like puzzles with tidy solutions. Outside those books, they are messy affairs. They often leave behind more questions than can be solved satisfactorily. A wise man had once said to me before I became a policeman that I should never be hasty in judging someone as a criminal. That right and wrong are quite often not simple matters of black and white.' Usha nodded, but her eyes continued to look profoundly sad.

Turning to Sukanta, Dhananjoy asked, 'Sukanta babu, since we are clearing up all our confusion, let me ask you one question that's been bothering me. On that evening while returning from the village, did you not see Sarala's corpse?'

Usha's body tensed, but she controlled her impulse to jump to her brother's defence and kept quiet. It was clear to her that Sukanta had been keeping quite a few secrets from her.

'It was quite late by the time I finished what I had gone to do at the village,' Sukanta said. 'I asked the man I had gone to meet if I could lie down in the courtyard of his house. He had no objections. Early next morning, I returned to the Rajbari using the other route that you mentioned. The one that leads to the uttor dorja.'

It was now Usha's turn to cast a reproachful glance at her brother. When she tried to extricate her hand from his fingers, Sukanta tightened his grip and said, 'No, don't feel upset, Usha. I want to say this to you in front of all these people. I have lied to you and not been a good brother. You deserve much better than this. I promise that I will tell you everything. It will be ugly, and it will shock you. But lies – especially those you tell your loved ones – only fester inside one's mind like a raw, untreated wound. I need to come clean to you, and I will. And I hope you will forgive this brother of yours after you have heard me out.'

When it was time for the two detectives to go up and meet Thakurani for one last time, Bansi couldn't help but notice a quick exchange of glances between his friend and Usha. It made him hope that Dhananjoy's ties with the village might be strengthened in the near future. Surely there was no harm in indulging in a bit of fantasy. Daroga Bansidhar Gupta thought with a little smile to himself as he hurried behind the man without whose help he could never have cracked the case. Bansi, however, had one final question.

'So, did you solve the all-important mystery of the stolen coconuts, Joy?'

'Indeed, I did, Bansi. I'll tell you about it over dinner tonight.'

Late that night, after Dhananjoy had had his dinner and answered each of Saroja's probing questions about the solving of the murder, he heaved a sigh and reclined on his bed with the letter that Rakhal had left for him. The writing was small and painstakingly neat. Dhananjoy could imagine him composing a few drafts before being satisfied with the final piece of writing. Even while writing what he knew could very well be his last letter.

Dear Dhananjoy babu,

I nearly got away with it, didn't I? But if you are reading this letter, I know I haven't. I had feared this as soon as we had met. I was proud of all the careful planning that I had undertaken. That I didn't let my emotions get the better of me and make a hash of everything. That I stayed awake at night thinking of all the possible ways I could be caught and then taking care of each of them. Would you believe that I stole coconuts from the Rajbari kitchen and practised hitting them with a brick so that I would be able to kill Sarala with a single blow? I practised and I practised till I perfected the right amount of force that would be required to crack open a skull. How utterly insane that sounds when I write it. But believe me, somehow it had felt like the right thing to do.

But you know all that already, don't you? You know that the murder could only have been committed by someone who took pride in his ability to plan and second-guess every kind of eventuality. Perhaps the only eventuality I couldn't have planned for was the sudden arrival of Daroga Bansidhar Gupta's friend from Calcutta!

My life, in any case, has been so full of unexpected twists and turns. So unlike the maths problems I love to solve and where I know the end of my journey, where I can be sure of it. Life's not quite like that, is it? Perhaps that's why I became such an obsessive planner. Always fearing the worst. And yet, never able to predict that one thing life would keep up its sleeve. As if my father's sudden decision to kill himself, leaving me stranded, was not enough of a shock to last me a lifetime! When I thought I would spend my life in Badalgram, all by myself, hunched over the table where the gomashtas sat and work my fingers to the bone, my employer, the taluqdar, got me married to Sushila. Then just when I had reconciled myself to spending my life with a woman I couldn't love, indeed, to spending my life without ever knowing love, the gods above laughed and threw me right into the path of love.

I was not prepared for what I felt. I was blinded, dazzled by the emotions that ricocheted inside me. I felt euphoric and nauseous at the same time. How could this have happened to me? Nothing could have prepared me for that turmoil I felt every time I looked at him! Or heard his voice talking about the ideals of swadeshi. Have I shocked you, Dhananjoy babu? I shocked myself initially. How was it even possible, I wondered. And yet there it was! The more I tried to stamp on the love I felt, the more it behaved like a trapped fish, flailing about and refusing to die! Each time Sukanta walked into the room, talked to me about the andolan and rehearsed his speeches, my heart hammered inside my chest like something that would explode out of my chest one day. I knew my love was always going to be one-sided and unrequited. It was a mirage. And yet, it gave me so much more joy than the reality of my marriage to Sushila. Would you call it some kind of sickness, a perversion, Dhananjoy babu?

All I know is it gave me happiness, the kind that I had never ever felt in my life. Surely, I deserved it after all that I had endured. How was I harming anyone if I spent a few stolen moments admiring those chiselled features? Or lurked in corners simply to be able to gaze at him while he worked in one of the rooms downstairs near the kitchen? Just looking at the delightful way his wayward locks fell over his eyes. Or the way he tapped his lip or scratched his temple when troubled by a thought. What did it matter that I had stooped so low as to steal his handkerchief and kept it close to my heart? (Then I dropped it one day, and poor Puti got an earful from Sushila for being careless.)

And then, life threw me off course again when Sushila announced she was pregnant. I felt ecstatic but also confused. Would I be betraying my child if I could not destroy that which raged in my heart? So, I tried once again to crush that love which consumed me day and night. I tried and I tried and then realized the fruitlessness of it. The only way to kill those feelings would be to kill myself, and I wasn't ready for that. I had to carry on with my incongruent existence. Dutiful husband, father-to-be, everyone's dependable Rakhal-da but also a man who craved the sight of another, day and night, like it were a powerful, forbidden drug. How ironic that when I finally began to understand what poets and songwriters have raved about, I had to keep trying to deny its very existence, even to myself.

Are you judging me, Dhananjoy babu? Are you recoiling in horror? Well, what do I care? I'm dead, and it's an enormous relief to unburden my darkest secrets.

But what, you might ask, does any of this have to do with Sarala? Be patient, my friend, I'm coming to that.

A couple of months ago, I began to get the feeling that my one true love was becoming increasingly drawn to the attractive widow who worked as a cook in our household. It could well have been my lovesick mind playing tricks on me, but it seemed as though they were laughing and chatting with each other at every given opportunity. Every time I thought of their being together, it was like a glass splinter slicing away at my ribs. Maybe, in my lovelorn state, I imagined all kinds of things that weren't there. Soon, I had convinced myself that the damned girl had seduced Sukanta and that they were meeting secretly. Her need to stay at the Rajbari was part of the plan to be close to him. My insides roiled with rage when I saw the impudent wretch flash him bashful smiles and heard her ask him about Vidyasagar and the remarriage of widows. How dare she, I thought to myself. As though he were mine! The girl had lately become all puffed up with self-importance – a far cry from the stuttering, wide-eyed creature who had entered the kitchen as Kamini's assistant. I wanted to wring the saucy wretch's neck.

And then, a few weeks ago, I noticed something else that made me realize she had to go. I had gone out for a walk in the morning as I sometimes do, to clear my head before the day begins in earnest. I saw her standing next to a tree, holding it for support, and even as I looked, she vomited. When she turned around and saw me, her face became all flushed. She shook her head and ran away from there, leaving me feeling utterly bemused. Soon, the penny dropped. Of course, there could be only one explanation! I had seen Sushila feeling sick in that manner soon after her pregnancy was confirmed.

That was all the proof I needed. It felt like a monster had embedded its talons in my brain, raking them back and forth till I felt I would go mad! Mad with jealousy. Finally, I made the decision. My adversary – for I thought of her that way – had to die. Of course, I tried to tell myself it was largely because she had distracted Sukanta from the noble cause of the andolan. But the truth was that my very existence felt blighted every time I imagined her in his arms and then carrying his child. The only antidote to that pain was her death. And so, as you know, I started planning, and you'll have to admit, it was a good plan. A brilliant plan, even though I say so myself. There was no way your friend would have solved the case without your help.

This letter has become so much longer than I expected. Sushila has started complaining, asking me to stop working and prepare for bed. Little does she know it might only be a matter of a few hours now. Will I live to see my child? Who knows? All I know is once you unveil me as the killer, I won't hang around for an arrest and all the rest of it. I'll decide my own punishment. For once, it'll be my decision. I just hope I see my beloved's face one last time before I go.

Please destroy the letter after you have read it, Dhananjoy babu. And if possible, don't talk about my shameful secret to anyone. That is my one final request, and I know you are too decent a man to ignore it.

Rakhal Bagchi

EPILOGUE

A FEW DAYS LATER

Dhananjoy sat on the daaoa of Bansidhar's house, sipping tea, smoking a cigarette and remembering the weeks that had gone by. This had become his favourite place to sit with Bansi in the evenings. Going over their investigation, asking each other frenetic questions or, at times, simply gazing at the coconut trees and the blue yonder in companionable silence. *Tempus fugit*. He remembered that phrase from one of his Latin lessons in the missionary school he had studied in Calcutta. Time had really flown. He was waiting for Bansi to come out of the house so they could walk together to the station.

Dhananjoy felt as though he was already missing the village and the people he had met here. Since early morning, there had been visitors who had come in to say their goodbyes. Sijad had come with Daktar babu and assured Dhananjoy that he would see him again very soon in the city. Sukanta had arrived slightly later, bearing gifts from Thakurani, and had sat with him to talk about his plans related to the andolan. The pompous manner had gone, replaced by a solemn, more thoughtful air. Hopefully, also a finer understanding of the cause that did not involve rash actions against perceived 'enemies of the nation'. When asked about the members of the Rajbari, he said that everyone was still trying to come to grips with all that had happened. The shock had yet to wear off. But life, he said, always, found a way of limping back to its usual rhythm, didn't it? Even Sushila had gradually begun to step out of her room and sit down with the rest of the family. She rarely smiled or talked, but at least she didn't feel the need to be solitary all the time.

Dhananjoy's last visitor was Bama, and after seeking his blessings, she had asked him if he would put in a word on her behalf with his boss in the Calcutta office. She wanted to become a detective in the city. She was prepared for all the exciting challenges, as well as the mundane grunt work. Dhananjoy had smiled and nodded. He didn't disbelieve her. He couldn't wait to see the expression on Smithson's face when he told him about a meye goyenda.

With his arms folded, he now sat gazing at the iridescent horizon. The sun had begun its preparations to set, and the mellow colours of the evening skies soothed his very soul. He listened carefully to the songs that the birds around him were singing, putting their very heart and soul into them, as if to impress him one last time. Sadly, these sights and sounds would all be lost again once his train dropped him back in the bustling city he thought of as home. He had never dwelt on this before, but he was sure this was his favourite time of the day. Who was it who had told him it was called the godhuli hour? Was it his mother? Thinking about her no longer brought that pain churning and twisting inside him. Or the need to clamp down on the tidal waves of emotions and memories. So many memories! Ma crouched on her heels watching the water bubble in a pot on the stove and stirring the rice from time to time. Or pushing back the end of the sari covering her head to get a better view of things. Washing the big grinding stone to remove all traces of spices on it and then storing it carefully in one corner of the kitchen. Anxiously removing the tiniest bones from his ilish so he could eat his favourite fish without having to fret about something getting stuck in his throat.

'Ki re? Should we go?' Lost in his thoughts, he hadn't seen Bansi come and stand next to him. Saroja stood near the door wiping her tears. The food she had packed for his journey would feed most of the passengers on the train. Both Bansi and she had promised they would visit him soon. But they all knew that fulfilling such promises often took time. Till then, there was always the wait and the anticipation.

Trunk in hand, Dhananjoy walked towards the station with his friend. The desultory chatter they kept up while walking was just a way to keep their actual emotions in abeyance. Suddenly, Dhananjoy felt Bansi's hand on his arm.

'Joy, wait. I wanted to ask you something before you leave.'

'What is it, Bansi?'

'I have been waiting to ask you this ever since you came. Somehow, I could never find the right moment. Well, it's this. Would you like to see your ancestral bhhite on your way to the station, Joy? Where you spent the first ten years of your life. It's falling to pieces, but it's still there.'

Bansi had sounded a little nervous while broaching the question. Dhananjoy looked at him, eyes brimming with affection for his childhood friend. 'Yes, Bansi. Yes, I would really like to see it. Can you take me there?'

AFTERWORD

The seed of this novel was planted some years ago when I began my postdoctoral research on Bangla crime writings, that featured women as victims of assaults and murder, and were produced in late nineteenth century and early twentieth century colonized Bengal. The research, among other things, revealed to me that several decades before fictional detectives like Byomkesh Bakshi seized the readers' imagination, there were real-life darogas like Bankaullah and Priyanath Mukhopadhyay who were publishing accounts of actual cases that they had investigated and solved. The daroga accounts are the first manifestations of a dedicated crime-centred genre in Bangla and were extremely popular at the time they were published. These writings emerged in the years following the establishment of a police department in Calcutta and the development of modern, 'scientific' techniques of investigation such as fingerprinting and forensic post-mortems.*

---

* In 1868, a dedicated Detective Department was set up in Calcutta by the Commissioner of Police, Stuart Hogg, almost a decade before the emergence of the same in Scotland Yard.

For researchers like me the non-fictional daroga accounts are invaluable material, not only for being pioneering writings about crime-and-investigation, but also for providing a window into many aspects of life and society of the time – the late nineteenth, early twentieth-century period – that remain excluded from mainstream literature. For instance, they often provide glimpses of actual female lives and actions that offer a startlingly different perspective from the way women were represented and stereotyped in popular culture of the time.

It is true that from the 1860s, 'women's reform' was a hotly debated issue in Bengal and that subsequently the efforts of certain reform-minded individuals helped to enhance the roles and opportunities of women of dominant castes or class. But, at the same time, an overwhelming amount of prescriptive writings as well as popular farces, tracts, fictions and journals condemned/ridiculed female agency and sexuality and upheld silent, chaste, self-effacing and passive femininity as quintessentially Hindu, or Indian, or Bengali. Epithets like *Sati-lakshmi* and *Griha-lakshmi* were routinely deployed to remind women of the duties and ideals of 'good' femininity.

But despite powerful cultural distinctions between 'good' and 'bad' women that were prevalent in society, one finds, in Bankaullah and Mukhopadhyay's daroga accounts, an astonishing number of real-life cases that involve women who had rebelled against patriarchal strictures and taboos and attempted to explore different worlds of social and sexual relationships. Needless to say their 'audacious' desires and transgressions resulted in harsh familial and/or spousal punishments in the form of verbal abuse, threats, assault, murder or exile from home.

And yet there's no denying the evidence of the boldness and resourcefulness with which so many of them (including young 'upper'-caste widows whose lives were the most severely bound by shastric norms of austerity and celibacy) took risks and sought fulfillment on their own terms. It was in the memoirs of Daroga Bankaullah that I encountered the reference to a *meye-goyenda* (a female detective) who assisted the police in an informal manner. Not much is mentioned about her, except that she was a young widow who was extremely dexterous in her work.

Sarala's story – as well as that of some other women in the novel – although completely fictional, is inspired by the buried real-life accounts of those forgotten, often silenced courageous women.

ACKNOWLEDGEMENTS

The journey from an idea to a complete narrative is a long and tortuous one, especially for first time writers like me, who are constantly assailed by doubts and worries about whether it is a journey worth making. Without the support and encouragement of friends and family, this book would perhaps have never seen the light of day.

I've been incredibly lucky to work with my editor, Anupama Manral, and the team at Hachette India. Thank you, Anupama, for your kindness, wisdom and faith in the novel. Your thoughtful comments and suggestions make the novel what it is.

I owe a great deal of gratitude to many of my students and to our classroom discussions of the crime genre that made me realize its tremendous potential for entertainment and social commentary.

Thank you to Stewart King, Henry Sutton, Suzanne Solomon, Deepika Tandon, Srimanjari, Sengmei, Shweta Sachdeva Jha, Snigdha Singh, Gorvika Rao and Geeta Gangadharan Shrivastav for their unfailing kindness and encouragement. A special shout-out to Jeevanjot Nagpal for her help with certain technical matters.

Many thanks to my sister Sangeeta and my friend Sharmila Purkayastha, who have been a steady support through all ups and downs and with whom I can talk about everything good, bad and ugly.

To my entire family I owe thanks for always being available for help, advice and heart-warming or funny messages and videos. A special thanks to my daughter Shreyasi who would be very annoyed if I didn't give her a special mention and to Harshil and his wonderful parents, Pavan and Nita, who are also now part of the family.

A huge thanks to Saswati Sengupta, whose insights, candour, ideas, always on-point suggestions and unflagging support have meant the world to me.

And finally to Rajarshi, my first reader and brainstorming partner, who is as creative as he is good at number-crunching and excel sheets! Love and thanks.